Nick McDowell

Nick McDowell's first novel, THE WRONG GIRL, was published in 1995. He has also had short stories and poetry published. He works in publishing and lives in London with his wife and their three daughters.

SCEPTRE

Also by Nick McDowell

The Wrong Girl

Four
in the
Morning

NICK McDOWELL

SCEPTRE

The author wishes to express his gratitude to MIT Press
for granting permission to quote George Santayana.

First published in 1997 by Hodder and Stoughton
A division of Hodder Headline PLC
A Sceptre Paperback

10 9 8 7 6 5 4 3 2 1

British Library Cataloguing in Publication Data

McDowell, Nick
  Four in the morning
  1. English fiction – 20th century
  I. Title
  823.9′14 [F]

  ISBN 0 340 65734 0

Typeset by Palimpsest Book Production Limited,
Polmont, Stirlingshire
Printed and bound in Great Britain by
Clays Ltd, St Ives plc, Bungay, Suffolk

Hodder and Stoughton
A division of Hodder Headline PLC
338 Euston Road
London NW1 3BH

For Sarah, Natasha and Anna

For never can true courage dwell with them,
Who, playing tricks with conscience, dare not look
At their own vices. We have been too long
Dupes of a deep delusion!

Samuel Taylor Coleridge

Accidents are accidents only to ignorance

George Santayana

Part One

Fourteen Years

1

Two Secrets

The rain came in the night. Matthew woke to the sound of water pouring from a flooded gutter on to the ledge outside his dormitory window, slapping against the stone with drumming urgency. He looked at his watch. Its luminous hands told him that the time was three minutes to four. He listened to the hissing and gurgling, all the warmer in bed for the noises outside, knowing he had the whole of his birthday to come and none of it yet used up. He went back to sleep.

Matthew never doubted that his mother loved him. But he could not understand why she was late. The mid-morning break lasted from twenty to eleven until twenty past. By Matthew's watch, eight of these precious minutes had passed. Either side of the tall front door to the school were leaded windows with deep sills. Matthew, in his uniform of grey shorts and a grey flannel shirt, hopped on to the sill to the right of the door. Sitting there was permitted so long as a boy's feet did not touch the paintwork below the sill or the varnished wood of the sill itself, and on one day per year per boy. The seats were known as Birthday-sills.

'Double figures, I hear.' The English master strode past. His tenth birthday had become a cricket score.

'Yes, sir.'

'Well done, Kerrigan.'

'Thank you, sir.'

Matthew had received congratulations on his birthday from the French master, the matron, the music master (Matthew's friend) and from the English master who was really the cricket master but taught English too. Sports teachers had to occupy themselves when it rained. Matthew rubbed a hole in the steamed window and looked through the water running down the pane at a distorted view of the gravelled courtyard and the black drive hedged by rhododendron bushes as big as houses. The rain had come after ten days of afternoon cricket and sandals allowed in the grounds at break-time.

In his pocket, he had a piece of paper on which he had written the names of the boys with whom he would share his cake. He fingered the curled edges of the quarter-folded piece of blue Basildon Bond. He looked at his watch. Ten fifty-two. Which meant she was twelve minutes late and there were thirty-eight, no, twenty-eight minutes left. Less than half an hour. He rubbed the glass again and gazed at the torrent of rain drenching the stone walls of the courtyard, peppering the puddles in the gravel, running in muddy streams from the lawns on to the black drive. He heard water gushing down pipes from the guttering, to drains either side of the steps outside the front door.

Patterson Minor put his head around the door between the library and the hall. He was number two on Matthew's cake list.

'Your mater's late.'

'Says who?'

'Bet she doesn't come.' Patterson Minor's blond head disappeared behind the library door. Matthew pulled pieces of paper from his pocket. He found and unfolded his mother's letter of the previous week and reread the words – *Darling, I shall be at the school at 10.40 precisely, as you ask.*

He refolded the letter and unfolded the cake list. He touched his tongue to a stub of pencil and made a wavy line through Patterson Minor's name. Ten fifty-nine. Now there could be no more than twenty minutes sitting in the passenger seat of the car beside his mother. He watched the rhododendron bush beyond which the driveway curved out of sight. He saw the bumper, the headlights, the windscreen of a car appear there. But they turned into small movements of water and leaf.

He jumped down from the sill, opened the heavy oak door and ran to the bottom of the steps. He looked to left and right, rain blotching his shirt, to be sure that his parents' car had not slipped past without his noticing. The headmaster's Austin Princess was the only vehicle in the courtyard. A window creaked open above him.

'You.' Matron's voice carried from one of the dormitories at the top of the school. 'Get inside out of that rain this minute.'

Seven minutes past eleven. He could not stay still. He walked in circles. He rubbed the window and looked out on the courtyard. He read his mother's letter again. *Darling, I shall be at the school at 10.40 precisely, as you ask. Dad may take the morning off work to join me. He sends his love.* There was no doubting the words – round and solid, made of blue ink from her fountain pen. For his ninth birthday, she baked him a chocolate cake and the boys with whom he shared it said the icing was better than any icing ever, except Toland who insisted his mother's lemon cake was better. He saved the nine candles and used them to illuminate a bamboo camp that he and his friends made by the lower lake. He had not been able to use the Scalextrix cars because his track was at home, but he had been proud of the red

Ferrari and the green Jaguar and the cricket bat signed by Ted Dexter, although Toland said it wasn't his real signature.

The front door opened. A collapsing umbrella showered him. The headmaster's wife, Mrs Hunter, stood before him. Her left hand squeezed on some small object in her palm. She lowered her fist to her side and gazed at Matthew. Instead of sheathing the umbrella in the stand by the door, she let it drop at Matthew's feet and strode off in the direction of the headmaster's study. Matthew smelt the sour severity of polish as he reached down to the floor. He picked up the umbrella and flourished it for a dripping moment before stabbing it home into the rack.

Eleven-sixteen. In four minutes the waiting would be over. Perhaps the music master could be persuaded to buy something at the bakery in the village. Without his cake, Matthew was in trouble. He forced himself to sit still on the window-sill for those last few minutes. His stomach played host to a lizard which had woken at ten-fifty and now skittered and writhed inside him. He cleaned the glass again, rubbing with the sleeve of his flannel shirt which was now soaked. A car appeared and he jumped up on the sill, breaking the rules. At first, he thought it must be his mother's Volkswagen. Then it seemed possible that it was his father's blue Jaguar. But it was a car he did not recognise, a make he did not know.

The bell rang for lessons. He jumped from the sill to the wooden floor, turning to obliterate the mucky print of his sandals with the forearm of his shirt.

Mr Dartmouth could not say the word 'isthmus'. It clung to his tongue, refusing to leave his mouth. The boys around Matthew sniggered. 'Peninsula' slipped from Mr Dartmouth's tongue unmangled. He repeated the word, confirming his victory over it, stretching the final syllable with a conquering roll. Peninsulaaaa-r. Matthew heard the door of the classroom open behind him.

'Mr Dartmouth.' The headmaster's voice was quiet, almost a whisper. 'Could you spare Kerrigan for a minute?' The entire class turned to look at him.

'Of course, Headmaster.' Mr Dartmouth then asked Matthew to go with the headmaster, as if he could have failed to hear the exchange which had taken place over his head. He would follow the headmaster to the hall and kiss his mother. He would ask her for the cake. He would receive the presents and open them later, at lunch-time perhaps. The headmaster stood aside for Matthew to enter the study, a place of pipe-smoke and reprimand. Mrs Hunter sat in one of the leather chairs. The headmaster indicated that Matthew should sit in the other. Then he retreated behind his desk to stand beside the music master. In the silence, Matthew realised that the rain had stopped. Light expanded behind the two men standing in front of the window, their silhouettes fringed by a glowing edge. Matthew had never been asked to sit in the headmaster's study, nor had he heard of any boy being asked to do so. He continued to stand.

'Kerrigan,' the headmaster began. Then he glanced down at his desk. 'Matthew. It is with the greatest regret that I find myself in the position of being the person obliged to tell you—' The headmaster paused. Matthew looked at the sunshine on the lawn and in the trees around the lake.

'There has been an accident,' Mrs Hunter said. Her hand was gripped tightly by her side, as it had been during their silent encounter in the hall. She reached out her other hand towards Matthew. He approached her, banging bare knees on the low table. Magazines toppled and poured from the table. 'Sorry, sir.' Matthew dropped to his knees and piled the magazines back on to the table, one by one.

'We had a call from your grandmother.' Mrs Hunter held his hand. 'Your parents were both in the car.'

Matthew failed to banish thoughts of the cake from his mind. Perhaps it was on the back seat, or in the boot.

'There was no pain,' Mrs Hunter said.

'When can I see them?' Matthew wanted to let go of Mrs Hunter's hand. 'Are they in hospital?'

Someone knocked on the door of the headmaster's study.

'Enter.'

Matthew looked around to see the chaplain standing in the doorway. 'It's my birthday,' Matthew said. 'I'm ten.' He felt the hands of the chaplain on his shoulders.

'Love never dies,' the chaplain said.

'You must remember,' the music master said, 'that there would have been no pain.' Matthew tried to imagine the pain of a car accident but he could only visualise broken glass, jagged metal and people stepping gingerly from a crushed wreck.

The music master pushed past the chaplain, lifted Matthew in his big arms and gave him a rough hug. His beard tickled Matthew's cheek. The music master put him down and left the room. The hands of Mrs Hunter and the chaplain were on him. The news about his parents had convicted him of a crime. He was a prisoner who must be restrained.

'I want to go to my mother,' Matthew said. 'I want my mother.'

'I know that you will honour the memory of your parents,' the headmaster said. 'The chaplain will help you commend them to God.'

Matthew fell over. He had lost all sensation in his legs and feet, hands and arms. They carried him to the sick room and took off his uniform. He slumped naked on a bed while matron went to his dormitory to fetch his pyjamas. Then she slipped him under the covers and closed the curtains.

He stared at the ceiling, quarantined with a loss in which he did not believe.

It was evening when his grandmother's voice woke him. He heard the click of claws on the linoleum and knew that if the school had allowed Gran to bring his dog, a major breach of the rules was being overlooked. At school, Matthew described the black retriever, whose name was Banjo, as 'his'. At home, Banjo belonged to Matthew, his mother and his father, equally. He did not like the idea of the dog being on her own. He allowed her to nuzzle between his hand and the bedcovers on which it lay. The silk snout and the velvet forehead moved under his palm.

His eyes were still closed. His hand remained impassive. Matthew was not ready to be awake.

'The shock he's had,' matron said.

'He's not the only one to have lost someone,' Matthew heard his grandmother say. 'His father was my only child.'

'No one is underestimating your loss, Mrs Kerrigan,' matron said. 'Matthew's a boy. Just a boy.' Matthew had always thought of 'Mrs Kerrigan' as describing his mother.

'What on earth am I going to do with him?' his grandmother asked. 'What am I going to tell him?'

'That his mother and father are in the arms of God,' matron said. 'For ever.'

'Will he believe that, do you suppose?'

'I believe it,' matron said.

The black retriever made a low groan and Matthew, unable to staunch his instinct, reached his arms out and clasped the dog's head, to comfort her.

'He's awake,' matron said. 'I'll be leaving you now, Mrs Kerrigan.'

'Please—' Matthew opened his eyes to see his grandmother reaching out her hand, but matron had left the room. Banjo climbed half on to Matthew's bed. 'I'm sorry, Gran.'

'There's no undoing it.' His grandmother wore a raincoat and a black cotton scarf, knotted under her chin.

'There was no pain,' Matthew told her. The dog's long tongue lolled and salivated on the portion of white sheet which was turned over the blanket, close to Matthew's face. Hot meaty breath made his cheek damp. 'What will happen to Mum and Dad?'

'They will go to Heaven.'

'I mean, will there be a funeral?'

'Can you remember the name of the vet's wife?' his grandmother asked. 'The one who does the flowers in the church?'

'Enright,' Matthew said. 'Mrs Enright.'

'Thank you, Arthur,' his grandmother said. At the sound of the word Arthur the dog twitched, muscles taut.

'Matthew.' Arthur was his father's name. 'You mean Matthew.'

'Oh goodness.' His grandmother pushed the dog aside to embrace Matthew. He thought she was saying 'you poor boy', but as she raised her head from his, unmuffling her words, he realised that she was saying 'my poor boy'.

'I didn't ask them to come.' He must not ask her about the cake and the presents. 'They just said they would.'

'Your parents are in the arms of God, for ever,' his grandmother said.

Matthew tried to imagine it now, the vast biceps of a giant, much bigger than the music master's, big enough to embrace all the dead. Would the cake, he wondered, be in the arms of God? 'I should have asked them not to come,' he said.

His grandmother stood and walked to the window. The dog licked his face. Why was his grandmother looking through the crack in the curtains? What was she staring at? No one could be using the cricket nets after that much rain. He remembered lying on a similar bed, listening to rain in the night, his birthday like a tree-lined avenue before him.

'We're going to be friends, the two of us.' The grandmother turned back to Matthew. 'Later on we will give you an unbirthday party.'

'I should like that,' he said in an effort to please her. 'I'm sorry, Gran.'

'No one is to blame, Arthur,' she said. 'It was an accident.'

This time, it took Matthew Kerrigan a moment to notice his grandmother's mistake. Perhaps it was not a mistake in the usual sense of being correct or incorrect, earning a tick or a cross.

'There won't be any cake for my friends.'

'There will be other cakes,' his grandmother said.

Matthew did not care about other cakes. What he wanted was a cake that day, that minute, and a knife for cutting and matches for lighting candles. His grandmother sat on the edge of the bed beside him. The dog laid her snout in his grandmother's lap. She pushed Banjo's head from her coat and brushed at a string of saliva which looped from the material to the dog's jowl. Banjo began to bark.

His grandmother's hand covered Matthew's. Together they watched the dog barking until Matthew realised that if anyone was going to soothe Banjo it would have to be him. He made a squeaking noise, drawing air through lips pressed tight together. He felt the snout against his shoulder and pulled his hand free of his grandmother's to stroke the dog's head. 'Where will Banjo live, Gran?'

'You'll come to me, for the moment,' she said. 'Then we'll see.'

The smells in his grandmother's cottage were old, like in a museum.

'Who will walk Banjo?'

'I don't know,' his grandmother said. 'I don't know everything.'

'Her bed and her bowl are in the back kitchen,' Matthew said. 'She has a biscuit last thing at night. A round dog biscuit. You get a bag of them, all different colours. Black and red and yellowy.'

'You love that dog, don't you?'

'I was just telling you,' Matthew said. 'So you knew.'

'Do all the parents visit boys on their birthdays?' his grandmother asked.

'Unless they live overseas,' Matthew said. 'Or have birthdays in the holidays.'

'Are there any boys you particularly like?' she asked. 'Do you have a best friend?'

Matthew immediately thought of Felshaw, who had been made headboy at the beginning of the term. Felshaw was a fast-bowler and had a girlfriend. He and Matthew could not be proper friends because Felshaw was thirteen and allowed to wear long trousers in summer. 'Not just one,' he replied. 'There's Toland and McFall. Sturgis Major and Hancock and—'

'There is a friend you would like to have with you? Just one?'

Matthew could not think of just one, apart from Felshaw. 'Did she actually make a cake?' he asked. 'Do you know?'

His grandmother stood again and stepped back from the bed.

'I think it was the last thing your mother said to me,' his grandmother said. 'She said she must be going because she had to put the icing on your cake.'

'When was that?'

'It doesn't matter when it was.'

'I want to be able to imagine it.'

'Last night,' his grandmother said. 'She came to the cottage last night.'

'Where was Dad?'

'He came to the cottage too.'

'Why?' Matthew asked.

'Your father often visited me at the cottage.'

'Where did they put the cake, do you think?' Matthew remembered his father's visits to the cottage as unwilling and infrequent.

'I don't know,' the grandmother said.

'Maybe they put it in the boot.' He waited for his grand-mother to reply, stroking the dog's head.

'Tell me, when do you have your morning break?'

'Twenty minutes to eleven until twenty minutes after.'

'Meet me down by the front door?' his grandmother said.

'Tomorrow morning? At twenty to eleven?'

'You'll bring Banjo?'

'Bring your friends and I'll bring Banjo,' his grandmother said.

'Oh, Gran!' He failed to suppress excitement.

'Ask matron to pack your Sunday suit. And some shirts.'

'Gran?'

'What is it now?'

'Can I leave school for ever and ever?'

'We'll talk about that tomorrow.' She moved into the doorway of the sick room and looked down the corridor.

'Do you think they might let Banjo stay tonight?' Matthew asked.

It was the headboy's privilege to watch television in matron's room between lights-out and the time, half an hour later, when he toured the dormitories to tell the other boys to stop talking and go to sleep. After his grandmother left, Matthew was installed on the sofa in matron's room. The black retriever slept on a blue rug between the sofa and an armchair with a white doily on the headrest. Matthew watched television. He heard the bell go for lights-out in the corridor. Soon afterwards, Felshaw slipped into matron's room.

'Stand up, Kerrigan.' He did as he was told. The tartan travel-rug which matron had tucked around him fell on the sleeping dog in a tenting crumple.

'I pretended that my parents were dead once,' Felshaw said. 'To see what it was like. But I couldn't forget I was pretending. So it didn't work.'

Felshaw stepped towards Matthew and put his arms around his shoulders, pulling him in close. Matthew was confused by the good things which were happening to him as consequences of the bad thing which had happened to his mother and father. Felshaw's embrace was the richest prize he could imagine. The dog slipped from between their legs and walked to the open window to sniff the air.

'Now.' Felshaw released Matthew from the hug. 'Stand in the doorway and look down the corridor. See if anyone's coming.' Glancing between the deserted linoleum alley and the interior of matron's room, Matthew saw Felshaw open the cabinet under the television set and remove a bottle.

'All clear,' Matthew whispered. Then he chewed on the words, tasting the idea of being in the clear. Felshaw unscrewed the brass cap from the clear-glass bottle. Holding it by the neck he lifted it to his mouth, placed his lips halfway over the opening, as if preparing to blow a trumpet, upended the bottle and drank. He reached for Matthew's arm, pulled him back into the room and took his place in the doorway. 'Just a little.' Felshaw handed the bottle to Matthew.

'I don't want any.'

'You don't know what you want,' Felshaw said.

Matthew did not want to complain, or choke, as he had seen people do on television. He drew a breath deep into his lungs – 'Just a little. It's strong.' – swigged from the bottle and then exhaled.

'Quick.' Felshaw grabbed the bottle from his hands and, replacing the cap, returned it to its place in the cabinet. 'Under the blanket.'

'David?'

Matthew had never heard anyone call Felshaw by his Christian name. Felshaw gave matron a glorious, mischievous, winning grin. He was suddenly another little boy, not an almost-grown-up at all.

'Cocoa, Matthew?' He nodded. Matron left the room.

'Now we have a secret,' David said.

'Two secrets,' Matthew said.

Matron said it was better to go to lessons but that he could just sit if he wanted to and the masters would understand. After assembly was maths, taken by the headmaster. At the end of the class, Matthew approached McFall and Toland and asked them to meet him in the front hall at the beginning of break. Toland blushed.

'It's all right,' Matthew said. 'I'm all right. Tell Sturgis and Hancock.'

At the start of the English lesson, after he had handed back their essays (Kerrigan got eight out of ten), the English master asked them all to say a prayer for Mr and Mrs Kerrigan. There were some moments of silence as each boy thought of his prayer and said it to himself. Matthew prayed that his grandmother would not be late. The bell took forever to ring. When it did, Matthew ran to the front hall where he found his grandmother talking to matron. On the polished wooden floor at matron's feet were a suitcase and his dog. He looked around the room in panic as his friends gathered about him. Felshaw opened the library door and gestured to Matthew to come in.

As he entered the library, he saw that the newspapers and reference books had been cleared from the long table by the window. Apart from the cake, which was chocolate and enormous, there were plates and napkins and a bottle of lemonade. Felshaw struck a match and kissed it to the wicks of five candles before shaking out the flame. The second match completed the ceremony. Matthew felt the heat rising from the candles, the knife gripped in both hands, ready to cut down into the centre of the cake. He read the words, Happy Birthday Matthew, made out of blue icing.

Thinking that they would not have the heart to sing to him, he inhaled deeply in preparation for the blowing out of the candles. But as his lungs filled, Felshaw's voice cracked the silence. Matthew let his breath out carefully, watching the flames wobble. Soon the other boys joined in with the headboy's deeper voice. He heard the words 'Happy Birthday, dear Kerrigan,' with the voices of matron and his grandmother singing Matthew underneath the louder Kerrigan. Banjo barked at the singing and continued to bark as Matthew blew once, extinguishing all the candles.

He made no wish nor any shout as he pressed the knife through the crust of icing, letting it sink under the weight of his hands and arms into the sponge below. The give of the sponge was delicious after the hardness of the icing. He plunged the knife into the cake a second and a third time, once for his father and once for his mother. Felshaw came up behind him and stayed his arms, suspending the knife in the air above the punctured cake.

Matron cut slices. His grandmother poured lemonade into white plastic cups. Felshaw, draining the last of the lemonade straight from the bottle, caught Matthew's eye and smiled. The boys ate their cake in silence. Matthew could only sip at the lemonade.

Felshaw helped them carry things to the boot of Matthew's grandmother's green Renault. Then he shook the grandmother's hand in a grown-up way and said, 'Please let me know if there is anything, anything I can do to help.'

Matthew could not climb into the front seat. Felshaw persuaded him to share the back seat with Banjo. Matthew watched matron and Felshaw through the back window as the Renault pulled away. They did not wave.

2

Lost in Space

His grandmother's cottage stood at the end of a sandy lane where a long ridge marked the boundary of the village. In winter, Matthew could see his parents' house in the valley from the bedroom windows of the cottage. But in summer the chimneys, the eaves and the television aerial were all hidden by the foliage of tall trees. Beyond the valley's quilt of hedged fields the land rose again to the Downs. Behind the Downs was the sea. At the end of the summer term of the accident, Matthew Kerrigan – who began to think of himself as plain Matthew once his uniform had been cast aside – returned to the cottage with his grandmother, as if he were returning home.

He had often climbed the hill from the house in the valley to his grandmother's cottage on the ridge, prompted by his mother, who knew that the older woman was lonely. Sometimes Banjo accompanied him. More often he would discover her there already, offering canine adoration in exchange for a bowl of left-overs.

The dog was famous for her roving. She befriended people on every street. When bored or wearied by her wanderings,

Banjo would either amble home or settle on a doorstep until the occupant of the house telephoned the number etched on the chrome tag attached to her studded collar. Matthew's father had complained that a retriever should so often have to be retrieved. Banjo was shot at by farmers whose pregnant cows she terrorised and beloved by the village butcher whose back door she daily darkened in her quest for bones. When not on walkabout, Banjo was Matthew's chief companion.

Her tag had been changed so that it announced the address and phone number of his grandmother's cottage. Banjo did not understand that the cottage was no longer a port of call but home. During the first weeks after the accident his grandmother's letters complained of the dog's disappearances. Matthew wrote back to explain that Banjo would always return to his parents' house in the valley and that his grandmother should seek her there first. She wrote again to describe the agony of collecting the dog each evening.

On his return from school for the summer holidays his grandmother delegated to Matthew the task of reclaiming Banjo from the house in the valley. While he was grateful for the chore, he knew that she had not assigned it to him out of simple generosity. On the first evening of the holidays, after he had unpacked his tuck-box and his trunk in the guest bedroom of the cottage, he set out to collect his dog.

He walked along the ridge past a terrace of brick houses. The sandy lane made him think of beaches and swimming. He turned right, down a steep footpath between high hedges where nettles threatened to close ranks across the narrow thoroughfare. To his left, in the field below the hedge, he heard the bulky exhalations of cattle. At the end of the footpath he climbed a stile and walked under oaks to cross the banked stream on a bridge of flint and old brick. He walked carefully along the edge of the next field in order to avoid a herd of heifers standing on its far side. Another stile brought him to a rutted lane and, on the other side, his parents' house.

He reached his arm over the gate to wiggle the rusted bolt. While he had a perfect right to be there, he walked through the garden like a trespasser, wincing at the sudden flight of a bird from the weeping willow, confused by the deep drumming which sounded like it was outside him but might have been the thudding of his blood. He walked along the side of the house on a brick path beside a hedge. He hesitated before turning the corner into the courtyard.

Banjo stood in the porch of the house, tail thumping. As he approached her, the dog scratched at the oak door with one of her front paws. Matthew was not strong enough to drag Banjo across the courtyard and out into the lane. After several attempts to coax the dog away from the house, he gave up and lay on the lawn. The grass was longer than it should have been, tickling the back of his neck and his ears. He looked up at the windows of his parents' bedroom which reflected rectangular sections of sky.

He woke to the dog licking his cheek. Most of the light had drained from the sky. The windows reflected only differing degrees of darkness. He was damp from the rising dew. When he sat up his shirt stuck to his back. The exposed skin of his legs itched. He heard a car approaching and then saw, over the hedge, the top half of his grandmother's green Renault. The dog followed him now as he crossed the lawn and opened the gate. His grandmother was weeping as he climbed into the back of the car. Banjo jumped in beside him.

'Don't do this to me, Arthur.'

'I'm sorry, Gran.' It would only make things worse if he corrected her. 'I couldn't get her to move.'

Banjo had been consigned to sleep in the kitchen of his

grandmother's cottage. When Matthew woke on the first morning of the summer holidays, the dog was curled up on the floor beside his slippers. He heard the radio in his grandmother's bedroom as he passed her door on his way downstairs. The cottage had small windows and the dark furniture in the ground floor rooms swallowed up the light. He missed the morning chorus of boys' voices, the marshalling insistence of the breakfast bell, the pre-ordained school day – Latin, geography, break, English, maths, lunch.

His grandmother's hair was steel-grey and wavy. Her hands were knotted by arthritis. Her eyes were dark and piercing. Her smile had to be earned. She continued to wear black through the long weeks of the summer holidays. Matthew became self-conscious about the blue of his jeans, his red jumpers, his green shirt, the white of his T-shirts. Once he asked her if he too should be wearing black, but she did not reply. Perhaps she had not heard his question. He could not bring himself to repeat it.

During that summer Matthew was prey to two fears. The first came from a television programme called *Lost in Space*. In the episode which he replayed in his imagination, the heroes were captured on a strange planet by wart-faced aliens and strapped to stone altars in a murky dungeon. Water gushed from a pipe high on one of the dungeon walls. The camera showed the water-level rising. The heroes must have escaped to conquer new planets and protect the galaxy from wart-faced aliens, but Matthew remembered only the water rising over the stone altars, the clutch of the cold on his arms, the water closing over his mouth.

His second fear – of possession – had no obvious source. He toyed with the idea that a malign sprite had entered his being to direct his actions. The fear of possession kept him awake and when he had convinced himself that he was the unwilling agent of an evil genius, he allowed the dungeon to fill with water and, as the chief hero, drowned himself to sleep.

In the attic bedroom of his grandmother's cottage, Matthew's bouts of possession and drowning established their nocturnal pattern. She had nothing to offer as life-guard or exorcist. Disappointment oozed from her. He was its source and its recipient. He failed her to the extent that he was not his father, a shortcoming for which he could hardly be blamed. And yet it seemed natural to him that he should shoulder the responsibility. He focused his attention upon the smell of her face cream, the slick oiliness of it skidding against his cheek as she kissed him goodnight. She ran her hands through his hair calling him by his father's name: there, there, Arthur; there, there Arthur, dear.

As the tide of possession engulfed him, he became a puppet committing involuntary atrocities. He removed ten-shilling notes from his grandmother's purse and clogged the downstairs toilet with lavatory rolls. He let down the tyres of a neighbour's Volkswagen. He lied about letting the dog out. Banjo relieved herself in the house, fouling the carpets. The empire of disaster over which he held sway expanded to colonise his friends and their homes. On one occasion he and another boy decorated a toy battlefield with birthday candles and left them burning while they went down to lunch. Black smoke filled the friend's house. Matthew denied responsibility and did not believe that he had lied. He was cursed by an incubus. His actions were not his own.

In the populous silence of the attic bedroom, his world turned like a carousel in moonless night. He rode on his mother's knee. Then he watched his mother and father riding together, their faces swinging into view before the platform turned and whirled them out of sight. Gran never talked of his mother and her disapproval banned Matthew from doing so. In the police state of his grandmother's mind, his mother was one of the disappeared, tossed into an unmarked grave. Matthew would not allow his unmentionable mother to fade away. One night he woke in the hour before dawn and, with his grandmother's lipstick and kohl, played Frankenstein to his mother's Lazarus. As he tried a blusher on his cheek he was jolted by a glimpse of her. Then streaks of black ran through the blusher and her resurrection was ruined.

His grandmother could not come to terms with Matthew being Matthew. He was a coffin in which his father's memory lay rotting. Could she not call him Kerrigan – a family name which contained them both?

'That's what they call me at school,' he argued.

'You'll be looking forward to the beginning of term.'

'Not really.'

'You've only another week of me,' Gran said. 'And then I shall be alone again. With my memories.'

'I'll miss you.' What could he say? She was all the family he had.

'I'm not senile yet,' she said.

'What's senile, Gran?'

'When a person is too old to recognise a lie. When a person can no longer distinguish between the present and the past. When a person becomes incontinent.'

'Incontinent?'

'Your father was always inquisitive.'

'Teachers say it's good to be inquisitive,' Matthew said. 'But not too inquisitive.'

He became plain Kerrigan by trading Matthew for Arthur, cancelling himself to slip free of his father. He boxed up his Christian name and put it into storage with the contents of his parents' house. After that, time passed more quickly. Kerrigan travelled lightly across the border of puberty. David Felshaw moved on to another school. He wrote to Kerrigan, sending news from the world which the latter would one day inhabit.

He read that David was confused by his transition from headboy of one school to lowest of the low in another. He shared his junior status with an autumn intake of boys who had, only two months before, been the kings of their respective preparatory schools. Except David, adopting the language of his new environment, wrote of his peers as men. Their correspondence continued until Kerrigan left prep school, another headboy on his way to becoming a junior man at the public school where David was already bowling for the first eleven and embarking on A levels a year ahead of his peers.

On his first day at the new school, Matthew followed other boys through unfamiliar streets. Streams of pupils from other residential houses merged as they neared the walled medieval campus in which the chapel, the classrooms and the sanatorium were enclosed. The crowd carried Matthew into the cloistered ante-chamber of the campus, the roar of echoed footsteps and exclamations pressing on his ears like generations of ancestors. He was a new conscript in an army, following a leader he would never meet, into an unsought battle with unknown enemies. He thought of his father, making the same daily pilgrimage twenty-five years before.

As the pressure of the crowd behind him disgorged Matthew from the cloister, he stepped off the pavement. Once separate from the mass of boys he did not rejoin it. He stood on the dewed grass beside the ancient flagstones and watched the school pass, glancing up, then lowering his gaze, inspecting each stranger, face by face. The flow slackened. Stragglers and late-comers hurried through the arched entrance of the cloister. The sun edged over the high wall of the campus, filtering gold into the bands of mist over the playing fields.

David approached, accompanied by two other boys.

Matthew raised his hand in greeting. David stared straight through him, muttered to one of his companions and walked on without breaking his stride. Matthew identified one of David's companions as Bill Braxton, a senior in Matthew's dormitory.

The next morning, as Matthew stood at the entrance to the cloister, David and his friends walked straight towards him, but without acknowledging him. Perhaps he was becoming as invisible as he felt, melting into nothing like the morning mist. He stepped aside, to avoid being tumbled over, but the three seniors adjusted their course, following him.

'What do you think you're doing?' David's chest was no more than an inch from Matthew's face. When Matthew tried to back away, he felt the press of another boy's hands on his shoulders.

'Nothing.'

'He's waiting.' David turned to Bill. 'Who's he waiting for?'

'Who are you waiting for?' Bill asked.

'What's he waiting for?' David said. 'Why is he waiting?'

'Why are you waiting?' Bill said.

'But what's he waiting for?' David pushed Matthew, who stumbled backwards, catching the heel of his shoe on the raised edge of a flagstone. 'Why the fuck do you wait?'

'He's a new man,' Bill said. 'Leave him alone.'

'What did you say?'

'He's new. Leave him.' Bill and the third senior walked away, following the last of the other boys towards the chapel.

'You're waiting for me.'

'No.'

'What are you waiting for?'

'Nothing.'

'You know what?'

'We'll be late,' Matthew said.

'They're never coming back.'

'I'm waiting for a friend,' Matthew said.

'I can't make them come back,' David said. 'And nor can you.'

A week later, in the hour between supper and evening prep, Bill stopped Matthew in the hall. 'Get your coat.'

'What did I do?'

'Nothing. Yet.'

Matthew followed Bill into the kitchen – which was out of bounds to the boys – then through the scullery door into a dank yard of dustbins and catering trolleys. Bill shoved his shoulder against a wooden door and led Matthew out on to a backstreet. They walked in silence, Matthew three paces behind the taller boy. Bill turned left, to ascend a hill which would take them off limits. Matthew heard footfalls behind him. He turned and saw David. The three walked on, Bill setting the pace, Matthew breathless in his effort to match the bigger boys' strides. He followed as Bill made turning after turning. Soon he lost his bearings, walking through a strange part of the town on unlit streets.

Bill stopped outside a pub. David's hands gripped Matthew's shoulders. 'Stand here.' David indicated the place, against the wall, under the high frosted-glass window of the lounge bar. 'If you see any masters, tap on the window three times.' David and Bill went into the pub. Matthew stood on the pavement, looking to left and right, shivering in his thin overcoat. He walked on the spot in an attempt to keep warm. A group of men loomed out of the dark and entered the pub. Matthew stood his ground.

An Alsatian trotted up to him. He offered his palm for the dog to sniff. He pushed at the dog's muzzle, trying to persuade it to leave him be. The attempted rejection increased the dog's appetite for love. As the dog's owner approached, Matthew recognised the biology master. He knocked on the window three times.

'Who's in there?'

'I don't know, sir.'

'Name and house?'

'Kerrigan,' Matthew said. 'F house.'

'Kerrigan,' the master stooped to look at his face. 'Major or minor?'

'There's just me, sir.'

'Watch my dog.' As the master entered the lounge bar, Matthew tapped on the window again. A second later, David and Bill emerged from another entrance, further up the hill. They ran without looking back and turned down a side-street. Matthew made to follow but the Alsatian tensed and emitted a low growl. He stood still.

'What sort of man do you want to be, Kerrigan?' The biology master walked down the hill beside Matthew. 'Do you know how much it costs your parents to send you to this school?'

'No, sir.'

'Do you think your father would be proud of you? Standing outside a pub, in the seamier part of town, in your very first term?'

'I was lost, sir.'

'I remember your father,' the master said. 'He ran up some impressive debts at Oxford.'

'Was he a friend of yours?'

'No,' the master said. 'Arthur Kerrigan was not my friend.'

The biology master walked Matthew back to his house. 'You won't want your parents to hear about this,' the master said as he opened the front door of F house. 'What have you got to say for yourself?'

'Nothing, sir.'

'Nothing will come of nothing, Kerrigan.' The biology

master ushered him through the door. 'Every schoolboy should know that.'

'King Lear, sir.'

'Let this be a warning to you,' the master said. '*Monitus estis*.'

'That's plural, sir.'

Matthew's grammatical acuity was rewarded by a spell in detention. He was told to write a three-page essay on 'The Uses of Treachery'. The following Saturday, after lunch, Bill Braxton cornered Matthew in the hall and took him to the bike shed. They rode along a narrow tow-path beside the river, stopping and pulling their bikes to one side when a master approached from the opposite direction, shouting out loud, apparently to himself. 'Heave, lift, wrists, forward, stretch-and-heave, lift, wrists, forward—' A rowing eight rounded a bend in the river. The master pedalled by, pipe clamped between bared teeth, gown flapping above his back wheel.

Kerrigan followed Bill Braxton to a stretch of disused railway line. Piles of rotting sleepers were netted by brambles. In a derelict signal hut, David handed out cigarettes and miniature bottles of whisky.

'What did you write?' David offered a match to Matthew's cigarette.

'I said there were three uses of betrayal.' Matthew exhaled through his nose. The sharp smoke stung his nostrils, pricking tears in the corners of his eyes.

'Only three?'

'The first is to destroy the state, the second is to fool enemies. And the third is to make new alliances.'

'Never let them know what you're thinking,' David said.

'I didn't.' Matthew tried drawing the smoke into his lungs and suppressed a cough.

'So what were you thinking?'

'About loyalty,' Matthew said.

'He's not waiting any more, is he?'

'He never meant to wait,' Bill said.

'I was never really waiting,' Matthew said. 'There's nothing to wait for.'

Nurturing Matthew did not suit his grandmother. She had raised his father. Why should she raise his son? Matthew sympathised with her when she told him how exhausting it was for a woman in her sixties to be guiding a boy through adolescence. By chance, answering the telephone when she was out, Matthew discovered her plan to relocate him with cousins in Devon. Despite his best efforts to bring it about, the scheme failed to get off the ground. His grandmother gave him extra piano lessons at the upright which stood in the dimmest corner of her dining room. Matthew's concentration was poor. He sensed other fingers moving over the keys beside his own. He stopped in mid-scale, forgetting where he was.

'Arthur was so quick,' his grandmother said. 'So clever and so quick.'

'I don't remember.'

'We shall look at the photos?' His grandmother had a habit of tailing her commands with a questioning lilt. She promoted the possibility of a negative response. She was confident of being denied. Her only grandchild did not disappoint her. She shuffled towards the desk in which the leather-bound photo-albums were stored.

'I don't want to.'

'I must look at them alone?'

He knew the photograph albums off by heart: the images, their order, the tug of her mournful commentary. Watching her weep over pictures of his father, he failed to assuage the loss which he had learnt to think of as, primarily, hers.

'I don't have to look at them.'

'You are an unnatural boy.'

'I can see them,' Matthew said. 'I don't need reminding.'

'You think only of yourself.'

'I love you.' Once Kerrigan had stumbled upon the magic effect of this phrase, it became his lifeboat, his means of escape. His world was a minefield in which one wrong move could trigger obliteration. He made maps on which he plotted the course which would guarantee him the greatest safety. He knew that his grandmother did not trust him. When he told her he loved her, he clouded her judgement. He lied in recompense for the protection she was obliged, but did not wish, to give. He kept a list in his wallet: tell Gran you love her; remember Mum; I hate school; Man U are great.

In one of his reports, the biology master (who had, it transpired, lent money to his father at Oxford and never had it repaid) described Matthew as sly. 'Now that's an interesting word,' his grandmother said, interrupting her ritual of reading each report aloud. Kerrigan could only feign interest at each assessment of his character and ability, having steamed open and perused the report before surrendering it into her hands.

'Is it good or bad?'

'They have taught you nothing?'

'I've learnt things they didn't mean to teach me.' He told her about the biology master and his long-standing resentment of Arthur Kerrigan.

'We must repay him,' she said. 'It will not be the first time I have had to settle your debts.'

'You mean Arthur's.'

'I know what I mean.'

The gesture would have been grander had it preceded the settling of his father's estate. He and his grandmother were now financially secure. She did not like the fact that the money was Matthew's, entrusted to her to disburse. She explained to him with bitter clarity that when he reached eighteen, whatever money remained in the trust would become his to spend. She sent a cheque to the biology master. He wrote back by return and explained that he had awarded himself compound interest over the fifteen year period between the loan and its repayment. He wanted more.

With the settling of the estate Kerrigan put into action a plan he had been brewing for some time. He proposed to his grandmother that she might pay someone to cook and clean, to entertain him, so that she would have more time to play bridge and go to the hairdresser. He had heard stories in the school dorm about continental au pair girls. The conception of his plan coincided with the appearance of straggles of dark hairs above his penis and under his arms.

Birgitta, a Dane of heavy haunch and loaflike personality, failed to satisfy. He froze her into misery and she left after two weeks of the spring holidays preceding his fourteenth birthday. Claudette, bony but presentable, arrived in July, when Kerrigan returned from school. She discovered evidence of life in the dreary region of Sussex which surrounded the village. Kerrigan and Claudette took the bus to Shoreham and swam off a beach of foot-punishing stones. In Brighton, they visited the cinema and the pier. Claudette found a pub on the edge of the village where the publican was prepared to overlook Kerrigan's unshaven minority. They sipped red wine in the twilight beer-garden. While she pretended that Kerrigan was eighteen for the sake of the publican, Claudette was also prepared to suppose him a child at bath-time. She soaped his skin and washed his hair.

Testosterone continued to work its monstrous miracle on Kerrigan's body and its urges. He entered a phase of waking each night in the hour before dawn. An alarm clock buried in the wall of his psyche jerked him from sleep. His erection pointed into the wide spaciousness of the night hours. Darkness spread like a blanket over memory's entrails.

Claudette's bedroom consisted of the other half of his grandmother's attic. Kerrigan navigated a course across the landing which avoided creaking floorboards. He hovered in darkness, an arm's length from Claudette's sleeping form. He shivered in vigil over a French girl only six years his senior. He smelt the milky sweetness of her sleeping body. As his eyes adjusted to the darkness in her room after the light on the landing, he could see her knickers atop a pile of other clothes.

On one such night, the threads of the thin carpet under his bare toes, pyjama top unbuttoned, pyjama bottoms turned teepee, Claudette reached out and took his hand. He did not know for how long she had been awake or if, on previous nights, she had pretended sleep, unsure what to do with the boy standing to attention by her bed. She made room for him, moving across the mattress and opening the covers so that he could slip in beside her. Her blue nightdress was rucked up to halfway between her knees and her belly. She manoeuvred his body so that he lay on his side, his erection directed away from her. Claudette pressed herself to his back, important parts of her touching his shoulder-blades and buttocks.

Drowsing in her arms, he had his first experience of disembodiment. The manner in which she received him under the covers made it clear that he was not the sexual predator he had built himself up to be, but a sleepless boy. Her fingers reached around him, searching only for his hand, which she held in hers. She whispered things in French and he knew from the tone rather than the words that she considered him a bereft person in need of her comfort. Man and child, he was annoyed at her disregard of his excited flesh and flummoxed by the unfamiliarity of her affectionate hugs. His limbs numbed. Sensation drained from legs, arms, penis. Only the parts of his body in direct contact with hers continued to send nervy messages to his cortex. His face became rubbery and impassive. He turned his head and tasted salt running over his upper lip on to his tongue.

Kerrigan stood beside the bed, looking down at the pyjamaed Matthew with the big front teeth and the face that half-smiled in repose. He did not marry up with his body again until the light began to press against the curtains and Claudette nudged him out of her bed. That's why people think I'm all right, he thought as he slipped back inside himself. They think I'm smiling.

He knelt on the floor beside Claudette's bed.

'Go now.' She hugged him. 'Before the grandmother comes.'

'Something happened.'

'You are a good boy,' she said. 'You will go well.'

'Maman,' he said.

'*Vas-y, mon petit.*'

In the last week of the summer holidays, Matthew's grandmother threw a cocktail party. In the drinks cabinet, Kerrigan's incubus had turned whisky into apple juice, rum into cold tea, vodka and gin into tap water, yellow chartreuse into urine. Even the Dubonnet had been swapped for Ribena, the dilutions carefully calculated to achieve the right shade of red. Only the sherry – his grandmother's invariable crepuscular tipple – remained what it seemed. Weeks of gradual metamorphosis would take only a moment to discover. Before the guests arrived, Kerrigan left the cottage with Banjo. He walked in the valley until after dark.

'Just like your father,' his grandmother told him, on his return. 'And his father before that.'

'I haven't touched your bottles,' Kerrigan said, betraying the innocence he had been determined to uphold.

'It's the drink that made them lie,' his grandmother said. 'Just the drink.'

'Was Dad a drunk?'

'Your father was never a drunk.'

'You just said he was, Gran.'

'Shut up, boy.'

Claudette entered the hall from the sitting room where she had been clearing up after the party. She had three glasses crooked on the fingers of each hand. Kerrigan followed her into the kitchen and sat down. He was remembering something familiar, from before the accident. Claudette placed the six tumblers in the sink, the chinking of glass on glass echoing an evening long before, the sound of ice clinking and ringing in a glass in his father's hand. One hand on the wheel, pinkie ring tapping in time to music from the radio, the other hand holding the glass, ice clicking and chiming in clear liquid. A snapshot of his father's face, a memory of the seat-belt tight across his stomach. And then nothing.

'You have taught him to lie, Claudette?' His grandmother entered the kitchen. 'That is the best you could do for him?'

'Madame Kerrigan, your boy speaks the truth.'

'All drinkers lie.'

Claudette looked at Kerrigan. 'How does she say you have done?'

The grandmother replied before Kerrigan could speak. 'He's been taking nips from the bottles. Mr Forester almost choked.'

'Ah, madame,' Claudette said, still looking at Kerrigan. 'I have been saving to make replacements. In France we like to drink sometimes.'

Kerrigan shook his head.

'In England we call it theft.' His grandmother attached herself to the idea that Claudette was the secret drinker and would not be separated from it despite Kerrigan's repeated confessions.

His grandmother refused to drive Claudette to Brighton where she might catch a train to her ferry. Instead, Kerrigan walked the girl to the bus-stop at the other end of the village. They shared the carrying of her big suitcase, swapping the burden every hundred yards. Banjo strolled a few yards behind them.

'I'll convince her it was me,' Kerrigan said. 'You can come back.'

'I go,' Claudette said. 'It is better if I go.'

'Better for who?'

'Be careful for the dog,' she said. 'I think your grandmother does not like her.'

'What will I do without you?'

'The time when you are at school is long,' Claudette said. 'It is too much time with her alone.'

'She hates me.'

'*Non, petit.*'

'Lie to her,' Kerrigan said. 'Not to me.'

'It was not only to take the blame from you.' Claudette dropped the suitcase on the tarmac. They stood at the side of the road with the suitcase between them.

'Why then?'

'I will miss my bus.'

'Yes.'

'You are dangerous to me, Matthew.'

Perhaps it was the sound of his Christian name on her lips which made it hard to understand the other words. They walked on in silence and reached the bus-stop by the grocery store where five other people were waiting. A group of teenage girls stood around a bench in front of the garage across the street, sullen and smirking.

'I will write to you,' Claudette said.

'Of course.'

'You must try to believe.'

'Don't go.' Kerrigan hugged her and felt the protrusion of her collar-bone against his forehead. She kissed his hair.

'*Je t'aime,*' she said.

'I love you.' The phrase surprised him, falling from his mouth on to her breast before the numbness could deaden his tongue.

3

Empty Train

A year later, Matthew met Jenny, Bill Braxton's younger sister. They were introduced before a cricket match against a rival school to which boys were encouraged to invite their families. David Felshaw and Bill Braxton were the opening batsmen. Bill, aware that Kerrigan would have no relatives at the event, asked him to chaperone Jenny. She was two years older than Kerrigan. Her blond hair was heavy and straight, hanging dull and perfect to her shoulders. Kerrigan wanted to tug and disarrange it.

Once the openers were off the mark (David with a regal late cut to the boundary, Bill with a well-judged single), Jenny asked Kerrigan to take her for a walk. 'I hate it when they get bowled out,' she said.

Matthew escorted her across the water-meadows, along the river and up on to the old railway line. She accepted one of his cigarettes.

'David used to smoke these,' she said.

One night, during a bragging session in the dormitory, Kerrigan told those within hearing that he had shagged

Jenny Braxton under a bush, while rowing eights slid past. What started as a deception contrived to impress his friends became truer each time he used the fantasy scene as an aid to masturbation. By the start of the summer holidays he and the disembodied Jenny Braxton were regular bedfellows. He was a little ashamed when he received an invitation to her seventeenth birthday dinner and surprised when she phoned to check that he was available. He promised to be there.

'Black tie,' Jenny said. 'Don't forget.'

Kerrigan had many ruses for extracting from his grandmother the money which she held on his behalf. His bicycle required constant repairs and refinements; he joined but did not attend a sailing club in Shoreham; he requested bus fares to Brighton to see films and concerts, the reviews of which he scanned so as to give the old woman accounts of the performances he had pretended to attend.

His advantage over her grew as her memory faltered. When she supposed him to be his father, he allowed himself to become the dead man. He wondered what he might discover about Arthur Kerrigan from the things his grandmother said when she mistook grandson for son. There was an element of danger in the game. His grandmother could surface into lucidity as rapidly as she plunged into confusion. Her temporal fugues often misled Matthew into thinking her stupid. She had not altogether lost her nose for sniffing out a lie.

He persuaded her that he would need funds to make his way, by train and taxi, to Jenny's house in Hampshire. 'And I should buy her a present,' he added.

'Don't knock her up, Arthur.'

'She doesn't care for me, mama.' He adopted the endearment which he remembered his father using with his grandmother, pronouncing it to rhyme with cigar.

'You called her Tricia when you thought you were in

love.' The old woman's hands lay on her lap. They looked like the twisted roots of vines. 'Patricia was never the girl for you.' Patricia was Kerrigan's mother.

'I loved her.'

'A mother knows.'

He did not reply, leaving her to whichever decade she was revisiting.

To avoid wasting money on an unnecessary taxi, he arranged to be met. He slept in the empty train and almost missed his stop. Weeds grew in the cracks between the paved platform edge and the tarmac beyond it. He stood outside the station, watching the line of trees on the far side of a field of wheat. Beyond a shallow incline, he saw the roofs of a barn and the tower of a grain silo.

Bill and Jenny Braxton pulled up beside him in an estate car slashed by streaks of dry mud. Jenny climbed out of the front seat, kissed him and sat herself in the back. His gift to her was a bracelet of Mexican silver which another girl had given him as a keepsake. The money which might have gone on a first-hand birthday present, along with the unused taxi fare, he had invested in a bottle of whisky which could be heard gurgling in his overnight bag.

Bill, still in his first month as a qualified driver, rounded the corners of the narrow high-hedged lanes with alarming speed. Jenny had been eager and a little proprietorial in her greeting. Her pleasure at seeing him was transparent. Now that she was relegated to the back seat, Bill and Matthew made no effort to include her in their conversation. Just before they arrived at the house Matthew remembered to utter a Happy Birthday.

Passing through the hall, he glanced into the dining room where a long table was laid for two-dozen guests. The sun through the french windows stretched rectangles of light and shade across white linen, gold sparking on glass and silver.

Jenny's father insisted on carrying Matthew's overnight bag. He followed the older man up the stairs, and was left to change in a dim room where the floor sloped downwards from the door to a low deep-silled window. Matthew sat by the window, gazing at a paddock where ponies had nibbled the grass down to a pale carpet. He heard fast-moving water under the wind.

He knelt at the low window, elbows canted on the cool stone sill and thought about Jenny Braxton changing in another room. After a time, he heard cars arriving on the other side of the house, voices expanding as car doors opened. He had no wish to dislodge himself from the window-sill. He sipped from the bottle, watching the stand of trees in the distance, listening to the water and wind behind the nearer voices and engines. The sounds merged like the decades and generations in his grandmother's memory. In the weave of gushing water and humming engines he heard the thread of David Felshaw's voice. The subsiding sun now illuminated only the high boughs. Long shadows reached towards him across the smooth paddocks. He was paralysed by the sound of water and did not respond to the knocking on the door.

'Can I come in?' Jenny's blue dress was made of heavy satin, strapless and tight. Her flesh leaked from it, as if she had swollen since she last wore it. Matthew remained kneeling by the window.

'We're ready downstairs.' Jenny stood by the bed.

'You look good.' The dress really was too tight.

'Can I have some of that?' she asked.

'What's behind those trees?'

She stooped to look through the window.

'Will you show me?' He handed her the bottle. 'Later on?'

He gave her the silver bangle, unwrapped, warm from his jeans pocket. Tears formed in the corners of her eyes. 'You shouldn't have.'

'I know.'

'Do you need help getting dressed?'

'I'm fine,' he said. 'I'll be down in a minute.'

After she quit the room he fell over in an attempt to aim his foot into his trousers. The uncapped whisky toppled from the sill. He grabbed at the chugging bottle, saving half of what he had not yet drunk. He used a hand-towel to wipe up the spillage. He heard some of the whisky drip between the floorboards and imagined it seeping through the ceiling of the room below.

After the trial of fitting studs into his shirt he was incapable of tying his bow-tie. Even when he turned from the mirror and talked himself through the required manoeuvres with his eyes closed, the slithery material refused to take shape under his fingers. He slumped, defeated, on to the floor, one arm on the window-sill to support himself. With each passing moment of immobility the prospect of movement became more remote.

He did not hear the door open. 'Told you it was strong, didn't I?'

'Can you smell it?' Matthew asked.

'Jenny sent me up to sort you out.'

'I heard your voice.' Matthew struggled to stand up. 'I thought I was imagining it.'

'I'm no ghost.' David Felshaw lifted the bottle from the sill and drank. 'I'm flesh, blood and appetite.'

'I don't believe in ghosts.'

'Get dressed, then.'

'Why should I?' Matthew reached for the bottle, but David held it away from the outstretched hand.

'Can't you let them rest in peace?' David said.

'They won't leave me alone,' Matthew said. 'It's not me doing it.'

David slapped Kerrigan across the face, once on each cheek. 'Stand up.' David steadied him, holding his shoulders lightly until Kerrigan nodded that he had found his balance. 'Keep still while I do this.' David knotted Kerrigan's bow-tie at the first attempt, nudged Kerrigan's chin up with his knuckles and leant back to check the look of the younger man's collar. Kerrigan keeled towards the window-sill. David grabbed his lapels and held him upright.

'You didn't have to hit me.'

David laughed. 'You didn't have to get legless.'

'You don't know anything.' Kerrigan practised standing up straight and keeping his balance while David worked intently over a hand mirror which he had placed on the bedside table. 'What are you doing?'

'Try to be cool,' David said. 'Don't go telling matron.'

'I'm not going down there.'

'Don't spoil her party,' David said.

'I hardly know her.'

'I'm not bothered about Jenny.' David swept the white powder into two long ridges with a razor blade.

'What makes you think you understand?'

'I don't have to think about it,' David said. 'Watch me and then do the same.' David took a short plastic drinking straw from his waistcoat pocket and used it to snort one of the ridges of powder up his nostril. 'Breathe out before you get close to the mirror.'

Matthew snorted the powder. Someone grabbed his slouched resolve and stood it to attention. Slack muscles tightened. A zinging clarity wiped all the muzziness from his mind. Five minutes later, he had become an incredibly interesting person of whom the dinner party should by no means be deprived. This conviction, along with the energy which accompanied it, lasted long enough to get him down the stairs, seated and into conversation with Jenny Braxton, on whose right he was placed. As the main course was served his state of dreamy anaesthesia returned along with the impression that immense physical effort was required to simply sit upright and listen to the story Jenny was telling him about a friend of hers who had walked across Wales for charity. He clung to an image of a girl walking across the mammal rather than the country and, stifling a giggle, was suddenly conscious of being the youngest person in the room. He was flattered and intimidated to be included in a group which harboured David Felshaw and Bill Braxton.

At the other end of the table, David talked to a dark-haired girl with a Gypsy complexion. Her pretty shoulders were thrown into relief by the narrow silk straps which held up her black dress. Matthew imagined being the dark-haired girl, close to the flame of David's attention, or being David, singeing the girl as he drew her closer. David caught his eye, smiled and shook his head. Was it David's conceit which enabled him to sense not just when he was being talked about but when he was being thought about, too?

'—and when she arrived in Gloucester, half the town was out on the street to greet her. How anyone could have the willpower to walk on their own like that for days simply amazes me.' It did not seem particularly amazing to Matthew, who could think of nothing to say in reply.

The girl next to David was smiling. Her straight teeth, bared in a wide smile, suggested other hidden perfections which might be revealed at any moment. As she leant forward and turned away from Matthew, hair falling to conceal her face, he glimpsed the deep shadow beyond her exposed shoulder-blade. Now David was telling her something, glancing at Matthew as he spoke. The girl looked down the table and grinned directly at Matthew just as he was beginning to chew on a mouthful of food. He attempted to smile back at her but saw, from the look on her face, that his crammed cheeks had rendered his expression absurd.

As soon as he had finished the food on his plate, the lights were extinguished. Mrs Braxton walked into the room carrying a cake on which the seventeen candles were glow-worms which might, at any moment, fly free of the icing. Matthew's numbness, a familiar visitation like toothache or desire, intensified as the party sang 'Happy Birthday', peaking at the scream with which Jenny accompanied her first stab at the cake. As life returned to his limbs he promised himself that he would be kind, wondering what form his kindness might have to take. Part of it would involve matching her attentiveness to him with an equivalent concentration upon her. He applied himself to this task. He noticed that the olive-skinned girl's black straps had slipped off her shoulders. David made her laugh, simply by raising his eyebrow. She leant close to him, laughter shaking her body, her breasts swaying under silk.

After dinner, Bill caught Matthew's eye and gestured that he should follow him upstairs. David and the girl lay sprawled on Bill's bed, sharing a joint. She passed it to Matthew. He saw and then tasted her red lipstick on the filter. She wore a solemn expression now, as if sharing the joint required a ritual attention which could not admit of frivolity. Matthew drew hard and held the smoke in his lungs until he let out an involuntary squeak. David and the girl lay beside one another, not touching, staring at the ceiling.

'Go to it, Kerrigan,' David said. Matthew returned down-stairs, found Jenny and sat near her.

When the party broke up, David hugged Matthew, whispering *courage* in his ear. Matthew sat alone in the dining room while Jenny said goodbye to the last guests. Only Matthew, too young to drive and with no parents nearby to collect him, would be staying the night at the Braxtons' house. For the first time that evening he was more sober than he wanted to be. He took a half-empty wine bottle from the middle of the table and walked through the open french windows on to a wide expanse of lawn. In his mind he repeated the question he could not ask Jenny Braxton.

Standing in the night garden, he looked back at the lit windows and saw Jenny enter the dining room, smooth her hair, check herself in the mirror over the mantelpiece and wipe something from her lower lip with her middle finger. He sat on the grass and drank from the bottle. Who was the girl who had left with David Felshaw? David had failed, either by design or indifference, to give away anything about her. Matthew lit a cigarette, holding the match until the flame nipped his fingertips. Jenny approached across the lawn, lifting the hem of her long dress above her ankles. 'Can I have one?'

He lit her cigarette and listened as she told him how the image of his face blooming under the match-light had been beautiful, a pool of warmth expanding and then contracting to the pinprick glow of the cigarette's orange tip, floating above the lawn in darkness. Christ, Matthew thought. I make her feel poetic.

'The dew,' she said. 'You must be soaking.'

'It was a good party.'

'I can't sit down here,' Jenny said. 'I'll ruin my dress.'

'Let's go inside,' he said.

'That's not what I meant.' She walked further into the darkness, away from the house. Matthew rolled over on to all fours and pushed himself on to his feet.

'I love my present,' she said as he caught up with her. He stifled the urge to tell her where it came from, to describe the other girl. 'Don't you love birthdays?'

'Of course.'

'I'm so glad you came.' She was very close to him as they walked, her bare shoulder bucking against his jacketed arm. He could see an obstacle up ahead in the darkness. She maintained her course. They reached a hedge and stopped. 'You were very drunk.'

'Not now,' he said.

'No?' she asked. 'Not now?'

'Look—'

'What?' Her face was close to his. There was nothing for it but to kiss her. He touched his lips to her cheek, far back, near her temple. She placed her fingertips on his white shirt-front and waited.

'I'm sorry.' The anaesthetic flooded his arms and legs. He fell forward but her palms, flat against his shirt-front, forced him to remain almost upright against her.

'Don't be.' She put her arms around him. He was propped against her like a grandfather clock tipped against a workman's shoulder. 'You're here.'

Matthew certainly appeared to be there with her on the night lawn, the thickness of her perfume catching in his throat. He could think of no gentle words with which to explain. 'Your Mum and Dad?'

'They've gone to bed,' Jenny said. 'They trust me.'

'I really like you.' He closed his eyes and saw an image of David and the olive-skinned girl walking across the paddock towards the trees, David's hair invisible against the back of his dinner jacket, the girl's mane stark against the exposed skin of her back.

'Do you remember what you said to me?' Jenny asked. 'When we walked by the river that afternoon?'

He could remember nothing that had been said that afternoon. It was all buried under the things which he had subsequently invented.

'You said you loved the countryside in summer, but in darkness, when there were only shapes and shadows, not colours.'

'Like now,' he said.

'Is now what you were trying to describe?'

'Something like now,' he lied.

'Well?' She stepped back to avoid falling under the weight

of him, assuming that he had the power to right himself. He fell to his knees in front of her like an arcane suitor.

'You don't have to be nice, you know.' She pulled the tight part of the dress higher up her thighs so as to squat in front of him. 'That's not why I invited you.'

Matthew's skin began to prickle.

'I've ruined it now,' she said. 'I have, haven't I?'

'You didn't mean to,' he said.

'Jesus.' She stood up abruptly and stomped towards the house.

'It's my fault,' he said, aiming the words at the back of her head. She turned but he could not see the expression on her face. 'It's my fault,' he repeated.

In the morning, breakfasting with Colonel and Mrs Braxton, Matthew and Jenny observed the rituals of friendship, enquiring after each other's soundness of sleep, exclaiming at the success of the dinner party. Jenny's dour expression aggravated Matthew's hangover.

'I hope your bed was comfortable.' Jenny's tone prompted her mother and father to exchange a look. In fact, Matthew had woken before dawn and been unable to recapture sleep.

'It was a surprise to see David again,' Matthew said.

'It's Alison I know. They're inseparable.' Jenny seemed to regret this fact. Or was she telling Matthew something else? 'When people first meet them they think she's his girlfriend.'

'Isn't she?' Matthew wanted to smoke a cigarette.

'They're brother and sister,' Jenny said. 'But they like to come across as an item. Can you imagine that, Matthew? Pretending to be someone's *boyfriend* when you're no such thing?'

4 ∫

Spangled

David Felshaw and Bill Braxton left school together at the end of the autumn term. Kerrigan returned, in the new year, to the society of other fifteen year olds who still resented his friendship with the departed seniors.

In the first week of the following summer term, Kerrigan woke before dawn and rose in time to intercept the post. Determined that his sixteenth birthday should go unmarked, he had to be sure that no one in his house became aware of it. The day before his birthday, he received a letter from Bill Braxton, instructing him to be at the derelict signal hut at three o'clock the following afternoon. Matthew cycled to the rendezvous on the tow-path beside the river, remembering the acts which his sexual imagination had performed with Jenny Braxton.

As he crossed the road to reach the old railway line, he saw Bill standing beside an orange VW Beetle. Matthew waved and approached. Bill continued to stare across the water-meadows at the school. 'Dump your bike in the hedge.'

Matthew peered through the side-windows of the VW.

David was in the driving seat. There were two girls in the back. He recognised one of them as David's sister, Alison. The other he did not know. David leant across and opened the passenger door. Matthew pulled down the seat and squeezed in next to David's sister. 'He's way behind us, Ali. Give him the sacrament.'

'My heart's gone strange,' the other girl said. 'Why is my heart all curly-up?'

'Stretch your legs,' Alison said.

Bill climbed into the passenger seat and slammed the door. David started the engine. Beside Matthew, in the back of the car, Alison dug deep in her handbag, pulling things out and handing them to the other girl, who thanked Alison object by object. 'Comb.' ('Thanks.') 'Lipstick. Crystal. Post-card. Cigarettes.' Matthew was conscious of Alison's thigh against his own. Despite being pressed against him, she had not yet acknowledged his presence. David turned on to the main road which ran east, away from the school.

'I can't find it,' Alison said. 'I must have dropped it.'

David slowed down and pulled over. They all climbed out of the car. It began to rain. The others raised their faces to the sky. Matthew watched as raindrops fell on Alison's cheeks.

'I'm crying from the outside,' Alison said.

David put his arm around Matthew's shoulder. 'She's dropped the box. Little silver pill-box. Look in the back, on the floor.'

'Won't they get wet?'

'Doesn't everything?' David said.

Matthew found the pill-box wedged between the horizontal and the vertical cushions of the back seat. He handed it to David, who opened it and unfolded a piece of black paper. Inside were three tiny nuggets of a red crystalline substance. 'Take this, which is my flesh. And this' – he handed Matthew a carton of orange juice – 'which is my blood.' Matthew pinched one of the nuggets between thumb and forefinger, placed it on his tongue and swallowed it down with a slug of juice. David watched, and when the ingestion was complete, kissed him on the cheek, his hands in Matthew's hair. Then he turned Matthew towards his sister. 'He's joining us, Ali,' he said. 'Matthew will be with us soon.'

She dropped her chin, dragging her attention away from the raindrops. She placed her hand, palm outstretched, flat against Matthew's chest. Then her arm went limp and the hand slid off him. David walked Matthew along the verge to the fence against which the other girl was now leaning. 'Josephine,' he said, 'Matthew's coming with us. We're folding him in.'

'Don't bunch up,' Josephine said. 'We need intervals.'

'Evenly spaced.' David backed away from her.

'Like—'

'Bollards?' Matthew suggested.

David drove. Matthew sat next to him in the front. In the back, Alison, Bill and Josephine dried each other's hair with wads of kitchen roll. The rain fell across the windscreen in thick sheets. Matthew lost his sense of direction and could no longer guess where David might be taking them. They drove into a corridor of swirling water, deeper into rain, further into the drumming on the roof and the bonnet, into the sizzle and rush of water under the tyres.

Matthew's body grew lighter, as if he had shucked a loaded rucksack after a day's walk. His shoulders wanted to rise above his neck and press against the roof of the car. His gravitational ballast had been drained by the crystal he had eaten from Alison's pill-box. Seat-belt fastened, he prepared for take-off, muscles tightened in anticipation, toying with the threat that the aircraft might fail to tear itself from the pull of the earth before tarmac turned to grass, grass to trees. A vortical giddiness accompanied his every movement – reaching forward to tip ash into the ashtray, turning to change the pressure of the seat-belt across his chest – a liquefying desire to twist to the left. The boundaries of his body crumbled as he melted into the seat, feet thawing on to the floor.

'Happy Birthday, Matthew,' David shouted above the music.

'When do I come down?'

'In the morning,' David said. 'With the light.'

Matthew tried to read the hands on his watch but could not make out the time. Then he realised that he could not read the watch because darkness had, in fact, fallen. 'When did it get dark?' He turned down the volume on the tape machine. 'Where are we going?'

'Too many questions,' David said.

'Hey,' Bill said. 'Be careful.' David steered the car back on to the left-hand side of the road.

'I'm your brother,' David said.

'I'm all spangled,' Josephine said.

'I'll be all of your mother,' Alison giggled. 'I'll be mother to all of you.'

'Drop it, Ali.' David slowed the car down. Matthew struggled to undo his seat-belt.

'Who wants some apple?' Alison held the half-eaten fruit close to Matthew's face, her arm extended through the gap between the front seats. He could smell her skin. He wanted to lick it. 'It's made of ash,' he said. Alison dropped the apple, which fell on David's thigh and rolled on to the floor at his feet.

'Fuck.' David reached a hand below the steering wheel to sweep the floor in search of the fruit.

'Watch out!' Bill slammed his palms against the back of David's seat. The VW lumbered on to the wide grass verge. Matthew lurched forward, banging his cheek against the dashboard. The car came to a halt under the broad canopy of an oak tree, front bumper nuzzled into a hedge.

'Wow,' Josephine said.

'It's stopped raining.' Alison wiped mist from the window beside her face. 'I can't hear the rain.'

Matthew closed his eyes and listened for the fall of water beyond the canopy of leaves. The low hiss of an approaching vehicle transformed into a splashing roar as a lorry steamed past. In the darkness, Matthew imagined that the VW, rather than sliding off the road, had slipped out of orbit and was tumbling, as weightless as he, into emptiness.

'Well, I'm going for a pee,' Alison said. 'Let me out.'

Matthew stood in a row with the others, the long grass soaking his trouser legs, to form a barrier behind which Alison could squat. Beams of light angled into the distant sky, puncturing the low clouds and then, with the sound of an approaching car, veered to shine on the four of them. Matthew shielded his eyes with his arm. He glanced over his shoulder at Alison, crouched by the tree, her bare legs revealed in disjointed sections by the corridors of light which passed between the standing bodies. Out of the corner of his eye, Matthew saw that Bill was also gazing at Alison. The car passed, Alison disappeared. The trace of the headlamps was branded on to Matthew's retinae. Wherever he looked, wobbling streaks of white light jumped across his vision.

'You're bleeding,' David said. 'Matthew, your mouth is bleeding.'

'Ali, have you got tissues?' Josephine asked. 'We need tissues.'

'I want to go home.' Matthew began to weep. The iron tang of his blood mingled with the salt of his tears. The combination tasted like barbeque-flavoured crisps. He was hungry. 'Take me home.'

Once the car was back on the road, Bill drove, Josephine

next to him. Matthew sat in the back between David and Alison, the arms of brother and sister overlapping behind his neck, their hands joined over his stomach. Matthew guided Bill, turning by turning, towards the village on the perimeter of which his grandmother's cottage stood. As they passed through the village under cover of darkness, Matthew directed Bill to take the road which wound down the hill into the valley below the cottage.

'Turn right here.'

Bill slowed the car and steered between puddled ruts. As the car rounded the first corner, the headlights revealed a lake, stretching across the lane. 'Where now?'

'The stream floods the road when there's heavy rain,' Matthew said. 'I know the way by heart.'

Bill edged the car forward according to Matthew's instructions. The VW glided across the lake. When the lane was visible again, Matthew turned and looked through the back window. The grey pallor of dawn, or perhaps moonlight behind cloud, polished the lake's surface. The rain had stopped. Matthew saw a succession of VWs, clones of the vehicle in which he sat, crossing the lake. One veered off the submerged lane and sank. The others followed as if, like the carriages of a train, they were linked. Car after car submerged beneath the lake. 'I'm losing it,' he said. David and Alison tightened their embrace around him.

The lane straightened. Bill accelerated. Then he slammed on the brakes. David, Matthew and Alison were thrown forward as one body. 'I think I hit it.' Bill switched off the engine and climbed out of the car. As Matthew followed, he saw that Josephine was asleep in the front seat. 'Banjo?' Matthew called. He felt the dog's coat slide under his hand, then hot breath on his knuckles.

The dawn stretched open a band of scarlet above the line of the hill. Matthew, Bill, David and Alison followed Banjo along the lane on foot. The black retriever ran ahead of them, then circled back, trotted up to Matthew, nuzzled his hand and bounded away again. They walked up the rise beyond the house in which Matthew had lived with his mother and father. Above the South Downs, the clouds were towering pink giants, solid as stalactites, suspended from Heaven. David and Alison stood either side of Matthew, their arms across his shoulders.

'It'll never look like this again,' Matthew said.

'It'll never be like this again,' David said. Banjo bolted down the hill, towards Matthew's parents' old home.

'I should go back to Josephine,' Bill said.

'She's sleeping,' Matthew said.

'She's our responsibility.' Bill turned to descend the hill.

'Let her sleep,' David said. 'She's stable now.'

'No,' Alison said, 'we should watch her.' She slipped her arm from Matthew's shoulder. His skin was suddenly cold now that hers no longer protected it. 'We should have stayed with her,' she said over her shoulder as she set off down the hill.

'Girls are strange,' Matthew said.

'She gets jealous,' David said. 'As soon as Bill takes an interest in anyone.'

'Bill and Alison?' Matthew asked.

'What's it to you?' David gave Matthew a playful shove.

'Should we go back?'

'You don't get it, do you?' David walked out into the field. 'Nobody goes back. There's no way back.'

'I'm going back,' Matthew said.

'You're not listening,' David said.

Matthew heard Banjo barking, urgent and forlorn, in the valley. He ran down the hill. He heard David running just behind him. As they approached the abandoned car, Matthew saw that the passenger door was open. Alison and Bill were wading towards it. Banjo splashed and plunged beyond them. A cigarette packet floated in the shallows at the edge of the lake. The tone of Banjo's barking changed, choked into a higher register. The dog plunged her head into the lake and emerged shaking water from her muzzle.

Bill surged through the water and dived beside Banjo. He rose from the cloudy water, juddering from the cold. 'There's nothing.' Banjo plunged her snout into the water again. 'Where the fuck is she?' Bill shouted. Matthew caught up with them and grabbed Banjo's collar, pulling the dog's head out of the water. Banjo twisted her head free of his grip and turned to snarl at him. 'It's me.' He offered the palm of his hand for the dog to sniff. 'It's Matthew.' Banjo snarled at him once more, then plunged her head into the lake. Matthew had to use all his strength to stop himself collapsing into the knee-high water.

He heard laughter and turned to see Josephine stumbling through shallow water towards him. She stopped by David, who was squatting on the bonnet of the car, and kissed his mouth. Alison found a tarpaulin in the boot of the car and wrapped it around Bill. Together with Josephine, they climbed into the back of the car. David settled behind the wheel. 'Come on, Kerrigan,' he said. 'The dog's crazy.'

'Wait.' Matthew was certain, in that moment, that Banjo possessed all the sanity there was in the dawn valley. He called gently to his dog. The animal stood her ground, legs submerged, back, tail and head sleek above the surface. 'Come, girl.' Banjo raised her head, howled at the clouds and then surged through the water, away from the car, towards Matthew's parents' house.

Matthew passed his A levels and secured a place at university. He chose to start his degree the following October, declining the opportunity to take a year off. He returned to his grandmother's cottage, laden with books, at the end of each university term. In his second year, he started wearing glasses, the prescription necessitated by his habit of smoking dope and then reading for hours at a time. He had to strain his eyes to keep the page in focus. With each successive visit to the cottage, he noticed his grandmother drawing closer to the time when she could no longer fend for herself. In the attic bedroom, where Matthew lay with Banjo at his feet, unassisted sleep evaded him. The childhood carousel on which he had ridden with his mother and father was replaced – on his many wakeful nights – by images of Alison, Bill, David and Josephine, and by a Matthew whom he did not recognise as himself, more an amalgam of Matthew and Banjo.

One evening during Matthew's finals term, he was telephoned by his grandmother's next-door neighbour. 'She can't manage no more,' the neighbour said.

Matthew arrived at his grandmother's cottage the following day. The stench of stale urine in the hallway wrinkled his nostrils. In the drawing room, it rendered the air unbreathable. In the kitchen, a yoghurt carton punctured by toothmarks lay under the table. Shredded and chewed food packaging littered the rest of the floor. The sink was brimful of greasy water, crockery submerged like the debris of a shipwreck.

He opened every window in the house and set about the business of clearing up. He asked the neighbour to come in and help his grandmother to change her clothes. He worked on the kitchen, emptying rotting food from the fridge, sweeping the charred remains of unidentifiable delicacies from the oven and the grill, carrying stacks of old newspapers and bin-loads of rubbish into the back garden. He piled them on the spot near the compost heap where he had buried Banjo the previous year.

His grandmother's favourite chair in the drawing room was the primary source of the stench. He moved her from the dished seat of the tawny velvet armchair and made her sit in its unsullied twin on the other side of the picture window. Then he picked up the chair and carried it through the hall, past the kitchen and out of the back door into the garden. He placed it like a throne on top of the pile of newspapers and bagged garbage. In her bedroom, the sheets were grey at the centre, white only where the linen ran down the side of the mattress or had been tucked under it. He stripped the mattress and flipped it over before fitting clean sheets. He made a bundle of her old bedclothes and carried it down the stairs. The fire in the garden smouldered and flared through the evening.

After he had helped his grandmother upstairs to bed, he laid out his books on the dining-room table and settled himself for an evening of revision. It was not long before he rose and wandered through the silent house, finding Banjo's old lead in the pantry and a brown envelope containing his school reports in a drawer in the hall. He lay on what had been Claudette's bed in the attic. He stood at the window of his old bedroom. In the moonlit valley, the trees concealed the house which had once belonged to his parents.

When he was sure his Gran was asleep he took the photo-albums from the bottom drawer of her desk. He watched from the back door as the moon cleared a cloud, unfurling a shadow of the house across the lawn in the back garden. The smoke from the fire was acrid and sweet and he wondered whether there were dead creatures being cremated along with yesterday's news and the linen the old lady had soiled. He tore sheets of heavy cream vellum from the album, pages on which the photographs were mounted. The vellum caught quickly on the embers of the dying fire. The photographs were slower to burn. Arthur Kerrigan and his sainted childhood melted and twisted before the flames wormed through the middle of each image, eating a widening hole all the way to the edge. That night he did not sleep.

He spent the afternoons of the next three days visiting nursing homes. In these converted country houses, the odour of micturition was only slightly better masked than in his grandmother's cottage. She would find it familiar, homely even. 'Yes,' he said to Mr Largesse, the proprietor of Longacres, 'I think she will like it here.' The pension fund which his father had started on her behalf had been topped up in his will. It would cover at least a decade of the fees. She was seventy and, stout as she was, he did not believe she could hold out beyond eighty.

At Longacres, she would have a private suite with alleged twenty-four-hour nursing care, meals brought to her room, a television and an orthopaedically-adjustable bed. She would be spared, unless she chose to partake of it, the television lounge where friable ancients gawped at eternity.

'Arthur, you promised?'

'You'll like it there,' he said. 'With people your own age.' His father had used the same phrase when persuading the young Matthew that he would be better off at boarding school.

'You promised I could come to live with you.' His grandmother stared out of the window.

For the first time in years, he rebelled against being mistaken for his father. 'Arthur is dead, Gran,' he said. 'He was killed in a car accident on his way to visit me at school.'

She smiled. 'All you could think of was cake.'

'I was ten years old,' Kerrigan said. 'I had to think about something.'

'You made me bake a cake the day after my son died.'

'It was the same day,' Kerrigan said.

'Haven't I been punished enough?'

'You'll have your own room,' Kerrigan said. 'People will come and visit you.'

'Arthur would never have let this happen,' she said.

Something stopped Matthew from disclosing that his father had planned exactly this fate for her. The pension scheme designed to pay for her retirement home had been set up when she was still in her fifties. Arthur Kerrigan had decided to salt his mother away in an oldsters' farm fifteen years before the need for it arose.

'There is ash all over the lawn?' Her eyesight – like her sense of time – was as suddenly acute as it was sometimes hazy.

'I've been burning your rubbish,' he said.

'And now you'll be going back down the hill,' the old woman said.

'Not anymore.'

'Arthur would have come more often,' the old lady said. 'But she wouldn't let him.'

'He loved you, Gran.'

'Don't force me to go.'

'Longacres is the best in the area,' Matthew said. 'Give it a chance.'

'I know how it will be,' the old woman said. 'Where's the other chair gone?'

'I got rid of it,' Matthew said.

'Did anyone give you permission?'

'It stank,' he said. 'The whole place stinks. You're like a child without a nappy.'

'Where did you learn to be so heartless?'

'Where do you think?'

They came for her in a private ambulance. Nurse Bradshaw, from Longacres, made a choice of clothes from his grandmother's wardrobe and packed them into suitcases. The old woman seemed unaware of what was happening until the nurse took her arm and asked her if she was ready.

'Photographs,' the grandmother said. 'I am allowed to take photographs?'

'Anything you like,' Nurse Bradshaw said. Matthew took

the framed pictures of his father from the mantelpiece, the table-tops, from the walls.

'The albums.'

'She lost the albums,' Matthew whispered to the nurse. 'Years ago.'

'We'll make sure you get your albums, dear.' Nurse Bradshaw led the old woman to the door of the cottage. 'Off we go, then.'

'I miss my Arthur,' the old woman said to no one in particular. 'I never should have let him go.'

'They all leave the nest, don't they?'

'I was a good mother.'

'Yes, dear.'

'And now he's throwing me out.' The old woman stopped on the garden path. Nurse Bradshaw turned to look at Matthew. He nodded his permission. Nurse Bradshaw put her arm around the old woman's shoulders and forced her towards the open doors of the ambulance. He heard the scrape and scuffle of his grandmother's shoes on the brick path.

5

Ten Quid

For a year after graduation, Matthew supplemented his inheritance by doing freelance research for a marketing consultancy. He bought a two-bedroom flat in Earl's Court, where occasional visitors included David but never Alison. He leavened his boredom with small, malicious acts. He humiliated a girlfriend at a dinner party, detailing her sexual peculiarities to the table. He bricked the windscreen of a neighbour's car. He crashed the computer network at the marketing consultancy. He baited waiters and bus conductors. He booked taxis to non-existent addresses on other people's accounts. He rang random phone numbers in the night, looking for others to share his vigil.

In the evenings, at the offices of the marketing consultancy, he entered data into the computer network, undisturbed by the daytime community of salaried employees. Silent Spanish cleaners emptied wastepaper baskets as he worked at the glimmering screen. Afterwards, he usually made his way to a squat in the World's End where a loose community of deadbeats and dissolutes included a teenager who believed he was Jimi Hendrix, an Australian biker who had broken his legs five times, a retired Hell's Angel who kept rabbits in the backyard and an American miniature called Annie, whose ankles were ulcerated from fixing speed. She drove a decommissioned black cab in which a porcelain vase affixed to the meter was daily replenished with stolen flowers. The squat offered a wide range of substances at prices as erratic as its tenants.

The ceiling of the first floor living room was lined with silver foil, fabled to enhance the effects of hallucinogens. A boom-box and a brown television, deposited by desperadoes in lieu of payment, provided entertainment. By mid-evening the room began to fill with punters. Some were immobilised by their purchases while others became hyper-animated. Gazers and gabblers, the giggling and the gauched, sat side-by-side on tattered cushions. Matthew, as a loyal customer, claimed a place near Mike, the retired Hell's Angel, from whom the better products could usually be had. While none of the squatters could claim any rights to the house, Mike was its self-elected landlord. His talent for enforcement guaranteed that his whims were accepted as imperatives.

One evening, Tony – an occasional resident and compulsive scrounger – turned up the sound on the television, overstepping one of Mike's most sensitive boundaries. Mike frogmarched Tony to the backyard and corrected him with a hammer. Later that night, Matthew waited for a consignment of Durban Poison. He watched television with Mike and the Australian, smoking the spliffs that were passed to him, doused in impatient anticipation of what might, or might not arrive.

'He needed sorting,' Mike said. Tony had stumbled out of the squat on recovering consciousness, blood trickling from his left ear.

'He'll be back,' the Australian said.

'He best not come back with me here,' Mike said. 'Where's that Dave?'

'Fuck knows,' the Australian said.

'What happened to the skins?' Mike asked.

'Don't look at me, man.'

'Say that again.'

'I said, I'm looking for them.' The Australian crawled across the floor, searching.

'That's what I thought you said.'

Matthew must have fallen asleep. The next time he was conscious, he heard a familiar voice.

'How are you going to understand Burroughs if you haven't read Nietzsche?'

'Who the fuck is Neecher?' Mike said.

'Who the fuck is Burroughs?' the Australian asked.

'Forget it,' David said. 'How much do you want?'

Matthew sat up. David glanced at him but gave no sign of recognition.

'Couple of ounces.' Mike reached into the front of his trousers.

'Can't you do better than that?' David asked.

'I'll have an ounce,' Matthew said.

'Do I know you?'

'Don't you?'

'Shut your mouth,' Mike said to Matthew in a quiet monotone. 'It's expensive, Dave.'

'It's come a long way to be here.'

Matthew stood up and nodded to Mike and the Australian.

'Where are you going?' David asked him.

'Home.'

'Don't you want your ounce?'

'Sure.'

'Wait for me downstairs.'

Matthew stood in the dark hall, looking at the deserted street through the cracks between the boards covering the windows.

When they were outside, David shook his head. 'I'm

disappointed.' He unlocked the door of a green Jaguar. 'Very second-rate.'

'I get by,' Matthew said.

'Don't hang out there.' David started the car. 'Come to me.'

'How was I supposed to know where you were?'

'Use your initiative, for fuck's sake.' David threw him a bag. 'Roll one. Those people are losers.'

'You don't return my calls,' Matthew said.

'What am I?' David said. 'Your boyfriend?'

'Stop the car.'

'Simmer down, Kerrigan.' David accelerated. 'I was out of the country.' They drove in silence for some moments while Matthew rolled a joint.

'How's Bill?'

'In love,' David said.

'Still?'

'My sister's his holy grail.'

'And Alison refuses to answer his prayers?'

'Bill doesn't have a love-nest in Trastevere,' David said. 'Bill lacks Latin qualities.'

'You're jealous.'

'I don't give a fuck about how she lives her life,' David said. 'Your place or mine?'

Matthew's flat in Earl's Court betrayed the evidence of David's compulsive charity. The Conran sofa, the brace of Trinitrons, the new towels and bed-linen, the antique kilim, were all flashy advertisements for David's underworld connections. It had cost him nothing more than ingenuity to furnish Matthew's flat. Matthew was the butt of David's generosity, trapped into gratitude.

David strolled through the modest rooms and found them wanting. 'Why don't you throw away the bottles when they're empty?'

'I was busy.'

'Get a cleaner,' David said. 'I go away for three weeks and you start living like a savage. There's a cigarette end in this shoe.'

'You haven't called me for six months.' Matthew sat on the green sofa while David collected bottles and dirty plates and put them in the kitchen. 'Your answering machine has run out of message space.'

'Want a beer?' David called out, as he opened the fridge door.

'There's vodka in the freezer.'

'Try this.' David dropped an envelope on the table and flopped down on the sofa beside Matthew.

'Who did that?' Matthew had noticed a cluster of circular scars on David's forearm.

'You really want to know?' David unsealed the envelope. Inside it were a dozen folds of paper. He opened one of the folds and tipped a quantity of magnolia-tinted powder on to the glass table-top. He used an Am-Ex card to shape the powder into four plump lines.

'I was scared.'

David rolled a ten-pound note into a tube and handed it to Matthew. 'What the fuck do you know about it?'

'We're not on the street,' Matthew said.

'Forget it.'

'So tell me.' Matthew snorted two lines of the powder.

'I delivered short. The guy I was acting for stiffed me on the money. So they took me upriver to a hut in the forest, left me to think it over. No water. No phone. Then they came back. Little Indian woman with a flat face started asking me questions in Spanish. What the fuck did I know? She offered me a cigarette. I hadn't had a smoke in a day and a half. She put the cigarette in my mouth, held a match for me, let me puff for a while. My hands and feet were tied so I was gripping the filter between my teeth as I smoked. Then she took the cigarette out of my mouth.'

David snorted the two remaining lines of powder. 'I think she had a good time.'

'And you?'

'I passed out after the third time.'

'Jesus.'

'When I came round, she was creaming this other guy with a spiked club.' David started to laugh.

'You liked that?'

'She was going to do it to somebody,' David said.

'You're winding me up,' Matthew said.

'You wish.'

A week later, after a business trip to Brighton, David arrived at Matthew's flat with a bundle in his arms.

'Saw your name on the pedigree. Great grandmother: Banjo, brackets, Kerrigan, close brackets.'

'I was asleep.' It was after midnight.

'She's yours, orphan.' David hoisted the puppy, wrapped in a white towel, into Matthew's arms. 'The dog of the dog of your dog. She's family.'

'I don't want this.' Matthew avoided looking at the stubby snout sticking out of the bundle.

'Trust me,' David said. 'I know what you need.'

'What's her name?'

'Char,' David said. 'Move over.' He stepped past Matthew into the flat. 'As in Charlotte. Girl I met.'

Matthew carried the warm bundle to the sofa and unwrapped it.

'Take this thing away,' he said.

'Which thing?'

'This—' Matthew paused. 'This animal.'

'I thought you meant the telly,' David said. 'Or maybe the sofa.'

'David.'

'What?'

'Nothing,' Matthew said. 'You surprised me.'

'Look, if you don't want the dog, don't have the dog.'

'I'm sorry,' Matthew said. 'You don't understand.'

'I should take the dog away,' David said.

'No,' Matthew said. 'I'm sorry.'

David stood up and smiled. 'What are you doing for the next couple of hours?'

'Going back to sleep.'

'Can I borrow your car?'

'I've got to visit the old woman in the morning,' Matthew said.

'I won't be long,' David said. 'Hang out at my place while I'm gone. Try the new brown.'

'How is it?'

'You had Chinese rocks?'

'Once.'

'Before they were stamped on?'

'Who knows?' Matthew said.

'Well, this is better,' David said. 'Eighty-five per cent.'

'Two hours?'

'Less, probably.' David held out his hand.

'What?'

'Wake up, orphan. I need your car keys.'

They climbed the stairs to David's flat, the dog bundled in Matthew's arms.

'A bloke named Silus is coming round with some money,' David said.

'The catch being?'

'You remember Base?'

'No, David.'

'The dude with the printed hair.'

'No way.'

'You don't have to let him in,' David said. 'Give it to him through the letter-box.'

'Absolutely not,' Matthew said. 'I can't handle people the way you can.'

David juggled a bunch of keys to unlock the door. 'He won't come before two and by that time you'll have the four grand from Silus.' David pulled the gas fire out from its surround and reached behind it. 'Silus may want a gram. Give it to him for eighty.' David handed him two folds of paper. 'This is strong, all right? There's milk in the fridge for the dog. Heat it and let it cool to sterilise. And give Base three grand. Whatever he says. Three grand.'

'David—'

'Feed your dog.' Matthew heard David running down the stairs in the wake of the door slamming.

The fifth floor flat on Hammersmith Grove had a shabby gentility. The rooms had struggled to retain the character given them by David's absent sister. Although Alison shared the place with David, Matthew could see her influence had been missing during the months in which she had been living in Italy. He had never been alone in the flat before. He took the opportunity to snoop, opening doors along the corridor, looking for Alison's room. Before he found it he entered a room which was evidently David's. Clothes were strewn on a half-folded futon mattress. Paperbacks were canted on the carpet like tents in a field. A mirror, flat on the floor beside the mattress, was smeared where wetted fingers had swabbed the remains of powders.

The walls were closely covered with framed photographs. It took Matthew a few moments to realise that they were all of Alison. He heard a low extended quack in the hallway. He turned off the light in David's room and walked along the corridor to pick up the Entryphone.

'Let me up.'

'Who's that?' Matthew asked.

'Who the fuck are you?'

'Never mind.'

'Let me the fuck in,' said the voice on the Entryphone. 'It's Base.'

'You're early.'

'You what?'

'Come back in an hour.'

'Don't shit me.'

'Come back later,' Matthew said. 'Come back after two.' He replaced the Entryphone on its wall-cradle. The extended quack sounded again. The telephone started shrilling in the living room. Matthew noticed that since his last visit the door had been fitted with four new locks. He turned keys in each to secure the flat.

As soon as he picked up the phone a female voice talked at him, as if its owner had been in the middle of a conversation on which Matthew was now eavesdropping: ' – can't believe you haven't phoned me and you're never in and Mum and Dad haven't had sight or sound of you in months, which may mean weeks, but still. David, you cannot go on like this! Do I have to fly home to get you to do anything? David? David?'

'Yes?' Matthew was accustomed to not being himself.

'I must have the wrong number.'

'It's me,' Matthew said. 'Matthew?'

'The one who trashes the flat?'

'I just got here.'

'That's what they all say.'

'You know me.' Matthew's free hand covered his ear to block the continuous quack.

'There's someone at the door,' Alison said.

'I'll wait.'

'At your end,' she said. 'I can hear the buzzer. Is David all right?'

'He went out for a while.'

'It's after midnight. Where is he? He's never there. What's he doing? Does he look ill?'

Matthew had an image of Base downstairs, leaning his palm against the button which made the quacking constant in the hallway.

'He seems fine.'

'Tell him to ring me,' Alison said. 'Say I'll ring him in an hour.'

'Which?'

'I can hear someone thumping on the door,' Alison said. 'What's going on? Is he in trouble?'

'I'll tell him, OK? Got to go.' The puppy was whimpering on the sofa. The thumping stopped and a hinge squeaked as someone pushed open the letter-box from the outside.

'I'm coming in.'

Matthew did not move.

'You hear me, Davey,' Base shouted. 'I want my fucking wedge. Not later or tomorrow or next week but right here and now.'

Keeping away from the opening of the letter-box, Matthew leant over, holding the doorframe, to peer through the fish-eye at the figure of Base. His head was shaved, except for a patch at the back where the barber had razored out the letters of his name. His skin was slick with sweat over swollen muscles. He leapt to the carpet by the door and shouted through the letter-box. 'Why'd I give you a chance, you cunt?' Pause. 'You ever learn respect, I'll fuck my mother.' And then, quietly, 'Let me in or I'm busting in.'

The quacking door-buzzer sounded. The phone started shrilling again. Matthew sat and then lay down on the carpet in the hall. Then he stood up and went to the phone in the living room.

'Davey, my man, what is the shake?'

'Yeah,' Matthew said.

'How it is, Silus suffer a delay, hear me now.'

'Yeah?'

'Davey, that you, bwoy?'

'David's back later. He told me you'd be round.'

'I will be,' Silus said. 'What can I tell you, man?'

Matthew heard a crashing thud in the hallway. The quacking doorbell sounded again. 'Bring the money,' Matthew said. 'Please.'

'Love to, man. Would just love to do that thing, but what can I say? Sylvia she jus' mash up my plans.'

Matthew slapped the phone down, the numbness starting in his mouth and his wrists. A terrible thundering crunch, accompanied by an ominous splintering, issued from the hallway. The phone rang again. The doorbell quacked. He took out of his pocket the two folds of paper David had given him, remembering other folds of paper in other pockets. He opened one of the packets and dipped his thumbnail into the magnolia-brown powder, raising his hand to his face to sniff. Then, hearing a new voice outside the door, Matthew went into the hallway.

'All right, man?'

'What you want?' Base's voice.

Matthew edged his face across the door towards the fish-eye. It was Tony, the squatter who had received the benefit of Mike's hammer.

'You spare me a cigarette, man?'

Base gave Tony a look of incredulous scorn. 'What you got for me?'

'My girlfriend's handbag was stolen,' Tony said, 'with all our money in it, right? Dave said he'd lend me enough to get the train tickets so we can go and see her kid in hospital in Oxford. He's got cancer, right? We have to, like, be there for him, man. Because the kid is going to die and my girlfriend is in a bad, bad way.'

'You scamming me?'

'I never,' Tony said. 'A man such as yourself.'

'You knock on the door now,' Base said.

'Sure,' Tony said. 'That's cool.'

'Nothing is cool,' Base said. 'Do it.'

Knock, knock, knock. 'Dave, it's Tony, right? You there, man?'

'He let you in,' Base whispered. 'Otherwise—'

'Whatever you're into is fine with me, man,' Tony said. 'Just a tenner would help. Can you spare a tenner?' And then turning back to the door – knock, knock, 'Dave, man, you have to help me out here. I've got assets I can draw on. Temporarily frozen but solid, right? Very solid.'

Matthew watched Base grab Tony from behind, pinning his arms against his sides in a bear-hug. He carried Tony to the banister and tipped him, forcing his head and shoulders over the rails.

'Respect, man,' Tony said. 'You have my respect.'

'Let me the fuck in,' Base shouted. 'Or down he goes.'

'Got to get to Oxford, man,' Tony squealed.

The phone continued to ring inside the flat.

'The money isn't here,' Matthew said. 'The guy who was supposed to bring the money didn't come.'

Base released Tony and punched him in the kidneys. Tony screamed. A female voice from a lower floor shouted, 'I'm calling the police.'

'You do that,' Base shouted back. 'See what happens, if you do that.'

Tony managed to break free and tumbled down the stairs. Base followed. Matthew inspected the bolts and the barrels on the doorjamb into which they were slotted. Everything appeared to have held. The puppy limped into the hallway. He scooped it up under his arm and went to the telephone. As he picked it up, he heard Tony wailing on a lower floor.

'How's the orphan?'

'Bastard.'

David laughed. 'What's up?'

'You bastard.'

'Silus fucked up.'

'You fucked up,' Matthew said. 'Never again, David.'

'Never say never.'

'Base is trying to bust the door down.' Matthew lit a cigarette. 'How could you do this to me? And Alison phoned.'

'Got to go, so listen up,' David said. 'The pine dresser in the kitchen. Up at the top on the left. There's a panel. Looks like facing but it slides back. Pay Base out of that. And tell Ali I'll call her in the morning. Love you, babe, and I'm out.'

'Bastard,' Matthew said, but the line was already dead. When he tried to stand up he was leaden-limbed. There was a coursing of warm honey inside the lead. The trials of conducting David's business-life now seemed less daunting. The renewed thumping on the door was muffled. Matthew placed a chair beside the kitchen dresser, moving slowly. Then he turned and vomited into the kitchen sink. Smiling, he wiped puke from his lip and climbed on to the chair. He found the sliding panel and pulled out a wedge of notes and a cylinder of silver foil.

Three thousand was how many fifties? Was it six or sixty or six hundreds? Did it really matter? Besides, the guy could bang on the door all night for all he cared. Fifty, a hundred, a hundred and fifty, what the fuck? Eight minutes to eleven. Six minutes past eleven. Start again. Fifty, a hundred, one fifty, two, two fifty, three –. The absurdity of it mattering. Matthew's legs were full of light. He could feel it even if he couldn't see it yet. Any minute now, though. He started to count again.

It was easier to crawl than walk. He met the puppy in the doorway of the kitchen and rubbed his nose to the miniature snout. At the front door he pulled himself up and looked through the fish-eye. Base leant against the banister working between molars with a tooth-pick.

'Want your money?'

When he had checked the money, Base stood up from the letter-box and folded the pile of notes in two before slipping them into the back-pocket of his training trousers.

'Sweet,' Base said. 'Tidy business. Next week.' And he bounded down the stairs.

Matthew crawled around the flat until he found the puppy. He lay in the corridor with the animal balanced on his chest. He was his mother and the dog was him and he was looking after the dog and really he should give it some milk but, hey, let's just rest awhile.

When he woke it was light, after seven in the morning. 'David?' His hands waved over his chest, searching for the puppy. 'David?' There was no one else in the flat. He unbolted the front door. The puppy was in the bathroom, lying beside a pool of its own urine.

He waited until nine before calling a cab. He replaced the cylinder of silver foil and all of the money in the stash. Then he changed his mind and took two fifties for himself. He wrapped the puppy, now full of warm milk, in a towel and turned keys in the four locks to secure the flat. At the bottom of the stairs, in the communal hallway, Tony sat against a wall.

'Scuse me and everything but maybe you can help me out,' Tony said. 'My girlfriend had her bag stolen with our tickets to Oxford and all our money.'

'And the little boy has cancer.'

Tony recognised Matthew. 'Sorry, man. Just a tenner, maybe? To get me by?'

6

Blue Dress

By the time the taxi turned through the gates into Longacres, Matthew had decided that he would never see David again. The ridiculous handicap of the puppy, needy and helpless in his lap, was a constant reminder of his absent friend. The taxi idled along the driveway between rhododendron bushes, flowering pink and purple. A chill juddered through his torso. He told himself that he was suffering no more than a sluicing of guilt at abandoning his grandmother unvisited for so long. A choking sensation clogged his throat. As the taxi entered the carpark he was drowning in air. This converted country house with its careful lawns and shrubs was a grotesque parody of his boarding school. The roles had been reversed: he was now the visitor rather than the visited.

'She's not allowed pets, you know,' Nurse Bradshaw said by way of greeting.

'It's not for her.'

'Let me settle it with Nurse Felton.' When Nurse Bradshaw came out of the office, Matthew followed her along the corridor.

'You may find her changed.' Nurse Bradshaw's thick tights sizzled as her thighs rubbed against each other. She walked ahead of Kerrigan into a dayroom dominated by a television which was attached to the wall by a black arm. A bundle, topped by spun-sugar hair, shouted, 'Is that you, Sebastian?'

'It's only Mr Kerrigan, Doris.' Nurse Bradshaw spoke with studied patience. 'Sebastian died four years ago.'

'When will Sebastian be here?' Doris seemed to direct the question at Matthew. He waved, the beneficent visitor, wanting to apologise for not being the ever-awaited husband or son.

Scanning the chairs, Matthew saw faces bespectacled and lined, eyes suspended in cobwebs of crinkled skin, mouths collapsed over departed teeth, liver-spotted hands clawing at knee-blankets. Halfway along the row, a pretty young woman sat in a pose of imitative impassivity. Matthew thought she must be asleep. The trespass of her youth into this garden of passing mocked the wrinkled, shrunken immobility of the women around her. After some moments he looked again at the young woman sitting in the midst of those whom it seemed impossible, in the passage of fifty years, she might come to resemble. Her loveliness and vitality mocked her surroundings. A low moaning issued from Doris.

'Come now, Mr Kerrigan,' Nurse Bradshaw said. 'Your grandmother is waiting.' At these words, the young woman looked up at Matthew and mouthed the word hello, making Matthew, who mouthed it back, her co-conspirator.

At the lifts, he hesitated, wanting to go back. Nurse Bradshaw was telling him how she hated Doris howling and spoiling things. How men in their twenties were all Sebastian to her; that his death was re-enacted for her by each of them not being Sebastian.

'And the young woman is a relative of—?'

'Mrs Calvin.' Bradshaw ushered him into the aluminium interior of the lift. 'Anne's such a nice girl. Here we are now.' The lift doors opened. 'Sometimes they get older very suddenly. Almost from one day to the next.'

Matthew imagined returning to the dayroom after visiting his grandmother to find Anne transformed into a lolling octogenarian.

'We're used to it.' Nurse Bradshaw patted his shoulder as she followed him into his grandmother's suite of rooms. 'Don't you be shocked.'

During the year of her residency at Longacres, his grandmother's skewed sense of time had become extravagantly random. She no longer dithered between generations and decades but flung herself between the scenes of her life like an epileptic in a Zimmer-framed Tardis. Last Tuesday and Christmas 1930 were no longer decades apart but neighbouring days, seeping into each other. As her bones became brittle and her skin shrivelled, Gran shuffled the cards of memory with no respect for sequence or suit. Matthew tried to visit every month and phoned the duty nurses for weekly reports. His last conversation with Nurse Bradshaw had warned him that Gran was despondent, not herself at all. Who wouldn't be, he wondered, living on a diet of television and cheery remarks from the long-suffering, insufferable staff?

'How are we today, Mrs Kerrigan?'

'We are very well, my dear,' his grandmother replied, the sarcasm light enough for Nurse Bradshaw to disregard it if she chose. 'We slept well, we dreamt. We did not wet the bed.' Perhaps, Matthew thought, the nurses pluralised their charges in an attempt to mitigate the loneliness that each must suffer.

'Arthur,' his grandmother greeted him. 'Back again so soon?'

'Thinks you were here yesterday,' Bradshaw whispered.

'I'm not Arthur,' Matthew whispered. 'It's me, Gran,' he said out loud, leaning over her blanketed knees. 'It's me.'

'Is she outside?' She held his forearm in the powerful clutch of her clawlike hand as he pressed his lips to her paper cheek. 'Bradshaw, go and fetch his wife from the car. I have something to tell her.'

'I'll be going now, Mr Kerrigan,' Nurse Bradshaw said. 'You ring the bell if you need me.'

'She's gone,' Matthew said. 'They're both gone.'

'Who's gone?' she asked. 'Are you there, still? Matthew, is that you?'

'It's me, Gran,' he said. 'Here I am.'

'You remember that blue dress? It was lovely but my step-mother never let me wear it. You met her? They don't answer when you ring the bell, you know. Try it. Go on, try. She killed him,' Gran said. 'My Arthur.'

'It was an accident,' Matthew said.

'She minced around him, like a cat on heat.'

'What medication do they have you on?'

'They think they can shut me up but I remember everything – all the names and dates and accusations.' She nodded in agreement with herself. He turned to switch off the television. 'Leave it,' she said. 'Please leave it on a little longer.'

'Shall we have a drink?' Matthew opened the cabinet beside the television set. 'Would you like a glass of sherry?' When she did not answer, he poured himself an inch from her whisky bottle.

'They're poisoning me,' she said. 'Take me home, Arthur. I must buy something for Matthew's supper. That French girl forgets to feed him. We can't have little Matthew going hungry.' She stood, the canary-yellow blanket falling away from her knees. He watched her wobble and totter. She banged her knee against the low table where last month's magazines parodied a dentist's waiting room.

He leapt up and grabbed her shoulders to stop her falling. His hands pressed to the bone through slack flesh. Her torso fell away from him and he had to stoop rapidly and hug her stout middle to save her from collapsing. 'My darling boy,' she whispered in his ear. 'Carry me away.'

They were stuck. The table between their knees made it impossible for Matthew to right her. Her smell – unguents, urine, mothballs, the ghosts of old meals, a cheesy odour of flesh ready to depart – thickened in his throat. He slid the table to one side with his foot until he could step closer to her and push her upright. Her arms encircled him. He held her. He held his breath. He counted to ten. The numbness in his hands and feet only increased and he had to push her away, back down into the chair with its damp patch where she had been sitting.

What had she meant about the accident?

It would be cheaper, more considerate, to transfer her to a psychiatric unit. He considered this possibility as he endured another half an hour in which the events and personalities poured from her in a jumbled torrent. He attempted to anchor her with questions relating to the present. He found himself repeating, like a mantra, the essential roster of family facts: that he was her grandson; that his parents, Arthur and Patricia, were dead; that her husband Sean was long dead; that the blue dress, for which she persisted in asking, was God knows where; that her step-mother – whom Matthew had never met – may or may not have sacked the stable boy.

'That girl. Claudette. She is dead too?'

'I don't know, Gran.'

'You had sex with her?'

'Please.'

'She was a vixen. All the filth you brought into the house, spending your aunt's savings on whores and champagne.'

Before the returning numbness got the better of him, he leant forward and shouted at her. 'They're all dead.'

She pushed the red buzzer on the wall beside her chair.

'What do you think I'm going to do?' Her defensive gesture encouraged him to consider the possibilities. Words fluffed in his mouth like cotton wool. 'They are all fucking well dead, do you hear?' He stumbled on balloon feet, hands bumping the walls, out of her room and on to the landing.

The lift doors opened to reveal Nurse Bradshaw. 'What has she done now, Mr Kerrigan?'

Matthew unlocked the door to David's flat, planning to wake him out of his late sleep. Even as he turned the keys, forming the phrases in his mind with which he would berate his mentor, he suspected that he would fail to voice the finalities he was concocting. David would brush aside Matthew's claims, as if Matthew – like the puppy – might pretend to freewill, but in the end would reveal his need for the shelter and guidance offered by a more powerful other. Matthew slammed his palm against the door to David's bedroom, intent on taking revenge for the borrowed car, the hobbling gift of the puppy and the episode with Base.

The futon mattress was folded in half as it had been the night before. The same clothes were draped over it. If David had returned to the flat he had not slept. Matthew unwrapped the puppy and placed it on the carpet. He sat on the folded futon. Studying the framed photographs of Alison which covered the walls, he saw that a loose chronology governed the display. On the left, by the door, was a little girl standing by a climbing frame, her soft dark hair fluffed by wind. Behind her, his hands curled around her shoulders, was David. He smiled straight at the camera, claiming its attention as his right. The skin around his eyes was tightened in sceptical amusement. His mouth smiled in unambiguous pleasure. Matthew scrutinised the walls, moving to the right until he came to a shot of brother and sister in evening dress. It could have been taken on the evening of Jenny Braxton's birthday party. In the photograph, they stood slightly apart. Her neck was inclined so that her hair fell on the shoulder of his jacket, merging with his long hair, her black eyes raised in the direction of his face. His fingertips were visible on the ridge of her bare shoulder. He remembered the evening when he had seen Alison for the first time and supposed, from the compelled complicity with which she had behaved towards David, that she was his girlfriend. He remembered the agony of paying court to Jenny, while the dark-haired girl smiled at David and touched his hand.

During the five years since the birthday outing, Matthew had often wondered whether David consciously avoided allowing him to meet Alison again. Contemplating the series of photographs, along with the hysterical phone call the night before, constituted the nearest approximations of intimacy between Matthew and his friend's sister.

Furthest to the right, on the wall beside the bed, were photographs of Alison alone. Matthew recognised the Forum in the background. Alison stood on a street-corner, staring directly at the camera. The set of her mouth was uncertain. Did the camera really mean to be pointing at her? Alison and David looked alike, their narrow, elegant noses from the same mould. The skin around her eyes tightened in his expression of doubting humour as if, checking David's response for all those years, she had learnt to simulate it. A close-up photograph revealed the thin white worm of a scar at the corner of her left nostril. David's disappearance might bring Alison back from Rome. The longer he was gone, the better.

Matthew sniffed more of the magnolia-brown powder from the paper packet. As he dozed and drifted, he opened his eyes from time to time, checking that he could still command the muscles which hauled heavy lids from unfocused eyes. Doubled images of the photographs lapped and overlapped so that the figures and faces of David and Alison wavered and merged before him in a flutter of super-impositions.

His hamstrings were stretched and relaxed. His neck was loose and flexible. Alison, infinitely gentle and kind, had massaged his limbs as he dozed. The warmth on his skin was a memory of her hands upon him. He heard the extended quacking of the doorbell and the rhythmic shrill of the telephone, but he did not stir in response. The sounds were too distant. Sunlight lanced and shimmered the rucked surface of the sea above him, then pulsated on his skin, kneading him like a baby's fisting hand. He heard, faintly, the mechanical snaps of the answering machine collecting the call. Then, drowning in joy, saturated by light, he let the currents waft him deeper, breathing rose-water.

He made a daily pilgrimage to the flat, drawn by the hope that David or Alison might one day greet him as he opened the front door. One morning he found fresh gouges and dents in the wood along the crack between door and jamb, scars left by a screwdriver or a crowbar. He thought of David, keyless, trying to re-enter his own flat, struggling to prise his way back into the life which, along with the puppy, he had pressed on Matthew.

The earth in the geranium pots had shrunk. The clods surrounding the plant's roots rattled as he brushed his hand over the leaves, petals showering the carpet. The red light flashed on the answering machine but he did not listen to the messages. He searched the flat until he found, in the pocket of a black pair of jeans, the keys to David's Jaguar. In Alison's room, where discoloured rectangles made a chessboard of the walls, he ran his hands along the rail of dresses and skirts in the wardrobe, spare hangers clattering and ringing against each other like untuned bells.

At the squat in the World's End everyone was out except

Mad Annie. She led him into the kitchen where she was making soup.

'You know Dave?'

'I don't know any Daves.'

'The one with the Durban Poison,' Matthew prompted.

'That was home-grown.' Annie stirred her foul-smelling soup. 'Heard he got busted.'

'Where?'

'Frisco.'

'Annie, we're in London,' Matthew said. 'That must be some other Dave.'

'You mean Gentleman Dave?'

'Maybe.'

'Where have you been, man?' Annie said. 'Roll a spliff, why don't you?'

'What happened?'

'That fucking guy.' Annie poured the remains of a bottle of Paul Newman salad dressing into the soup. 'You warn him, all he says is, I can handle it. Kind of people he does business with, any shit can happen.'

During a single evening at the squat, Matthew heard that David had left the country, died of an overdose, been sectioned, imprisoned, knifed, kneecapped and necklaced. Each version was as implausible and malicious as the last. Glee at David's misfortunes was ubiquitous. Shocked by David's unpopularity, Matthew defended him, reminding those who maligned his friend that they would have to swallow their words when David resurfaced.

A week after David's disappearance, Matthew moved into the Felshaw flat in Hammersmith Grove, unfolding the futon and sleeping under the photographs, the puppy at his side. The first time he climbed on to a chair in the kitchen to slide back the panel of the stash was also definitely the last. He told himself he was transgressing just this once, while knowing that the first trespass would guarantee a second and a third. He removed a small amount of the magnolia-brown powder from the sausage-shaped cylinder of foil. His fear of detection seemed to improve the chances of David's return.

He forced himself to work in the afternoons, driving David's Jaguar to the offices of Communications Unlimited. He loaded data on to the office computer, the conclusions of a survey of London tourists, their buying habits by gender and age. He returned, in David's car, to David's flat and listened, without bothering to write them down, to the names and numbers which spouted from David's answering machine. The mumbling of unknown voices was punctuated by the patter of Base and Silus. Alison called every day. She left no number. She talked of returning to England; quizzically, as if she hoped that David might encourage her to come or not to come. He became habituated to the daily dose of her 'David, it's Ali' played back on the tape, someone who made sense in the midst of the narcotic patois which encoded the other messages. The doorbell quacked in the night, but he did not respond.

The puppy roused him each morning, at a quarter to four. The animal's digestion operated by a clockwork which suited the pattern of Matthew's wakefulness. He carried the creature to the bathroom, where he had rigged up a litter-tray. He fed it milk or boiled chicken. Then he dosed himself back to sleep.

After a week, he stopped going to work, pleading illness. Time dribbled, oozing from light into darkness. His confinement in the flat melted the distinction between one day and the next. When he ran out of clean clothes, he wore David's. He forgot to eat. He forgot to listen to the answering machine. The regular rhythms of the puppy's hunger and Matthew's incursions into David's stash fostered the illusion that he lived the same day again and again.

7

Stand-in

When Alison Felshaw was seventeen she told her father what she thought of his brooding rages. Her presumption incited a venom in him so terrifying that she never dared criticise him again. He told her she had no right to judge his actions when she had no knowledge of the causal background which fed them. He was the only man she knew who could use a phrase like 'causal background' when he lost his temper. His rage – which she had learnt in the years since then to avoid detonating – made him super-eloquent. Alison's rendered her tongue-tied and hopeless. She was so busy trying to contain it that she had no energy left for expressing it to the person who had provoked it. She concluded that if she refused to acknowledge her father's rages, she would liberate herself from responding to them. She refined the art of not seeing what she saw, not hearing what she heard.

David had gone to ground again. If they had both been in the same city she could have run around looking for him. But since he was in London and she in Rome, she would have to track him down by telephone, or fly home into the rainy bit of the English spring.

It had been more than a fortnight since she had spoken to David. The last time he had been out of contact for that long, he had put himself through a clinic in the West Country where he had been dried out and cleaned up, instead of Alison having to nurse him, which she had done in the past and hoped she would never have to do again. Thank God their father was still paying David's BUPA sub. He had stayed clean for a while, gone to meetings. Then some friends of his turned up from Australia with a delivery.

Was she serious when she told herself – as she did that morning, sitting in the sunshine on her rooftop in Trastevere with coffee and white peaches – that she might leave Rome for David's sake? It would be hard to imagine circumstances more enviable than her own. And yet she envied her previous self, the Alison of nine months ago, who had allowed herself to be set up in a beautiful flat in a funky old building by a man who was married to a tennis nut and ran the Italian arm of one of the international record companies. Work and family kept Sergio busy, but not so busy that he couldn't visit her most weekdays and even stay over sometimes on the pretext that he was abroad. And he didn't mind her having girlfriends to stay. Tamsin had come out in October. Josephine had come at the end of November, which had been a nightmare. Bill Braxton had flown in for a week in February. Sergio took a less generous view of her men friends. But then he would, wouldn't he?

After Bill left, Sergio had asked her to give up her teaching job. 'Teach me to speak English,' he said in perfect English. 'Let me be your pupil.'

'What could I teach you that you don't already know?'

'You don't need the money, *cara*.'

He wanted her permanently available in the apartment in Trastevere – fragrant and welcoming – so that whenever his wife decided to knock up with her pro, he could slip away to the flat, sure that Alison would be there. But she refused to give up her pupils and her narrow margin of independence.

It was ten in the morning and already it was hot up on the roof terrace. The white peaches were to die for and she was listening to a bunch of CDs Sergio had dropped round, drinking coffee and managing not to smoke cigarettes. She pulled up her nightie so that the sun shone directly on to her legs. She was bored. Sergio had stopped sleeping with his wife – who must, Alison surmised, have started sleeping with someone else, probably her pro. Having spent months hoping that Sergio would stop sleeping with Floriana, Alison could not explain why his having finally done so filled her with disappointment.

She pressed re-dial on the cordless phone and heard David's voice on the answering machine of their flat in London. 'David, it's Ali. Call me.' I'll try him again in an hour, she decided. I won't let the cold feeling in my abdomen get the better of me. She pulled the nightie further up and then took it off altogether.

When David came to Rome, it turned out that he hadn't come to visit Ali at all – as he had made out – but because of some guy from Mexico who wouldn't fly into London. David used her apartment as his rendezvous. He and the Mexican argued about their deal for hours. Alison – who spoke some Spanish – was forced to translate. David had ordered three ounces of coke. The guy had brought only thirty grammes. David was refusing to pay, even for the thirty grammes. An extreme position to take, but typical. Some Italians David half-knew pitched up and everyone started taking the stuff and Alison had a few lines too, because what the hell. Sergio arrived. David refused to leave, despite her heavy hints. In the end, Sergio had a line to establish trust and then brokered an arrangement between David and the courier. David stayed and stayed. Sergio took David and Ali out to dinner. When David was

about to leave, Sergio had a call on his mobile from the
tennis nut who wanted to know why he was not home.
After Sergio's departure, Ali and David sat up all night
doing the coke. David left the next morning. Josephine
phoned from the airport at lunchtime. Alison listened to
her weeping and monologuing about David's callousness
for forty-eight tedious hours.

Why should she look after her older brother? Her cus-
todianship was entirely self-imposed. David only asked her
for things when no one else was around to provide them or
when she was the most suitable patsy for his latest scheme.
Maybe she would go to London for a week or so, find him,
get him fixed up and be back in time for the weekend in
Ponza with Sergio while Floriana went to Tivoli for her
mixed doubles tournament. And maybe she would have
dinner with Bill Braxton while she was there.

She lay in the morning sunshine, calling the flat in London
every hour and getting the machine, calling Josephine who
rang her back from work, calling Tamsin and Bill's answering
machine, which said he could be reached on a mobile number
which turned out to be unobtainable or the network was
overloaded or something. David had all sorts of mobiles and
pager numbers but he changed them every month because
of the business he was in and so she never had the right
numbers when she needed them, as she did now.

Sergio came round after lunch for his siesta. He must
have looked in the flat first and then come up to the
roof terrace, or maybe he knew she would be up there.
He walked across to the recliner. She told him she wanted
a swim and why didn't they go to the tennis club on the
Appia Antica. He announced that he was going downstairs
to have a shower. So they had a shower together and
then, as they made love, still wet, the phone rang and
she wanted to answer it in case it was David, or Josephine
with news of David's whereabouts, but she remained loyal

to the impassioned, sensual creature she had pretended to be since she stopped feeling impassioned and sensual about Sergio. After he came, he smiled at her for a minute or two before falling asleep. It must have meant something to him that she hadn't let the phone distract her from what they were doing.

She woke him at half past four. She had pupils coming to the flat at five. She waited until he was properly awake and then said, 'I might have to go back to London for a couple of days.'

'As you wish.'

'Don't—' she said. 'I never see you over the weekend.'

'I was making a plan.'

'We have Ponza to look forward to,' she said.

Sergio climbed off the bed and walked across the bedroom towards the shower. 'There may be a small problem with Ponza.'

When he had a problem to which he had no immediate solution, Sergio invariably described it as small. She waited until he had showered again and returned to the room with a towel wrapped round his middle which, for someone in his late forties, was still trim. 'There is a problem with David?'

'Perhaps,' she said. 'A small one.'

'He's a big boy, *cara*,' Sergio said. 'Big and quite bad, I think.'

'No one knows where he is,' she said.

'He has much luck.'

'He needs it.'

'To have you, I mean.' Sergio dropped the towel and began to dress.

'He doesn't have me.'

They kissed at the door and she climbed the stairs back to the roof terrace. She dialled British Airways and booked a flight. Then she left a message on the machine at the London flat with her flight details and time of arrival. Maybe David was taking messages off the machine. Maybe he would come to the airport.

One of the few things in which he had never failed her was collecting her off planes. She hated not being met at the airport. It was a phobia – he called it the existentialism of the arrivals lounge – which they shared. Her decision to fly home was based as much on the idea that David might be lured to the airport to meet her, as on any real hope that being in London would improve her chances of tracking him down.

After she finished teaching her English class, she had a couple of hours in which to pack and take a taxi to Leonardo da Vinci. She did the last of the coke David had given her because she didn't want to leave it in the apartment, which was in Sergio's name. She closed the shutters on the evening light, on the sounds of the street below.

By the time she was on the ground in London she had convinced herself that David would be standing at the barrier, a look of bored disdain setting his features. She snaked through the green channel without any pause for questioning, feeling guilty despite having nothing to declare. The mosaic of faces shimmering above the barrier in the arrivals hall was a backcloth against which David's surly features would materialise at any moment. There he was – no. He could have cut his hair. Watch out for that. A charge of recognition animated faces which seemed to look at her as they spotted some long-awaited relative or friend immediately behind her. She slowed, assessing the faces one by one.

She walked across the hall to the meeting point and had someone page David on the public address system. She waited for five minutes and then joined the queue for taxis. She counted more minutes passing by on the digital display boards of the office blocks either side of the Westway, jerked forward and back on the angled seat by the stop-start evening traffic, the door-locks clicking each time the cab-driver pressed the accelerator or came to a halt.

She had not seen David since February. Even as she told herself that he would have criticised and complained, demanded and bullied her from the moment they were in his car, still she wanted him beside her, just to know, just to be able to say to herself that her brother had come, as he always did, to meet her at the airport.

When she reached Hammersmith Grove, she saw his Jaguar parked in the street. She paid the cab, not waiting for her change. David was in, sleeping most probably. She left her green suitcase and her hold-all in the hallway, bounding up the stairs to the flat on the fifth floor. When she reached the door at the top of the stairs she remembered that her keys were in the hold-all. She banged on the door, partly in frustration, partly in the hope that David might let her in.

She returned to the hall and then, having shouldered the hold-all, commenced her second ascent. Climbing the five flights of stairs, she began to have doubts about the point of her journey. She turned keys in the four locks, annoyed with herself for no longer knowing which one slotted into which lock. Her innocent forgetfulness was a negation of David, of family, of the very idea that people need one another, that love counts for something, that coming home is important. Along with the sound of the barrels turning in the locks she heard the low whining of a creature in pain. 'David? David?' She hurried her attempt to undo the last lock, jamming the key, dropping the bunch of keys in her rush to be inside now that she realised why she had been right to obey her instinct and fly to London. 'I'm coming. It's all right, I'm here now.' At last she batted the door open and saw a black puppy lying belly-up on the hallway carpet, its stomach narrow and pink. The living room was empty, geraniums dying, dust thick on the top of the television, curtains half-drawn.

Edging open the door to David's room, she saw that he had taken all of her photographs and hung them in his room. She pushed the door further open. She saw the bottom half of his sleeping form on the futon. She paused, gulping down her relief. She knelt beside the mattress and leant over her beloved, infuriating brother. She pulled back the duvet from his – Christ, whose? – head.

The face was concrete grey, rubbished by a graffiti of stubble, eyes sealed with sleep crust, the skin around the nostrils red and raw, lips dry and rimmed with muck like a tideline on sand. Her fear that the impostor might be dead in her flat dispelled any concern about what he might do to her if he was alive. She pushed and prodded at his body until it began to roll, shying away from her hands. 'That's his T-shirt you're wearing.' The stranger said nothing in reply. 'Where is he?'

Matthew heard her racing from room to room, swinging doors open, thumping them closed. The sounds were more distant as she moved down the corridor, louder again as she ran past the room in which he lay. He heard faint voices, punctuated by the electronic beep of the answering machine as she played back old messages.

When she returned to the bedroom, she opened the curtains and stood by the window, keeping her distance.

'Why are you sleeping in my flat?'

Matthew considered telling her she was wrong, that actually it was his flat. Instead, he said, 'Have you brought David back?'

He watched as Alison arranged a response. Because her expressions were similar to David's, he was able to read on her features the passage from taut surprise through confused fear to glazed surrender.

'What have you done?' she asked him. 'What have you done to my brother?'

When Matthew attempted to recall the march of events,

the unfurling of time, he became perplexed. He tried to sit up but his body would only allow him to lift his head an inch off the pillow before his neck gave out. He closed his eyes. He fumbled on the floor beside the mattress, his hand crawling in search of cigarettes. His eyes closed, he saw an image of Alison's hair, but much longer, so long that it reached down in braided cords, out of the living-room window, towards the street. He climbed down the rope of her hair, shins coiling the braids for grip, hands sliding on the gloss of it, surrounded by the sweet smell of her hair, climbing down and down.

She decided to let him sleep, this man she knew she knew, but could not place. Should she phone her parents? Worrying them would create new problems. She could contain her anxiety more easily if she did not have to mollify theirs. She closed the bedroom door, wishing she could lock it from the outside. She ran water into a milk bottle at the sink and carried it through to the living room where she poured it over the cracked earth around the geraniums. She drew back the curtains and watched motes of dust swirling in the stale air. She opened the windows, feeling the stretch in tired shoulders as she pushed the frames out into nothingness, shuddering in the wash of cold spring air.

She pulled the Hoover from the cupboard in the hall, then jumped as she felt something slide past her calf. She gave milk to the puppy and closed it into the kitchen. The rhythm of the hoovering calmed her, the lawn of carpet darkening as the machine lifted dust and grit that had lain there God knows how long. She replaced the newspaper in the litter-tray and carried the puppy to the bathroom. As she set to work on the kitchen, pulling plates and cups and glasses from the cold greasy water in the sink and running fresh water to wash up, she saw a cylinder of foil on the table, open at one end, a pinkish-brown powder spilling from the package on to the blond wood. The thought came to her that this was another of David's games. He might arrive back any minute. The concrete man would leap from the bed, laughing with relief that the game was over. They would open champagne. David would hug her. The stand-in would disappear.

8

Cluck

She strode into David's room and squatted beside his bed. The stranger was blinking himself awake but otherwise immobile.

'Who are you?' Her voice sounding very loud after not talking for an hour. 'Who do you think you are?' she asked.

'I need something.' The stranger was sweating, bubbles of glass on his pasty forehead.

'I've chucked it.'

'Sure,' he said. 'Please, Ali.'

'Don't call me that.'

The stranger shook his head from side to side on the damp pillow. He stared at her. 'You haven't really, have you?'

'Maybe,' Alison said. 'Tell me your name.'

'David.'

'David?' Alison said. 'I don't understand.'

'I really need a hit,' he said. 'On the kitchen table.' The quartzed blue of his eyes was diminished by pupils so open that she seemed to be peering into darkness.

'He may be in danger,' she said. 'If you know where he is, just tell me.'

'You know me,' he said.

'Where's David?'

'I don't know,' the stranger said. 'If I just had—'

'Tell me where he is,' Alison said. 'I might give it to you.'

'He took my car. Said he was going out. Just for a couple of hours.'

'When was this?'

'I can't think straight,' the stranger said. 'I'm sick.'

'What else happened that night?' she asked.

'What night?' the stranger said. 'Aren't you going to help me out?'

'The night he borrowed your car.'

'You phoned,' he said. 'You thought I was going to trash the place.'

'Jesus,' Alison said, determined not to cry. 'That was three weeks ago.'

His hand reached towards her face but she pushed it away and stood up. 'Can't be,' the stranger said.

Alison telephoned a police station, registering David as a missing person and leaving her number. She phoned hospitals and psychiatric units and drug rehabilitation centres. She phoned all the people she knew who knew David – Johnny Bell and Martha, Angela, Jacqueline, Gina, the many friends of hers who had become his ex-girlfriends. She checked to see if Josephine had made any progress. None of the people she knew had seen David for weeks.

When she returned to the bedroom, the stranger's hand was scuttling over the floor beside the bed. It settled on a cigarette packet. He lifted it above his chest where he could see it without moving his head. His fingers did not seem to be working properly. She took the packet from his hands and offered the filter end of a cigarette to his lips. Then she held a match as he puffed. She wiped perspiration from his brow with the corner of the duvet cover. He smoked his cigarette, clenching the filter between his teeth. She was about to remove it to tip his ash when the column toppled and slid off his cheek to nestle by his neck on the pillow.

The sun bloomed from behind a cloud and light expanded through the window behind her head. She badly wanted to smoke a cigarette.

'You're an angel,' the stranger said.

'Don't count on it.'

'You'll sort me out.'

'I've thrown the stuff away,' she said.

He sat up. Then he lay back. She saw that he was crying.

'It was his trouble,' the stranger said. 'He landed me in it.'

'He does that.' Alison did not like his use of the past tense. 'He'll be back,' she said.

'I didn't realise he was in so deep,' the stranger said.

'Don't you know how to reach him?' Alison said. 'Who's he been running with?'

'I don't know,' he said. 'I know people who might know.'

'As if I was going to shop anyone.' Alison stood up. 'You're all paranoid.'

'All who?'

'Smackheads,' she said. 'Dealers. Whatever you are.'

'He fucked me over,' the stranger said. 'I could have killed him, I was that angry.'

'Or hurt,' Alison said.

'Speak for yourself.'

'It's all right to care about him.'

'I don't care about anyone.'

'But you stayed around,' she said. 'You were waiting for him.'

'He was like that.'

'Yes.' She removed the burnt-down cigarette from between his fingers and stubbed it out in the ashtray. 'That's what he's like.'

The stranger struggled to sit up. She made him drink a glass of water. He smelt the way David sometimes smelt – a smoky, chemical odour, sharp and rank in the nostrils, ammoniacal. He started to weep again. 'Alison,' he said.

His face was familiar but she could not give it a context. 'I can't remember your name.' She wanted to comfort him even though she knew, from the times when she had watched David going through this, that the sudden gusts of sorrow were part of the process of withdrawal. David called it the soul crying out for a lost haven, mocking himself afterwards, when he was strong again, for the tears he had shed.

'Kerrigan.' He grimaced as he sounded the 'K'.

'Just that?'

'Plain Kerrigan.'

She could not call him that. He reminded her of David, which was oddly comforting even if it underscored David's absence. He vomited a thin bile on to the duvet cover. A string of saliva dangled from his mouth. 'When did you last eat?' Alison asked.

'I'm not hungry.'

'You should eat,' Alison said. She went to the kitchen and, returning with a cloth, wiped the pond-sludge from the duvet. They sat for some moments in silence. She watched as he lay curled under the duvet in her brother's place.

'I could eat an apple,' he said.

'Goodness,' Alison said. 'I always wondered what happened to you.'

'I didn't think you'd remember.'

'That night,' Alison said. 'In the valley.'

'It was the morning,' Matthew said.

'Bill thought Josephine had drowned,' Alison said.

'It wasn't my fault,' Matthew said.

'After we dropped you back at the school, I sat in the front of the car with David.' There was a silence. Alison looked at him, struggling to remember his Christian name. 'The others were asleep in the back. We almost went back for you.'

'I wish you had,' Matthew said.

'David always turns up in the end.'

'You want him to come back?'

'Don't you?' Alison asked.

'I can't imagine him not,' Matthew said, prompting Alison to consider the empty horizon of a future which did not contain David. 'I really could get by on just a little. To tide me over.'

The puppy followed her to the bathroom. She searched the medicine cabinet and found a bottle of the codeine tablets David used – he called them DFs – to diminish the effects of heroin withdrawals.

'You can have one of these every four hours,' she told him.

'Matthew,' he said. 'My name's Matthew.' He reached his hand out for the bottle but she pulled back. She opened the bottle, shook out a pill and offered it to him in her palm. She asked him for the details of his car, realising that she should report its loss to the police in case it was a means to discovering David's whereabouts. As she phoned through the details she was conscious that if David was involved in some complicated deal rather than simply on a binge, she might be endangering his liberty. How angry he would be if he knew she was talking to the police. And yet he might be safer in jail.

Matthew woke to cooking smells. The paper packet he kept beside the bed had been empty last time he checked, and the time before that. He looked again. It was still empty.

He coughed, setting off a prickly itching in his throat. His penis was flaccid but sensitised, as if he was on the point of ejaculation. He shuddered and sat up. He crawled to the doorway of David's bedroom and listened.

Alison was talking on the phone in the living room. He edged forward into the corridor on jellied knees. David's T-shirt scratched at his skin like a cheese-grater. He held his breath to choke a cough. The puppy was curled up asleep on the carpet by the front door. On the kitchen table, the foil cylinder had been replaced by onion skins, a chopping board, the tops and tails of carrots and a packet of pasta. Steam wound from a simmering pan on the hob. He would have to move a chair to climb up to the stash at the top of the pine dresser. He pulled himself upright and stood still as a surge of faintness pumped through his head and chest.

He lifted the chair and shifted it a few inches before his strength gave out. Then he repeated the process, lifting and settling the chair-legs on the tiled floor as quietly as he could, half-knowing that even if he managed to stand on the chair to look in the stash, he would find nothing there.

He was squatting on the chair, preparing to stand, when he heard her footsteps on the tiles. Mustering the last of his strength he straightened his knees, lost his balance and swiped his hand along a shelf of crockery in an attempt to right himself. He tottered on the chair, clinging on to the dresser. 'I was looking for cigarettes.'

'I've been through this before,' she said.

'Honestly,' Matthew said.

'You won't find anything,' she said. 'I cleaned it out.'

He collapsed on to the chair, banging his knee on the dresser.

'Go back to bed,' she said.

He was weeping and, at the same time, experiencing a pre-orgasmic fluttering in his unerect penis. He was scared to move again in case the friction of his underpants against the sensitive skin triggered ejaculation. And now she was on her hands and knees, collecting together the shards and lumps of broken plates, and the front of her dress fell away from her skin so that he could see her breasts hanging unbrassiered. The curve of her hips was accentuated by her quadruped position, her buttocks raised as she reached forward under the chair to collect pieces of crockery.

'If I wasn't so sick, I could get about,' he said. 'Ask around.'

'You won't find him unless he wants you to.' She knelt before him. 'You've hurt yourself.' Her fingers pressed on the area around the wound, just below his kneecap.

She returned with cotton wool and plasters, pouring water from the kettle into a bowl. She dabbed away the blood. 'You're not on the needle.'

'I'm not going to infect you,' he said. 'I should go, anyway.'

'Sure.' She sat back on her haunches. 'Go.'

'Hey.' The wound began to sting. 'To look for him.'

'Go, then.'

'You don't want me to look for him?'

'I'm not a moron.'

'I'll find him,' Matthew said.

'There's only one thing you'll find.'

'I don't want to go,' he said. 'Apart from that.'

'You just said you did.' She went back to work on his cut knee. He winced and jerked his leg away as she pressed too hard.

'Hold me,' he said. 'Just for a moment.'

'Keep still.' She peeled the back off a plaster and sculpted it to his knee.

'Didn't you hear me?' Matthew said.

'Of course I heard.'

'Doesn't anyone ever hear me?' Matthew stood up, pushing the chair away. 'What's the point, if no one listens?' He was sobbing now, relieved to be out of control. 'No one ever hears. Or if they do it's just yeah, yeah, later, maybe, probably, possibly.'

'I don't know you well enough to mother you.'

'That's such a David remark,' Matthew said. 'That's typical fucking David.'

'Don't hate your friends,' Alison said. 'Save it for your enemies.'

'You don't understand.'

'I'm his sister,' she said. 'Remember?'

'Me, I mean.'

'You're not so different.' She leant forward on the tips of her toes and kissed his forehead quickly, ruffling the hair at the back of his head. 'Go back to bed. Take your dog with you.'

Later she brought him a tray on which she had laid out a bowl of chicken soup, slices of bread, a glass of apple juice ('for your liver'), salt, pepper and butter on a dish. The inclusion of a white linen napkin with a precise diagonal fold brought a tightness to his throat. Tears escaped over the rims of his eyelids. 'You're a strange man,' Alison said.

'I'm not like this,' he said.

'It's just what you're like,' she said. 'Don't be ashamed.'

'That scar by your nostril.'

'What of it?'

'I like it.'

He ate two bowls of the soup despite having no sensation of hunger. He lay on the bed, the dog at his feet. He could hear the murmur of Alison's voice in the living room, talking on the telephone. He touched himself, remembering her on her hands and knees. He came before he was erect. Then he slept. He woke to a churning in his bowels. He hobbled to the bathroom and relieved himself.

A day passed. She gave him codeine pills. She fed him. He slept. Once, when he woke, she was sitting beside the bed, looking at him. She smiled. He closed his eyes. He dreamt with a frenzy inside his shell of bodily torpor. Sometimes he surfaced clammy with cold sweat, calves cramped, throat itching. At other times he rolled on to the shore of consciousness, weary and calm.

Alison phoned her pupils in Rome and pleaded illness. She did not phone Sergio. Now that she was away from Trastevere, he faded from her attention like an astronaut unroped from his craft, receding into black nothing. When she was not cooking for Matthew she sat by the phone, talking to Josephine, or waiting for a call for David which would give her a clue as to his whereabouts. She did not want to phone her parents until David was back. She took the foil-wrapped package down to the fourth floor landing where a wooden box attached to the wall housed fuse boxes for the top two flats. She slid the package under one of the meters until it was no longer visible.

No institution – police stations, jails, psychiatric units, hospitals or treatment centres – within two hundred miles of London had any record of a David Felshaw. Twice the phone rang in the night but when she picked up the receiver the line went dead. The sealed world of David's operations closed her out. She had only Matthew.

She switched on the answering machine, hoping that someone might leave a telling message. Bill called and she was paralysed, unable to pick up the receiver as she listened to his voice on the machine. He had caught up with her messages, but he was in Glasgow, not back for another four days.

Alison looked up. Matthew was standing in the door-way of the living room, in his underpants and David's T-shirt.

'I don't have any clean clothes.' Matthew was smoking a cigarette. 'I can smell myself, even when I smoke.'

She ran a bath for him. He left the door open while he soaked. She walked past it four times before entering. 'I could wash you,' she said.

He sat up in the bath and leant forward while she wetted and washed his hair. David was always at his most tender when the physical symptoms of withdrawal were all but over, his self-possession defeated by the chemical riot which his body had endured. As she had bathed David, she now bathed Matthew. His hair needed cutting. A little colour had returned to his skin. She scrubbed his back. She made him lie back so she could wash his feet and calves.

'You'd better do the rest.' She held out the soap to him.

'Really?'

'Really.' She rinsed her hands in the bath.

'Did he ask you?'

She said nothing.

'You are as beautiful as it is possible to be.'

'I'm not at my best,' she said.

'Then I have something to look forward to.'

'I'm going back to Rome,' Alison said. 'As soon as we've found him.'

'There are things I want to tell you,' he said.

'I've heard enough confessions,' Alison said.

'You said not to be ashamed.'

He was right. She had said that. Why did she always encourage them? While he finished washing she looked in David's wardrobe and found clean underpants, the green linen shirt of his she particularly loved and a pair of blue jeans. She helped Matthew into the clothes, seeing that he was still weak, his fingers fumbling the buttons of the shirt.

'David often wore this,' he said.

'It suits you,' Alison said.

'I want him back just as much as you do,' he said.

'How soon?'

'We could try the squat,' Matthew said. 'There are people there who know him.'

He directed her through the side-streets of the World's End and had her park the Jaguar a few doors short of the house. It started to rain.

'Maybe I should go in alone,' Matthew said.

'Why would you want to do that?'

'You look, I don't know, too good.'

She was wearing a short black dress she had bought in Milan. Other than lipstick she was wearing no make-up. She had put a wide black elasticated band around her head to avoid the bother of putting her hair up.

'What are they going to do?' Alison asked. 'Eat me?'

'If they have any sense.'

'You think I'm uncool.'

'I want to be sure they tell me whatever they know.'

'Don't be forever.'

Sitting in David's car in the rain with Matthew gone, Alison wanted a cigarette all to herself. She had forgotten to ask Matthew to leave her one. Was it a bad sign that she was starting to smoke again? David had disappeared before, she had started to smoke before. Once, he had gone for a full month and, on his return, strolling into the garden of her parents' house in the country one Sunday lunchtime, had told her that he had been locked up for a week in a jail in Peru. On another occasion, he had phoned her from an island in Greece, asking her to join him at a cottage he had rented.

'Isn't it a pity,' her father once said, 'that David's intelligence can't be directed towards achieving something useful?' Alison experienced an inner rebellion, a feeling like being instantly drunk. But she said no more than, 'Yes,

Dad,' and 'True enough,' because David had made her into the one who behaved herself, the one her parents knew as the good girl, the nice girl, the kind girl. Being told she was kind and nice and good made her want to hit someone. For how much longer would she be glancing towards the touch-line of her life, to check that her mother and father were cheering? Her thoughts turned to Matthew, who was incidental, a means to the end of finding her brother. Like her, he was in orbit around Planet David. But that did not mean they had anything else in common.

Cursing herself, she shoved open the door of the car and ran down the street in the rain, trying to remember which house Matthew had entered. Number fourteen's ground floor windows were boarded up. Rubbish, bursting from a bin-liner, festooned the steps. She picked her way through cans and vegetable peelings and banged on the door. The man who opened it sported a tattoo of dried blood which curled down his face from the corner of his eyebrow.

'Got to get to the hospital,' the man said. 'Have you got wheels?'

Alison saw herself as a toy or a suitcase. 'I don't think so.'

'I've been concussed,' the man said. 'My wallet was stolen. Could you lend me five quid to get a cab?'

'It's raining,' Alison said. 'I'm getting soaked.' She had her purse out of her handbag and was looking for a small note but could find only twenties and Lire.

'Ten would be better,' the man said.

'Can you tell me if Matthew is here?'

'Ten quid,' the man said. 'Not much to a woman such as yourself.'

A mousy blonde girl who looked no more than fifteen appeared beside the man in the doorway with a hammer. 'I told you, out.'

Alison heard American West Coast in her accent.

'Easy, man.'

'You ripped me off.' She raised the hammer. 'And I'm not a man.' He tried to grab the mousy girl's arm. She lashed out, catching him on the side of the neck. Alison backed down the steps in time to avoid the man who slipped in the garbage and fell.

'Who in the fuck are you?'

'I'm looking for Matthew.'

'So?'

'And David,' Alison said. 'David Felshaw.'

'Everybody's after Gentleman Dave.' The girl twisted the hammer, rotating the head so that the handle turned like a key in the lock of her palm. 'What did he do to you?' The girl raised her hands to her face, still holding the hammer, and inspected the rings on her fingers. 'Don't tell me. I can guess.'

'He's my brother.'

'He was my brother, for a day or two.'

'Can't I come in?' Alison said. 'I'm soaked.'

'Or maybe that was the other Dave. Lot of Daves come through here. Lot of Daves, lot of Tonys. The fuck out of here,' she shouted at the man lying on the pavement. 'You sure you want to come in?' she said to Alison.

'I think Matthew's up there,' Alison said. 'I just spent the last three days cleaning him up.'

'Waste of time.'

'Should we do something?' Alison indicated the man still lying on the pavement.

'Fuck him,' the blonde girl said. 'Come on in.'

Alison hesitated and then, blanking her fear of the girl with the hammer, stepped inside the squat.

'Ever had crabs?' the girl asked her as they climbed the stairs.

'Only to eat.'

'Don't sit down,' the girl said. 'Don't sit your pretty ass down.'

Matthew stood up as soon as he saw her. Alison made out four other figures who were slumped on dirty cushions in the dimly lit room, curtains drawn against the day.

'Do I know you?' said one of the reclining casualties.

'It's cool, Mike,' Matthew said. 'We're going.'

'I know you,' Mike said. 'I think I like you.'

'She's David's sister,' Matthew said. 'Drop it.'

'Don't tell me what to drop,' Mike said. 'Some people came round looking for your brother.' Alison saw that Mike held a syringe in his hand.

'I slugged Tony,' the blonde girl said. 'I got him good.'

'What people?'

'Just people,' Mike said.

Matthew took Alison's arm and pulled her down the stairs. When they were through the front door she wrenched her elbow from his grasp. Tony was sitting on the pavement, holding his head in his hands. The rain had washed part of the tattoo of blood from his cheek and jaw.

'Should we do something?' Alison asked.

'He'd sell his grandmother.'

'Wouldn't you?'

'You don't want to get involved with Tony,' Matthew said.

'We can't leave him in the street.' She was thinking about David, lost or wounded, perhaps sitting on another pavement somewhere else in the city.

'Sure,' Matthew said.

'What do you mean?'

'Whatever.' He grinned at her.

'You fool,' she said.

'Lend me a tenner,' Tony muttered.

'What's the point in helping you?' she said to Matthew.

'I'm straight,' Matthew said. 'Honest.'

'Just a tenner,' Tony said.

'Fuck off, Tony,' Matthew said.

'Look at him,' Alison said. 'Is that what you want?'

Matthew said nothing.

'Throw your life away,' she said, pulling her purse from her bag. 'Chuck it away.' She crumpled paper money in her fist and threw it on the pavement beside Tony. 'Just chuck it all away.' Tony was on his hands and knees on the pavement, picking up the notes she was balling and dropping. 'I'm not staying around to watch.' Alison walked away.

'What the fuck am I going to do with fucking Lire?'

She ran the rest of the way to the car. Matthew caught up with her and banged on her window. She sat in the driver's seat, David's seat, the doors centrally locked, the keys still in her hand. 'Let me in.' She smeared tears across her face, feeling lipstick under the ball of her hand. She started the car and stalled putting it into reverse. The starter-motor choked and screeched. Matthew stood by the door, pulling at the door handle, saying her name – 'Ali. Ali. Ali.' At last, when she could bear him saying it no longer, the engine caught and she backed up and moved out of the parking space, the body of the big car brushing Matthew aside, leaving him to recede in the wing-mirror and then disappear altogether as she reached the corner of the street and turned into traffic.

By the time she was climbing the stairs to the flat, she had cleansed herself of all but the most practical considerations. She would phone Sergio and then go to the airport. Her guess was that Matthew would return to the flat and if he did then he could take care of the puppy. On the other hand, she did not want him there, making a mess, falling asleep with lit cigarettes, puking on carpets and inviting seedy people round. She had to go quickly if she was going to go at all. She started to pack and ordered a cab, planning to buy a seat on the first flight to Rome once she reached the terminal. The puppy whimpered under her feet as she folded clothes and placed them in her suitcase. She thought about giving her parents a ring but decided it was better for them to believe that she had not come at all than that she had been in England and not made time for them. She did not want to talk about David, or worry about him, or give him any tiny portion of any part of herself ever again. Each time she caught herself thinking about David, breaking the rule she had just set, she thought about Matthew too. She rushed around the flat, checking and double-checking. Then she changed into a loose skirt which would be comfortable in the plane. She tried Bill's number again, listened to his machine, phoned his mobile, was told that his phone may be switched off, please try later. She watered the geraniums, then petted the puppy until the cab arrived.

As the driver was hefting her suitcase into the cab, she heard her name being shouted. A figure was running towards her down Hammersmith Grove. She easily had time to climb into the cab and give her destination before he caught up with her, however fast he ran. And anyway, he had to slow down to squeeze between one of the trees and a woman with a pram. But no, he swerved out into the street so as to keep running at full tilt. He ignored a car which had to brake and swing out of his path.

She climbed into the taxi and sat well back, as the printed placard instructed, for safety and comfort. As the cab pulled away he drew level with the window beside her, looking in at her, panting, soaking wet, in an ecstasy of determination and speed and grace, and all of it was for her. She watched through the back window as the accelerating taxi put distance between them.

9

Treacle

She was not conscious of making a decision. The words rushed from her mouth, like a sneeze: 'Stop, please.' Through the back window of the taxi she saw Matthew look up. Then his head dropped again. He was catching his breath. She looked over her shoulder and caught the taxi driver eyeing her in his mirror. Matthew walked along the pavement towards the taxi. He climbed in without looking at her, as if she was not there. She could smell sweat – Matthew's, but David's too, coming from his clothes which Matthew still wore.

'The airport, is it?' the driver asked.

'No,' Alison said. And then, 'I don't know.'

'I'm booked for Heathrow,' the driver said.

'The airport,' Matthew said.

'Look—'

'What?'

'Can't we just drive around or something?'

'Drive around what?' the cabby said. 'I'm booked for Heathrow.'

'Do something,' Alison said.

'Hyde Park Corner.' Matthew closed the driver's partition window, sealing them off from the idea of the airport. 'What happened?'

'I should go,' she said. 'While I can.'

'You're free to go,' Matthew said.

'I don't want this any more,' she said. 'Not from you. Not from David.'

'He loves you.'

'What do you know about it?'

'He took all the photographs to his room.' Matthew paused. 'He arranged them like a pageant of your life.'

'It's not his to arrange,' she said. 'I don't want him running it.'

'We're the same, then,' Matthew said. 'That's our bond.'

Alison said nothing.

'I don't want to arrange your life,' Matthew said.

'Let me go,' she said, not looking at him.

'Tell me that you honestly want to leave,' he said. 'Say it out loud, so I can be sure.'

'Why shouldn't I leave?' she said. 'I was never with you so I'm not leaving you.'

'Don't go, then,' he said.

'You're confusing me.'

'I'll change,' he said. 'I'll stop.'

'You'll do whatever you do,' she said. 'Even if you don't mean to.'

'These are the things people say at the end.' Matthew lit a cigarette.

'I don't want to be hurt,' she said. 'Not by anyone.'

'He'll be all right,' Matthew said. 'He's a survivor.'

'And you?' They said nothing more until they reached Hyde Park Corner. Matthew told the driver to return to Hammersmith Grove.

'Do we have to go back?' Alison asked.

'We could to go my place.'

She knew that, for now, there was nothing to be done but return to the flat, that they had not yet reached a point where whatever had started to happen could be cut free from waiting (or even pretending not to be waiting) for David.

'I should have thrown you out,' she said. 'I didn't have to feed you.'

'You were kind to me,' he said. 'You were good.'

Alison grabbed a fistful of Matthew's hair, shaking his head, staring at him. Then she pulled his head forward to hers and kissed him, both hands on his head, no longer gripping his hair but cupping the back of his neck. Matthew's hands joined behind her back, his forearms closed around the slender sides of her waist. He could feel her backbone under his fingers, a slight tremor humming through it. She broke the kiss, leant her forehead against his chin and said, 'Goodbye.'

'Don't lie,' he said.

Matthew carried her suitcase while she paid the taxi. As they were climbing the stairs from the last half-landing up to the fifth floor, a middle-aged man in a green army-surplus jacket stepped from the shadows and took Matthew by the arm. The door to the flat was open. Alison screamed.

'Oi,' the army-surplus man shouted. 'Come here, Tel.'

Alison turned and ran down the stairs. The army-surplus man released Matthew and followed her, catching her as she tripped on the carpeting of the fourth floor landing. Hands gripped her upper arms, forcing her to re-ascend the stairs. While she was frightened, she was also relieved that someone was taking over, that someone else would determine the course of events.

Another man was searching Matthew, holding him against the wall with one hand, digging in his pockets with the other.

'Drug Squad,' said the man holding Alison's arms.

'You've found him?'

'We always find them,' the man said. 'In the end.' He pushed her through the doorway and guided her into the living room where three other men were searching through drawers, unzipping the cushion covers, emptying the geraniums out of their pots and breaking up the earth.

'Got something here, Guv.' The man who had been searching Matthew led him into the living room and stood by him, close to the doorway. He opened his palm to reveal a paper packet.

'What have you done with him?' Alison asked.

'Done with who?' asked the balding man.

Alison looked at Matthew, hoping for guidance, but he was staring at the floor, head hung limp. Then he broke away from the policeman and scrambled for the door. One of the searchers caught him by the leg and he fell, sprawling halfway into the hall.

'Your friend doesn't know what's good for him,' the army-surplus man said. 'Why not tell me who he is?'

'I met him on the stairs,' she said. 'I don't know his name.'

'Come now, miss.'

Matthew was being handcuffed.

'Nothing here, Boss,' said one of the searchers.

'Try the back.' The army-surplus man waved them away. 'Let's start with some names. You're the sister, if I'm not wrong.'

'Are you allowed to just crash in here?'

'Badge.' It read DS Cooper. 'Warrant to search the premises.' The print on the piece of paper was a blur.

'I'm Alison Felshaw.' She wished David were there. He would have known exactly what to do.

'When did you last see your brother, miss?'

'I was away,' she said. 'I came back to see him but he hasn't been around. Why are you looking for him?'

'Did I say we were looking for him?' Something had changed in the army-surplus man. 'I don't believe I ever said that, miss.' His tone had softened into what she took to be an affectation of regret. She feared the change, not understanding what it might signify. The phone started to ring.

'You pick it up, miss, and talk just as if we weren't here. Is that understood?'

She nodded. 'Hello?'

'Thank God.' It was her father, his voice gruff and strained. 'I've called half the numbers in the Rome telephone book.'

'Daddy?' She exhaled the word in a rising shriek, hearing some terrible absence in his voice, as if he were using the last of his breath to speak to her. She tingled with guilt at not having phoned her parents to tell them she had been – was – in England.

'Can you come home, darling?' her father said. 'There's something we must talk about.'

'Tell me, Dad,' she said. 'Just tell me.'

There was a long silence.

'Daddy, Daddy, are you there?'

And then her mother was on the line. 'Ali, darling, come home. Please come home.'

'It's David, isn't it?'

'Yes, it's David.'

'How bad is it?'

'It's very bad, darling.'

'Can I see him?'

'No, my darling.'

'But I have to see him.'

'They need to do an autopsy,' her mother said. 'Then we can see him.'

'No,' Alison said. 'No.' The army-surplus man took the telephone from her hand. 'You knew, didn't you?' she said to DS Cooper.

He looked away and spoke into the telephone. 'Mrs Felshaw? DS Cooper speaking. My sympathies for your loss.'

Alison did not listen to anything else that DS Cooper said to her mother. She walked across the room to join Matthew. She leant against his body and waited for his arms to enclose her. She had no right to demand comfort from her mother and father, having concealed her whereabouts from them. There was only Matthew, but his arms were not encircling her as she had hoped. She heard DS Cooper conclude his conversation with her mother. She reached for Matthew's hands and touched the metal of the handcuffs.

'Take them off,' she said. 'He's got nothing to do with this.'

'We don't know that,' DS Cooper said.

'I can vouch for him,' she said.

'And who is going to vouch for you?' DS Cooper said.

'I'm a teacher, for God's sake.' She needed to know exactly when he had died. She had to dispel the absurd but persistent idea that her moments of tenderness with Matthew had coincided with David's death.

One of the searchers handed Matthew's wallet to DS Cooper, who slipped out one of the credit cards and read 'Matthew Kerrigan.'

'The stolen car, sir,' said one of the other policemen.

'What do you like to be called, son?' DS Cooper asked. 'Substance abuser? Addict? Junkie?'

'He's got nothing to do with this,' Alison said.

'And what about you? Help your brother turn a tidy profit?' DS Cooper was detaching Alison from Kerrigan, pulling her arms away from him. 'Take this one down the station.'

Matthew was led away.

'David never meant any harm,' she said, wondering whether it was true.

'We're all victims nowadays,' DS Cooper said. 'No villains. Just victims.'

'How did it happen?'

'I want you to help me answer that question,' DS Cooper said. 'For his sake. For David.'

One of the policemen carried the puppy into the living room and Alison pulled it on to her lap. As the search continued, DS Cooper asked her questions about people called Base and Silus and Patch and Thread (or was it Fred?). Some of the names were familiar from the answering machine. As she gave an account of her ignorance, DS Cooper seemed to weary of his own questions.

'I knew he was in trouble,' she said. 'He stopped calling me.'

'Your friend—' DS Cooper consulted his notebook – 'Sergio. I'd like to talk to him. Informally.'

'Sergio never knew David.'

'But you did?'

'Do I need a lawyer?' Alison asked.

'I hope not,' DS Cooper said. 'I assume not. Your brother had a book of numbers, addresses?'

'He kept it with him.'

'We didn't find it.'

'It was you who found him?' Alison stood up.

'Lost him, more like.' DS Cooper turned the pages of his notebook. 'We'd been watching him. Then he disappeared.'

Alison said nothing, her attention absorbed by the idea that she, Sergio and Matthew had all been part of what DS Cooper had been watching.

'He owed someone a large sum of money,' DS Cooper said. 'Would you happen to know where I might find that money?'

'He never gave me money.' It was true. His gifts were never in the crude currency of cash. 'He was killed for money?'

'Did I say he was killed?'

'Can't you see I don't know anything? Can't you be decent and tell me how my brother died?'

'This Kerrigan fellow,' DS Cooper said. 'What's he about?'

'He's my friend.'

'Nice girl like you has a brother and a boyfriend both taking gear. Bit of a coincidence that.'

'Not if you stop to think about it,' Alison said. 'And I didn't say he was my boyfriend.'

'Who would have wanted to kill your brother?'

'Nobody,' she said. 'Everybody.'

'You're not including yourself?'

'He infuriated everyone,' Alison said. 'But we forgave him.'

The other policemen filed into the living room. She guessed from their expressions that they had failed to find what they were looking for. 'All right, lads?' DS Cooper glanced towards the hall. They began to leave. She heard their footsteps thumping down the stairs.

'Where did you find him?'

'He was in the car. Kerrigan's car,' DS Cooper said. 'Time of death not yet confirmed.'

She tried to swallow the indigestible knowledge that David was gone. Not just indigestible but impossible to taste or to swallow.

'You shouldn't be alone,' DS Cooper said. 'You should be with your parents.' Alison imagined their reaction – her mother on the sofa, arms crossed over her chest, hands on her own shoulders, holding herself; Dad standing by the window, staring out at the garden in which, for many years now, no children had played. She ran to the bathroom and vomited.

Policemen sat either side of Matthew in the van. His arrest appeared to be a matter of indifference to them. At the station, he was photographed and finger-printed. He signed a form on which a desk sergeant had laboriously itemised the contents of his pockets, placing them as he did so into see-through plastic bags. A drunk was hollering in a nearby cell. Matthew overheard two uniformed policemen mention a doctor as they passed through the lock-up area.

'I'm getting sick,' he said. To his surprise, the doctor was summoned. Matthew explained his condition and was given four twenty-milligram tablets of Valium, one of which he was supposed to take every two hours. He swallowed all of them as soon as the doctor left, pumping his cheeks in and out to manufacture saliva. He craved a cigarette.

When they asked him to take his belt off he supposed they were going to strip-search him. Then they told him to take the laces out of his sneakers and he remembered that these were customary precautions. The cell door closed behind him and the lock turned. Bright electric light made the little room vibrate. Would Alison stay at the flat? Would she go to the country or to Rome? He might remain in the cell for hours or days or weeks. They might tell him his likely fate or they might not. He stopped breathing, a swimmer pulled by a strong cold current: perhaps they had arrested him not so much for the small quantity of drugs they had found in his pocket but because they believed he had played some part in David's death.

The Valium turned his thoughts and movements to treacle. He stood by the door, leaning against it with his forehead, knees buckling and straightening. He longed for David, who would have turned the experience into an adventure instead of a penance to be endured. David would have helped him to be cool. He lay on the bed. They had not charged him with anything worse than possession of heroin. He could plead guilty and pay a fine. If only David had not borrowed his car that night—. He should have been stronger and refused to bend to David's wishes. He lay on the rough blanket and thought of his grandmother alone at the nursing home. He thought about Alison and the moment in the taxi when she had gripped his hair and kissed him. Then he fell asleep.

When they woke him, it was morning. Two uniformed policemen escorted him in a windowless van to his basement flat at Earl's Court. They found a pipe which he used to smoke hash but did not bother to take it with them. Then they drove him back to the police station and interviewed him. He told them that David had given him the drugs in the packet. They asked him about Base and Silus and a number of other people whose names were unfamiliar. He pleaded ignorance.

'Just a small-time junkie, then.'

'That's right.'

'With a Jaguar.'

'That was David's.'

'You were partners.'

'No,' Matthew said.

'You were living in his flat.'

'He asked me to look after things.'

'Things?'

'He was supposed to come back the same night.'

'Which night was that?'

'It must have been a Friday,' he said, remembering his visit to his grandmother the following day.

He was returned to the cell, to think up better answers to their questions. The Valium had worn off. Despite his not yet having a new habit, he was dogged by phantom sensations of withdrawal. He could only contemplate David's death within the frame of its impact upon Alison. He could imagine her grief, even if he was locked out of his own.

He slept again and woke to the smell of disinfectant, forgetting where he was until the bright light caged to the ceiling told him this was a cell and not a dormitory. In the afternoon, a detective in plain clothes asked him more questions. Matthew requested a cigarette.

'I stopped,' the detective said. 'You should give it a try. He was a good friend, this' – the policeman glanced at his notes – 'David Felshaw?'

'Yes and no,' Matthew said.

'Smashed up your car.'

'You can't prove that was him.'

'Why protect him?' said the policeman. 'He's dead. He never done you no favours.'

'But he did.'

'He landed you in it, Mr Kerrigan. Had you running his errands.'

'He was my friend,' Matthew said. 'It didn't matter to me what he did. I didn't ask.'

'So long as you got your gear,' the policeman said. 'He got you started on it, didn't he? Just another customer to him you was. Another source of income.'

'It wasn't like that.'

'You would've been happy to see the back of him.'

'No.'

'Shop him,' the policeman said. 'Get your own back.'

'I don't know the people he dealt with.'

'But you wanted to get your own back.'

'I didn't say that.'

'Think you can beat me at this game?'

'Is it a game?'

'Do you think it's a game?'

Matthew tried to concentrate. The policeman had picked up on his aura of culpability. But there were no substantive facts to attach to the impression of accountability he exuded. They told him he would be summoned to a magistrates' court to plead on the charge of possession. They gave him back his belt and his belongings. He walked out into the cool evening and for some moments as he strode along the pavement, the breathing of fresh air and the intoxication of physical liberty banished all thought. He walked to Hammersmith Grove.

By the time he arrived at the flat, it was dark. The door had been repaired. He unlocked it. The mess of the search had been cleared. The puppy was curled in a corner by the entrance to the kitchen and did not wake to his footsteps. He could see only by the bare bulb in the staircase which shone through the narrow rectangle of window above the front door. He quadruple-locked the door from the inside. He sat on the floor in the hall and picked up the puppy, stroking the plump black body. The light in the stairwell went out, cut by automatic timer. In the darkness, a strange odour leaked from his body. A stale smell he associated with the adrenalin which had pumped through him while he was under arrest.

The memory of wishing David dead drenched him in shame. He remembered how, on the day his parents had died, David had talked of trying and failing to imagine what it would be like if his own parents were to die. Matthew experienced no difficulty in imagining David dead. He was implicated in his friend's death by his failure of faith. The puppy scrambled to its feet and placed its front paws on his shoulder, peering into his face. His numb body shuddered involuntarily. The puppy licked his face. He tried to raise his arms to push the animal away, but he was incapable of movement. He heard the squeak of a floorboard somewhere in the flat. He tried to stand up but his arms would not raise him. His legs refused to respond. While he had been in the cell his whole being had focused upon his desire to be released. Now that he was free, time stretched before him like a sentence which no judge had imposed and no appeal could lift.

His body was a thing of liquid, a caul of warm blood. Floating within it he summoned and fingered images of his mother and father, of David and Alison. While he was able to touch these faces he had no fear of drowning. After a drifting hour they receded and he suffered a reprise of the childhood terror in which he was strapped to a stone altar in a dank prison, water gushing from a pipe, slowly filling the room. The sound of pouring water changed as the level rose, the note higher, tighter. Wetness seeped into his clothes. Ripples lapped against his arms and sides. As water closed over his chest and filtered into his ears, he shook his head with all the strength desperation could muster, breaking free of the amber numbness. Pins and needles prickled his skin.

The main door of the mansion block slammed shut five storeys below. Someone turned on the light in the stairwell. The puppy scrambled from Matthew's lap. He stood up and watched the landing through the fish-eye in the door. Footsteps approached. Alison's voice, another female voice. The backs of two heads, shoulders, and then the faces looming towards him as the two women turned in the stairwell to mount the last few steps to the fifth floor. He recognised Josephine. Matthew slipped into David's room and closed the door.

He heard locks turning.

'How come they didn't find anything?' Josephine asked.

'I moved it,' Alison said.

'You have the stuff? And the money?'

'Does it matter? It's no use to him now.'

The voices faded and became inaudible as Alison and Josephine went into the living room.

Josephine had driven Alison to the country and accompanied her back to London. Although it had been a help to share the parenting of her parents with a friend, now that it was over, Alison wanted to be alone. 'I think I could sleep now,' she said.

'And when Matthew comes back?'

'I don't know.'

'We should get rid of the stuff,' Josephine said. 'I could do that for you.'

'Josephine—'

'You don't want it around when Matthew gets back.'

'It's not around.'

'How much was there?'

'Are you taking your medication?'

'They'll section me if I don't,' Josephine said. 'That's what they said.'

'I don't want Matthew to know about the car,' Alison said.

'Maybe David was dead before they put him in Matthew's car,' Josephine suggested.

'They?'

'However the car got into the river, he might have been dead before that.'

'You think it's worse if someone else killed him?'

'It introduces the idea that he might have suffered, that he had no choice.'

'You're so calm.' Alison lit a cigarette. 'It scares me.'

'The magic of Lithium.'

'If you know something,' Alison asked, 'why don't you tell me?'

'You don't have to take a bunch of pills just to be normal. You're not in the bell-jar.'

'Perhaps I should be.'

'You don't want to be me.' Josephine coughed.

'He was with you, wasn't he?'

'Who?'

'When I phoned. You pretended not to know where he was. He was holed up with you.'

'Bill was with me,' Josephine said.

'Bill was in Scotland.'

'What's that noise?'

Alison followed Josephine into the corridor. The puppy was scratching at the door to David's room. Alison picked up the animal and opened the door. She saw the shape of a body on the bed and screamed. She backed against Josephine, thrusting them both into the wall of the corridor.

'What?' Josephine held her. 'What is it?'

Matthew lay on David's bed, still and silent, listening to the voices in the corridor.

'I should stay,' Josephine said.

'Really,' Alison replied. 'I'm all right now.'

'It's because I asked you about the stash, isn't it?'

'I need to be alone. I'm not rejecting you.'

'It amounts to the same thing,' Josephine said.

'How can you make it worse?' Alison asked. 'When it couldn't be any worse than it is?'

'You think it's less bad for me?'

'You said—'

'It's worse not to feel it.' Josephine's voice was fainter. Matthew heard the front door opening. 'Can you imagine what I would be feeling if I wasn't medicated?'

'He wasn't with you?'

'Bi-polarity or numb-out. Great choice,' Josephine said. 'I'll call you in the morning.'

'Yes, call me.'

The front door closed. Matthew listened as Alison turned the locks. She switched the light off in the corridor. In the near-darkness, he saw the faint silhouette of a body moving towards him, sinking to the floor. A hand reached out and brushed against his face.

'I'm sorry,' he said.

'They wanted me to go to the country.' She put her arms around him. 'How long have you been here?'

'A while.'

'Did they hurt you?'

'I didn't want to lend him the car—'

'I should have come back from Rome sooner,' Alison said. 'We all have something we wish we'd done differently. My mother said she should never have sent him away to school. Where do you start? Who made the first mistake?'

'But it was me,' Matthew said. 'It was my car.'

'It's nothing to do with whose car it was.' Alison stood up. 'My only brother. The only brother I will ever have.'

'I'm so sorry.'

'You and Josephine. It's as if he were your brother and I'm some distant cousin. Fuck it.' She dropped to her knees. He stroked her back. 'Don't.' She shuddered. 'I'll cry.'

'Let's not say anything.' He moved closer and touched her face. There were no tears.

'Come to bed.' She said it as if they had been sharing the same bed for many years, as if there was no other place for him to go. She led him to her bedroom, where an irregular chessboard of rectangular absences marked the places where the photographs had hung. Matthew allowed her to undress him out of David's clothes. They shared a cigarette.

'You make me smoke,' she said.

'Is that so bad?'

'Very,' she said. 'You're a bad influence.'

Matthew listened to her draw down the smoke.

'You're disappearing,' she said.

'I'm not going anywhere.' He took the cigarette from her fingers.

'In your head, I mean.'

'I can't help it.'

She began to touch him as he finished the cigarette. He reached across her in the darkness, dropping the cigarette in the ashtray without bothering to crush it out.

Then she was in his arms, rolling under him, swaying him.

The centurion who guarded Matthew's actions would not leave him alone as he made love to Alison. Part of him was glad that the controlling influence should direct his caresses and contain his excitement. He was participant and voyeur in the translation of his desire into touch and taste. Her skin was sweet, with a delicate perfume which was most intense on her breasts and under her chin. He kissed her there many times. There was a truce of words between them, an agreement not to break the swirling silence with its brisk traffic of unspoken tensions and truancies.

Alison could not unlock herself from the loneliness she had inhabited before finding Matthew in David's room. While she made love to Matthew, she thought about her parents. She continued to envisage them as people in their late thirties, faces tanned from some long-past holiday, animated by hope, untired by the years. When she arrived at their house, they seemed to have tumbled headlong into old age during the four months since Christmas. In the devastation which grief had wrought upon their faces she had seen reflected the bleak plain of her own, which one day she would have to cross. But not yet. Not yet.

The three of them had hugged in the hall, her father's shoulders tense in the clasp of an embrace which he would have preferred to duck. And yet, he had allowed Josephine to kiss him on both cheeks.

'I refuse to accept that my son was a drug addict.' Her father would not sit down, as if he must remain on the alert for some fresh crisis which might, at any moment, unfold.

She attempted to explain the sub-culture in which David had lived, a world which she had, until now, taken pains to conceal from them. 'Don't be ashamed of him,' she said.

'It'll come out in the coroner's report. It's better that you hear it from me.'

'He loved that life,' Josephine said. 'He was in his element.'

'We will never speak of this,' Alison's father said. 'I forbid it.'

'You'll stay with us, won't you?' her mother said.

'I'm not sure,' Alison said.

'What's wrong with you?' her father asked.

'Leave her be,' her mother said.

'We're all in shock,' Josephine said.

'A family must stay together,' he said. 'At a time like this.'

'Will you walk with me, Frank?' Josephine said to Alison's father. 'I need to stretch my legs.'

'I have a friend, Mummy,' Alison said when they were alone. 'He was David's friend too.'

'I understand, darling.' Her mother spoke very softly.

'Daddy's outside,' Alison said. 'You don't have to whisper.'

'You can bring your friend with you. If it would help.'

'I want to have a child,' Alison said. 'As soon as I can.'

'We all need time,' her mother said.

'I mean it,' Alison said.

Now that Matthew was in her arms she could not imagine where she would find the courage to open the curtains when morning came, let alone the strength of spirit to leave the room, the flat, the city, to return to her family home in Hampshire.

She knew that Matthew could not be as engaged in the moment as he seemed to be, that David's absence must overshadow his ardour, as it did hers. If they could sustain their truce, in which neither of them acknowledged what both of them must feel, everything else was bearable. Her determination to uphold her side of the truce made her afraid to speak, lest his name should issue from her lips. Determined to say nothing, she pressed her mouth to Matthew's. Then she thought of nothing at all, touching and being touched.

10

Redford

Alison knew he was close by. She sensed his trace or scent, in the next room, just around the corner of the street, beyond her reach. The day before his funeral she woke up and reached out across the sheet until she touched Matthew who slept beside her, unrousable, dead to the world. Her father had persuaded her to go home that evening. Matthew had work to finish off in London and it was agreed that he would travel down the following morning. Alison caught the train.

She woke to pitch darkness in the bed where she had dreamt away many childhood dawns, the bed in which she had lost her virginity. She stretched out her arms, but her fingers found only cool linen absence. It was just after three in the morning. The house was shrouded in zinging silence, with no small noises – other than her own tentative movements – to offset the hush of the night.

The dream drained from her mind even as the shock of so suddenly waking thudded in her chest. She climbed out of her bed and pulled on a large T-shirt, the hem of which fell to an inch above her knees. She opened the door to her room, stepped on to the landing and went into her brother's bedroom. The curtains were open, exposing the wide bay window which, in daylight, gave a view over the lawn to a pasture and a stand of trees by the river. Why had he forgotten to close the curtains? She turned to the bed. It had been stripped: no sheets, no underblanket, no duvet, no bedspread. Just the mattress, stained and naked, for all to see.

She stood in the bay and opened one of the windows. The silence was refracted through the distant chime of the river running over rocks. She reached below the sill of the window to the ledge on which David used to stub out and secrete his joints. She swept her hand along the ledge, gathering the mouldy cardboard filters and dropping them to the courtyard below. Looking into the pool of light from the carriage lamp, she knew that she would have to call Matthew. If Matthew had been sleeping beside her, his presence would have anchored her to things as they were, to the knowledge of who was living and who dead.

Char followed Matthew around the flat as he collected razor, toothbrush and pills from the bathroom, his suit from the wardrobe and underwear from the tumble-drier. In the sitting room, he rolled a spliff while Char, who recognised this act as a possible prelude to an outing, sniffed at the door in the hall.

Just after midnight, he put on his coat, placed Char's lead in her mouth and placed between his lips the spliff he would smoke on their walk. He heard a tentative knock on the door. Through the fish-eye, he recognised the woman who lived in the flat below, a divorced seamstress who kept cats. He opened the door.

'He's all right, you know.'

'Excuse me?'

'I was chanting,' the neighbour said. 'And now my electricity's gone.'

Char slipped between their legs and thumped down the stairs to the communal hall. Matthew and the chanting neighbour descended as far as the fourth floor landing. A wooden fuse-box was bracketed to the wall at shoulder height on the landing, immediately outside the neighbour's front door. By the dim light in the stairwell and some additional illumination from his lighter, Matthew opened it and peered in. There were two smaller metal boxes inside the wooden box. He opened one, established that it controlled the fifth floor flat, then the other. The trip-switch was off. He checked the row of fuses one by one and, having identified the break in the circuit, replaced the wire. Then he pushed the trip-switch back to the on position. Bach, washing-machine gurgles and a Hoover's urgent wheeze flooded through the doorway of the neighbour's flat, then were suddenly silent.

'Could you turn off those machines?' Matthew replaced the fuse-wire for a second time and flicked the trip-switch. Once again, the bright ceiling lights in her hallway revealed the interior of the fuse-box in stark detail.

'This never happened before,' the neighbour said. 'It must mean something.'

'It means you were using too many appliances.'

The neighbour stood in her doorway. 'Don't torture yourself.'

'I think you may have me confused with someone else.'

'There's no confusion. Come in. I'll make some tea if it's safe to use the kettle.'

'I should walk my dog.'

'As you wish.'

Once the neighbour had closed the door to her flat, Matthew reached beneath the fuse-boxes and pulled out the cylindrical package which he had seen wedged there.

He fetched Char from the hall and, dragging her up the stairs, returned to the fifth floor. Once he was inside Alison's flat, he tore at the cling-film which surrounded the package. Inside there were two rolls, one of bank-notes, the other of tin-foil. He sat on the hall floor and gazed at what he had found. Char moaned and cocked her ears. He shut her in the kitchen. Then he took his find into the living room.

There was the danger that her mother, who had always been a light sleeper, might wake to the sound of Alison's movements around the house. In those first seconds of consciousness, would her mother suppose (as Alison, half in dream, had supposed) that David were still alive, still near, still breathing? She tiptoed down the stairs, surprised at how clearly she remembered the position of each loose floorboard, which steps to skip, which to tread. She made one mistake. In the depth of the night the creaking wood sounded piercingly loud. She stood for a full minute, listening to the silence of the house, adrenalin jabbing her heart.

The door to her father's study, which always squeaked however often he oiled it, was open. She edged towards his desk in thick darkness, feeling her way until she settled her hand on the place where she knew the phone would be. She misdialled, hit the bar, dialled again. How many times, phoning the flat, had she listened impatiently to her own voice on the answering machine when the voice she had hoped to hear was David's? She pressed the bar to disconnect the call, then dialled again. She was too fast: the answering machine was processing her previous call. She dialled and dialled until she heard his voice.

'Mmm?'

'Matt, it's me.'

'What happened?'

'I need to talk,' she whispered.

'Speak up,' he said. 'I can't hear you.'

'I woke you.' She heard him light a cigarette. 'That sounds delicious.'

'Have one.'

'I never smoke,' she said. 'You're the one who makes me smoke.' She waited for him to respond. 'Matt?'

'Mmm?'

'You all right?'

'Sure,' he said. 'You sound furtive.'

'I don't know how you bear it,' she said. 'This time of night.'

'You get used to it,' Matthew said.

'Matthew?'

'Mmm?'

'Will you come?'

'Now?'

'I don't know how to spend the night away from you,' she said.

'I've been awake.'

'Thinking about him.'

'Thinking about you.'

'There'll be nothing on the road,' Alison said.

'I don't have a car.'

'Use his.'

'Imagine me,' Matthew said, 'arriving at your parents' place, in his car.'

'I'll warn them,' she said. 'You have to get here somehow.'

'What is it?' Matthew asked. 'What's happened?'

'I woke up and went into his room,' she said. 'I forgot. Can you believe? I forgot.'

'Where are the keys?'

'With Char's lead, in the left-hand drawer of the dresser.'

'You'll be awake when I get there?'

'Yes,' she said. 'And remember—'

'I always remember.'

'Good,' she said. 'And your suit. Don't forget your suit.'

The journey would take him an hour and a half, even this early. She put down the phone and made her way through the dark, familiar house to the kitchen where the stone floor made her bare feet ache with cold. She eased open the tap to fill the kettle, determined to wait, to save it for Matthew. She opened the kitchen door to smell the air and heard the nearby sound of the spring which trickled into an old stone trough in the backyard. She glanced up at the ridge of the hill behind the house, eager for the first bleaching of the sky. The click of the kettle turning itself off jerked her out of a shadowy reverie: a summer morning in childhood which had begun when David and she stole from the house, towels around their shoulders, to swim at dawn.

She made a cup of instant coffee and carried it with her into the television room. Two ruptured sofas, covered by old picnic blankets, were angled towards the screen. She sat, tucking her legs up under her as she did so. Her nipples had hardened in the chill air from the backyard. Her heel, under and between her legs, pressed into her from below and behind. She felt humid heat against the arch of her foot.

She searched for a channel which was as awake as she was, her mug of coffee perched on the curved arm of the sofa. Touching herself, she imagined her fingers being followed by her hand, her wrist, forearm, elbow. She would gradually insert her other hand until, up to the shoulders in herself, she could lean down, stretch herself open and squeeze the dome of her forehead into herself.

These thoughts, while not in themselves arousing, none the less caused her to touch the place where her body was involuntarily most alive. As she stroked herself, she thought of a night, years before, when she and David were younger, still living with their parents. Slumped on separate sofas, they had shared a joint and watched a late movie. Robert Redford starred in *The Sting*. She had touched herself in half-darkness, her hand under the rucked blanket, her knee raised, without David noticing. She could no longer remember if she had wanted him to notice.

The small movements of her fingertips settled into a rhythm. She was past the point of no return, thinking unthinkable thoughts. The clamping and fluttering, when it spread through her body, carried with it not pleasure, but shame. Thinking what, by daylight, was unthinkable. And when morning came she would have to embrace the consequence of having allowed herself those thoughts.

Alison crept upstairs, put on a warm dress and wrapped a shawl around her shoulders. Then she returned to the kitchen and let herself out of the back door. She slipped along the side of the house, past the tall yew hedge. A wide lawn unfurled from the crescent-shaped courtyard at the front of the house to a ha-ha five hundred yards away, where it appeared to merge with the rougher pasture which separated the garden from the river.

She had always turned to him. After her fling with Bill, when things were rough with Sergio, when her father was tormenting her, when she needed to be met at the airport. And now he seemed to be omnipresent, diffused through the air around her. She walked across the lawn in the silver light. When she looked back at the house, she half-expected to see him standing in the bay window.

All the unkind things she had thought about him, the bitter words she had said. These she now wanted to unsay, unthink, unpick the sentences, stitch by stitch, until the pattern of resentment unravelled. But she held off. Once the unravelling was complete, there might be nothing left of him. She listened to the silence of the garden, a silence more profound and empty for the distant thread of water over rocks. 'Bastard,' she said out loud. A bird began to sing. Then another.

It should have been easy – staying at her parents' house without him. The atmosphere had always been best when David was away. She remembered, with a new flush of shame, how she had nodded her agreement when her father had once blurted out that it was nice to be enjoying themselves without David's disruptive presence. They had been provoked into betrayal because David's absence diminished them. It was easier to deny him than miss him, curse him than mourn him. The garden which had been her childhood world would always be tainted by its missing heir. David had taught her to swim in the river. She caught her first trout from its banks. Once, she followed him as he climbed the cedar tree. At the top, paralysed by terror, she begged him to help her down. He soothed her with gentle words as she gripped his neck. As soon as she was safely on the ground, he teased her for being frightened.

Matthew drove at a steady fifty but the monotony made him drowsy. He lit a cigarette, lowered all the windows, and accelerated. On the Kingston by-pass the lanes seemed dangerously narrow. He stopped at a petrol station and drank a cup of coffee, scalding his tongue and the roof of his mouth. He passed rows of horse chestnuts in flower, the columns of blossom like candles waiting to be lit by summer.

He looked in the mirror, checking for police. When he returned his gaze to the road before him, he was rapidly approaching the back of a lorry. He swung into the outside lane to avoid a collision. A horn blared, headlights flashed in the mirror. He passed the lorry and moved into the near-side lane. The car he had narrowly avoided as he passed the lorry drew level with him. The driver wanked the air with his fist. Matthew focused on the road before him. The shock of the near-accident had sharpened his attention. As he had so often struggled with the curse of insomnia, now he battled with the seduction of sleep. His childhood incubus, the shades of his parents and David were passengers who chided their ferryman's carelessness. He evaluated his store of pharmaceuticals – Inderal, Haldol, Phiseptone, Valium, Librium, Ativan, Rohipnol, Azpav, Seroxat, Temgesic, Diaconal. The hues and shapes of the pills were variform, exotic, their nomenclature a poetry of derangement and restoration. And there was the package he had found in the fuse-box. He was rich in chemicals, driving a dead man's car.

Alison heard the sound of the approaching car and recognised the engine tone. She crossed the lawn and walked under the arbour to the tarmacked strip beside the tennis court. As Matthew parked, he failed to see her standing in the shadow of the woodshed. He turned off the engine, closed his eyes and was instantly asleep. She waited for some minutes before approaching the car and touching his cheek through the open window.

'My stranger,' she said. He opened his eyes and smiled at her. She reached inside the car and hugged him. 'You smell tobacco-y.'

'Don't cry.' He pushed her away to climb out of the car. 'Don't cry now.'

'Say, you love me,' she whispered.

'You love me.'

'Say, I love you.'

'You love me.' Matthew kissed her. 'You're freezing.'

'Warm me, then.'

'Let's go inside.'

She pulled up her skirt and guided his hand.

'Here?'

'And no more words.'

The funeral service took place at eleven o'clock. The coffin remained closed. Matthew sat next to Alison, in the same pew as her parents. After some well-turned platitudes from the vicar, David's father rose and walked to the pulpit.

'All of you here – many old friends, some new, some as yet unmet – will have particular memories of my son, some of which you have been good enough to convey to me in your letters of condolence. It was in this building, twenty-five years ago, that David was baptised. I had not thought to be burying him so soon. I planned to live long enough to witness his maturity, to embrace his children.'

There was a long pause.

From her seat in the congregation, Alison's mother spoke – 'Go on, darling.'

'I have struggled towards gratitude for David's life. I have raged. I will continue to rage. My son is dead. Nothing I say can bring him back. I remember his triumphs on the cricket field. A century and seven wickets taken in the same match. Captain of his Prep School. Sailing holidays. The school prize he won for a short story about rivers.' Frank Felshaw continued to list his son's achievements. Matthew knew that he did not have an inexhaustible fund from which to select. 'In his last years, we saw less of David than we would have wished. He became a stranger to us and, perhaps, to himself. When he did appear, there were still glimpses of his loveliness of spirit. Occasionally, the raw enthusiasm of old slipped out from behind his mask of wry detachment. You will all remember his quick intelligence, his roguish smile.'

When Frank Felshaw was finished, other members of the congregation stood and reminisced about the David they had known. Bill spoke briefly. Josephine stood up and then sat down again without saying anything. Matthew, anaesthetized by the cocktail of pills in his system, rose to his feet.

'I was ten—. He was the headboy. We had never spoken.' Matthew stared at the coffin. 'He was fearless. Too fearless. But he was kind, too.' Matthew surveyed the tapestry of faces in the congregation. Alison, who had been holding his hand, let go of it. 'There was a car accident. Both my parents died. David helped me through the first night. To know—' Unable to complete the sentence, he sat down.

Faces in the congregation turned to stare at Alison. She remained seated. David squandered his beauty and his intelligence, his charm and his advantages. He had squeezed favours from those who loved him. Anyone he helped became a target of his future need. His life was a catalogue of unreturned phone calls, forgotten birthdays, elaborate excuses, pleas for tolerance, and lies. Most of all, lies. Unless she could bring words to her lips soon, she would give her brother only her silence. She drew breath deep down into the pit of her lungs and stood up.

'I have grounds for bitterness. I know I am not the only one here who felt let down, at one time or another. You might argue that the uncertainty – would he turn up? would he break his promise? – enriched the times when he was there, when he was conscious, when he gave us his full attention. He loved excess. Excess for its own sake, for the hell of it. He exceeded in excess. If he were here, he would demand that we render ourselves unsafe to drive. I can no longer remonstrate with him, or mould him into the brother I supposed I wanted. Now he's gone.

'I loved his hair. His smile. The birthmark at the base of his spine. I loved his impulsiveness and his laziness. His voice on the telephone, calling at last, months late, offering excuses.'

Matthew fell asleep in the bathroom next to Alison's bedroom. He opened his eyes to the white porcelain base of the lavatory. His feet had wedged themselves between the bidet and the wall. He levered himself off the carpet and straightened his hair and his clothes. He unlocked and opened the bathroom door. A queue of four women waited on the landing. He hurried past them and shuffled down the stairs.

The wake had spilled into the garden. Suit jackets had been discarded and groups of mourners sat on the lawn in the afternoon sunshine. The scene reminded Matthew of a wedding party from which the bride and groom have recently departed. There was no sign of Alison, either on the lawn or in the house. Alison's mother was in the kitchen. 'I think they went down to the river. Go to the end of the lawn, then cross the field.'

When he reached the pasture beyond the garden, he saw Alison, Bill and Josephine lying on the grass under the shade of a tree. Char sat panting nearby.

'Well?' Alison said.

'I wanted to make sure you were all right,' he said.

'I'm not all right,' Alison said. 'All right?'

'Ali—' Josephine touched her shoulder but she shrugged the hand away.

'How could you?'

'What?'

'All that shit they were talking in church.' Alison stood up and then collapsed back on to the grass. Unseen by Alison, Josephine mimed drinking from a glass. 'And you joined in.'

'What he said was true,' Bill said.

'What about the things you didn't say?' Alison lay down in the long grass. 'Am I going to be left with all of it?' Matthew knelt on the ground beside her and took her hand in his.

'We're all left with it,' Bill said. 'It's what we have left of him.'

'There's nothing left,' Alison said.

'There's us,' Matthew said. 'All of us.'

'I don't hate him,' Alison said. 'I don't remember what he looks like. He's nothing.'

Bill stared at the flattened grass before him. 'I won't listen to this,' he said. 'I won't deny him.' One hand covering his eyes and part of his cheek, Bill sat silent and shuddering. Matthew put an arm around his shoulder.

Alison struggled, and failed, to sit up. 'What the fuck d'you want, Bill? What does he want, Josephine?'

'Nothing,' Bill said. 'Just don't deny him.'

∫ 11

Bi-polar

Matthew and Alison packed her brother's clothes and books into reinforced cardboard boxes which were to be stored in the Felshaws' house in Hampshire. Alison wrapped each of the framed photographs of brother and sister in newspaper.

'Can't we keep them?' Matthew asked.

'What are you going to do?' Alison said, taping up the box in which she had laid the photos. 'Build a shrine?'

'I like them,' Matthew said.

'My parents want them.'

'They have other pictures.'

'I'm going to burn them.'

'And that's going to help?'

'It'll help me.'

No substance, prescribed or otherwise, could silence or mute the monotone buzz – Entryphone, telephone, school bell – which rang constantly in Matthew's ears. At night, he heard the synaptic bustle inside his brain, the frantic translations of his body chemistry, the suck and push of pulses and veins beneath his skin. He did not mention the noises to Alison.

He guarded them as secret proof that he had been changed
by his friend's death.

The weeks after the funeral were punctuated by visits
from Alison's friends. Those who were not old flames were
aspirants to the fire. Constantine parked his blue Bentley on
Hammersmith Grove and reminded Alison of the weekend
in Manhattan to which he had treated her the year before.
He refused to acknowledge Matthew with either word or
gesture until Alison wrapped her arms around Matthew
and sustained the embrace until Constantine departed with
a petulant flourish.

At the squat, no reference was made to David's death.

'Who's serving you?' Mike touched a few grains of the
powder to his tongue.

'There's more.' Matthew took back the paper fold containing the powder. 'If you want it.'

'Must come from somewhere.'

'Friend of David's,' Matthew said.

'Who's that, man?' Annie asked.

'You know,' Matthew said. 'Dave.'

'Fuck him,' Mike said.

'He's dead.' Matthew flattened a piece of silver foil and
tipped some of the powder on to its centre.

'Didn't he total your car?' Annie reminded him.

'It was insured.'

'He had it coming,' Mike said, scratching his stomach.

'They say he overdosed.' Matthew twisted a tissue until it
was wound tight enough to be used as a taper.

'They say that?' Mike scratched his forearms.

'Didn't he?' Matthew lit the taper and held it under the foil
until the powder transformed into a blob of brown liquid.

'He overdosed,' Mike said. 'Ain't that right, Annie?'

'That's how it is,' Annie said.

The next day, while Alison was out having lunch with Tamsin, Josephine called round at the flat. 'Aren't you going to ask me in?' she asked. Matthew opened the door wide.

'So?' Josephine stooped and picked up a letter, addressed to Matthew, which had been lying on the doormat. She handed it to him and then walked straight through the hall into the kitchen. She peered around the room with inquisitive urgency. 'You've found it.' Josephine put down her Joseph Sale bag on the kitchen table and looked up towards the top shelf of the pine dresser.

'Found what?' Matthew opened the blue envelope and pulled out a card.

'You've got it, haven't you?' Josephine said.

'Search me.' Matthew leant against the sink.

'Don't be coy.' Josephine fiddled with a heavy wooden bracelet, pulling it over her wrist, then forcing it back past her thumb.

Matthew read – *To my darling boy, Happy Birthday, from your loving grandmother* – in her seismic biro scrawl.

'Happy Birthday.' Josephine had been looking over his shoulder. 'Anniversary of the trip, and my first bi-polar cycling tour. No wonder I feel weird.'

'The card's three weeks late,' Matthew said.

'If you've found it,' Josephine said, 'I can help you.'

'You lied to her,' Matthew said. 'About her brother.'

'Let's not compete about honesty.'

'Something happened before he died,' Matthew said.

'What about the package?'

'She trashed it before the bust,' Matthew said. 'You want to tell me, don't you?'

'You're pinned to fuck.'

'Methadone,' Matthew said. 'Doctor's orders.'

'Does Ali know you're at it still?' Josephine said.

'That's a matter for conjecture,' Matthew said. 'Was David with you?'

'I'm her friend,' Josephine said. 'You're her friend.'

'You won't say anything?'

'I'll be quiet as the grave.' Josephine opened the door. 'Let her know I called by.'

Later that afternoon, after Alison's return, a painter called Ronald announced himself over the Entryphone. He and Alison talked for hours about friends in common, none of whom Matthew knew. The following evening a Frenchman whose greying hair sorted ill with a complexion distilled from alcohol lectured Matthew on Joyce, Rilke, Wittgenstein's one-armed brother, Ravel and pasta shapes. He was on the verge of making a professional breakthrough, had been on the verge for some years. He traded on the vestiges of a youthful promise which, when the light was kind, he still appeared to possess. On departure, he borrowed ten pounds from Alison to pay for the taxi which would convey him to the recital he was giving in a church in Lewisham.

The phone rang with monotonous regularity – Constantine, Paul, Henri, Bill, Tamsin, Josephine, Sergio, Ronald, Angelo, Cristina, Edward, Nick. When Matthew was in and Alison out, he wrote lists of names and numbers for her on the backs of envelopes. Alison accepted the visitors and the phone calls as resignedly as the vagaries of the May weather. The suitors bore gifts – flowers, books, drugs – which she received in exchange for their pleasure in her company.

Matthew woke before dawn, icicles dangling from his throat into his stomach. He looked across at Alison. She lay staring at the ceiling. He touched her shoulder. She turned towards him and embraced him.

'What?' She stroked the skin over the knotted muscles of his neck.

'My summons,' Matthew said. 'It's today.'

While waiting for his own case to be heard, Matthew

witnessed two unchampioned young men of poor character and background being sent down for custodial sentences. Matthew was represented by an ancient barrister who dithered in his presentation of the accused as a first offender of good character and background. Matthew's palm sweated in Alison's. When called upon, he stood and admitted his guilt. The moment came for the magistrates to deliberate his sentence. He was led across the courtroom to a windowless holding cell where three other men sat on benches, watched by a policeman. He was at the top of the funnel down which, if the magistrates chose, he would spiral to incarceration. His twenty-four hours in a cell at Paddington had given him a foretaste of the torpor of imprisonment. He stood and paced the holding cell.

'What you up for?' The man who spoke was a red-headed Scot in his fifties.

'Gear,' Kerrigan said. 'Possession.'

'First offence?' Kerrigan realised the man was wearing a wig.

'Yup.'

'Three months,' the Scot said. 'That's what you'll get.' Matthew was silent. The Scot watched him.

'They can't lock me up,' Kerrigan said.

'Suspended, laddie. Suspended. Kid cannae take a fuckin joke,' the Scot said. 'Pish on you, Sonny.'

He was led back into the courtroom. His lack of previous convictions and his record of attendance at a drug dependency clinic were, the presiding magistrate said, to be taken into account. He was given a conditional discharge. He did not understand the term and looked to his ancient brief for guidance. Only when he was not taken back to the holding room did he realise that the condition was not custodial.

12

Frank's Cigar

It was a Felshaw tradition that the family should gather in the country for the bank holiday weekend at the end of May. Alison's parents assumed that she would be coming as usual.

'Let them misunderstand,' Matthew said.

'Don't make me choose.'

'They think it's my fault, anyway.'

'They blame themselves,' Alison said. 'Only themselves.'

'Look at me,' Matthew said.

'I know,' Alison said. 'I know.'

'Doesn't that help?'

'Not with them,' Alison said. 'You don't know about parents.'

'Well, fuck me for trying.'

There was silence between them for some moments. Alison carried the last box of her brother's belongings down to the hall. Matthew helped her pack the boot of the Jaguar. She opened the driver's door and stood aside for him.

'You want me to drive?' Matthew asked.

'That's right,' she said.

Matthew played tapes. Alison slept. Char lay curled on the back seat. When they hit the motorway, an hour ahead of the Friday-evening traffic, Matthew lowered the windows. The rumble of passing air drowned the music. Alison took off her seat-belt and rested her head on Matthew's lap. He drove, one hand on the wheel, the other resting on her neck.

When they arrived, the afternoon was still hot. He parked beside the tennis court. Alison was asleep, her head on his lap. He shook her shoulder. 'Here we are.'

She sat up and stared at him. 'Stay close to me, won't you?' They walked through the arbour of climbing roses to the crescent of courtyard in front of the house. Char followed, walking to heel. Alison's mother and father lay on white-painted recliners in the shade of a broad-branched horse-chestnut tree at the far edge of the lawn.

'You'll swim,' Alison's father said.

'No, Dad.'

'You always swim,' her father insisted. 'Someone caught a trout last week. The river's—'

'—cleaner this year than ever before.' For every year she could remember, far back into her childhood, the river had become cleaner.

'I'll fetch some towels.' Alison's mother rose from her recliner. 'Come with me, Matthew. I'll show you your room.' He followed her across the courtyard, into the carpeted hall and up the staircase. 'I've given you the one next to Alison's.' Joan Felshaw did not look back as she spoke. She opened the door on to a large room. 'We've left it as it was.' Wide windows, bowed above the courtyard, were stained ochre by late afternoon light. Char, who had followed them up the stairs, trotted into the room, jumped on the bed, wheeled around in pursuit of her tail, then flopped on to the bedspread.

'Down,' Matthew ordered.

'I don't mind,' Joan Felshaw said.

'Lovely room,' Matthew said.

'They argued over it,' Joan Felshaw said. 'Frank won't let me move anything.' She walked into the room. 'Not even the posters.' Pictures of Southampton football players, in tight shorts and shoulder-length feathered hair – vintage 1979 – covered the walls. 'No one else has slept in here,' she said.

'Thank you,' Matthew said.

'You'll change now.' Alison's mother backed out of the room. Matthew put on swimming shorts and a T-shirt, then slipped trainers on to unsocked feet. He took his sponge-bag into the adjoining bathroom, locked the door, shook four Phiseptone and a Valium from brown bottles and swallowed them with water scooped from the cold tap into the cupped palm of his hand. He unfolded a square of silver foil, lit a match under it and – opening his mouth wide – gulped the smoke which unfurled from the stream of brown liquid which melted down the gutter-fold of the foil.

Watched by her father, Matthew and Alison walked across the lawn. As they descended the stone steps into the field below the garden, Matthew took Alison's hand. Her fingers were limp in his grip. He released them. Thistles pricked at their ankles.

'We don't have to do this, do we?'

'Don't we?' She walked on ahead of him. Matthew turned and looked back at her father, who stood above the field, at the edge of the lawn. Matthew waved. The older man either did not see the gesture or felt no need to acknowledge it. Matthew caught up with Alison.

'You'll tell him I went in,' she said.

'Why?'

'I can't lie to him.'

'But why not swim?' He heard the sound of water moving

over rocks before he saw the river. When they came to the edge of the field, he looked down the slope to a curve in the river where sand had banked up into a narrow beach. The shadows of leaves were dark in the brown water. Matthew climbed down to the beach and took off his T-shirt. He dipped his hand in the icy water. He heard Alison's approach but did not have time to brace himself before she pushed. He toppled forward, diving head-first into the shock of the water, plunging through bars of tawny light until his hands gripped mulch. He swam under water until he reached the far bank, then broke the surface and turned to her.

'Don't ask me.'

'Please?'

'He'll see us.'

'Swim to me.'

She dropped her skirt and her shirt on the sand. Then she stood up straight and twirled before crouching to take off her knickers. Across the water from him, sun on her hair and on her skin, she raised her arms in readiness. He tried to commit every colour, every contour to memory. Then she dived.

They were walking across the courtyard to the front door when her father called out. 'How was the water?'

'Cold,' Matthew said. 'Clean.'

'I found the stumps,' her father said. 'We'll play before supper.'

'I should help with dinner,' Alison said.

'The hell with dinner.'

They walked on into the house. 'I can't face it,' Alison said.

'Tell him.'

'He'll sulk.'

On the landing, Matthew reached for the door of his bedroom.

'You're going to sleep in there?' Alison stood away from him.

'Your mother—'

'She did?' Alison shook her head, went into her own room and closed the door. Matthew showered and then, wrapped in a towel, stood at the window, looking out over the lawn towards the river.

Faint pocking noises came from the direction of the tennis court. He leant out of the window, peering to the left, saw Alison's father break into a stiff trot, whirl his arms and bowl a tennis ball at the stumps. The old man walked to the perimeter net at the far end of the court, lowered himself to his knees, picked up the green ball, pushed himself slowly back to his feet and strolled back to prepare another delivery.

Matthew dressed and walked out into the garden. 'I'm rusty,' he said as he approached the tennis court. Alison's father wore yellowy whites and a pair of plimsolls grey with dust. 'See what you can do.' Matthew took the proffered bat. On the flat of the wood, just below the grip, the initials *DF* were branded. Matthew stood before the stumps.

'What would you like?'

Matthew looked up. 'I'm not sure that I want anything.'

'Middle and off?' the father asked.

'Oh, middle.' He held the bat perpendicular to the ground and watched as Alison's father directed him until the bat was positioned before middle stump. Matthew marked the ground with the base of the bat, pressing the wood into soft turf.

'You have to run, that's the rule,' Alison's father said. 'Put the ball over the nets and you're out. No boundaries.'

Bemused, Matthew readied himself. Alison's father turned and walked away from him. Then he turned, galloped down the court and released the ball. Matthew swung and missed. He leant down, picked up the ball and threw it back.

'Fielders,' Frank Felshaw said. 'I'll get the women.' He limped off the court. Matthew dropped the bat and sat down on the grass, the cut scent of it thick in his nostrils. Some minutes later, Frank returned with his wife and daughter. The game continued until dusk, when Joan Felshaw declared bad light. The dew was rising as they walked across the lawn to the house.

At dinner, Frank Felshaw quizzed Matthew about market research. After the main course, the old man left the table to fetch more wine from the cellar. Joan and Alison cleared the plates. Matthew lit a cigarette. Alison flitted back into the dining room, plucked the cigarette from his fingers and took a drag. 'He likes you.' She handed back the cigarette.

'I'm being made to feel at home,' Matthew said.

'You are at home,' she said.

That night, when Matthew returned to his room from Alison's, he lay awake smoking until dawn. The next day, they swam and drove into the local village to shop. After lunch, Alison's father proposed that they play cricket at five o'clock, and then retired to his study. Matthew slept out the afternoon on a recliner in the shade. Alison's father did not reappear. No further reference was made to the planned game of cricket.

Dinner was served on a slatted wooden table at the edge of the courtyard. Matthew was placed opposite Alison. Her father did not come to table until after the food had been served. As he sat down, he banged his knee against one of the table legs. Wine wobbled in his glass and splashed on his shirt-front.

'Sort of car do you drive, Matthew?'

'Dad—'

'I don't have a car at the moment.'

'How d'you get here?'

'Frank.' Alison's mother placed her knife and fork on her plate.

'Who said he could use that car?'

Matthew watched candle-flames wavering in the almost motionless air. Across the table, Alison looked at her mother. A creature moved in the high boughs of the chestnut tree. A car passed slowly on the lane.

'Let's eat.' Alison's mother picked up her fork.

'Great thing about cars,' Alison's father said. 'Replace them. Start again. New model. Same with all machines.'

'Why don't you go inside, Frank?' Alison's mother said.

'Nothing to go inside for.'

'Let's talk about something else,' Alison's mother said.

'Not in front of the children?' Frank asked. 'I don't see any children.'

Alison stood up.

'No one leaves this table.'

'Please, Frank.' Joan Felshaw pulled at Alison's sleeve. 'Not tonight.'

'Not tonight what?'

'Nothing,' Alison's mother said.

'My table. My permission.' Frank backed against his chair as he stood up. 'Now, who needs more wine?' He walked around the table filling their glasses. Matthew lit a match and, as the flame flared in the night garden, he thought of Jenny Braxton and the night he had first seen Alison. Frank Felshaw set the bottle down on the table with elaborate care and walked away across the courtyard. Matthew put his cigarette between his lips, reached across the table and took Alison's hands in his own.

'You promised.' Alison looked at her mother.

'He promised,' her mother said. Then she turned to Matthew. 'He's been looking forward to you coming all week.'

'He won't remember in the morning,' Alison said. 'And we'll pretend nothing has happened. Because nothing has happened. Nothing.'

'Should I go?' Matthew asked.

'I don't think that's necessary,' Alison's mother said.

'To talk to him.' Matthew rose from the table.

'Tread lightly,' Alison said.

Matthew approached the house. Through the uncurtained window of the study, he saw Alison's father at his desk, a glass of wine in one hand, a cigar in the other. Matthew knocked on the study door. Receiving no response, he entered. The only light in the room was behind Alison's father. He faced away from Matthew, deep in shadow.

'Grab a jar,' Frank Felshaw said.

Matthew went to the drinks cabinet and poured himself a whisky.

'Help yourself.' The old man struck a match and waved it near the tip of the cigar. 'Spent my life with women. Don't know what they want. Never have. Child's banging an Italian.'

'That's over,' Matthew said.

'Been over before.' The old man dropped the match in the ashtray. 'Come into the light. Let me look at you.'

Matthew approached the desk with his lighter and touched the flame to Frank's cigar.

'Never did a day's work in his life,' Frank said between puffs. 'Never came home. Never saw him.'

'He wanted you to be proud of him.'

'Tosh.' Frank Felshaw puffed on his cigar. 'He was a wastrel.'

'He told me you were an old fool—'

'That's more like it.'

'He said you were an old fool and he loved you.' Matthew lit a cigarette. 'He said that made him a fool, too. He said you were the only person he allowed to make a fool of him.'

Frank Felshaw drew on his cigar until the glowing coal at its tip illuminated his alert blue eyes and his close-shaven cheeks. The two men smoked in silence. Matthew stubbed out his cigarette and stood up. 'There's no answer.'

'I'm going to bed,' said Frank Felshaw. 'Don't let me drive you away.'

Matthew was forbidden to help Alison and her mother clear the plates. He climbed the stairs to his bathroom, sluiced down three Phiseptone and two Valium with the remains of his whisky, then rolled a joint. He left the lights off in the bedroom and knelt by the open window to smoke. A carriage lamp, fixed to the external wall a foot below the window-sill, spread a pool of light over the courtyard. Moths circled the lamp, then flung themselves at the glass to strike it with audible pings. The stunned creatures tumbled, singed wings fluttering, to the paving stones below. Matthew leant out of the window, smoking, to observe the kamikaze procession.

He heard the door open behind him. Alison pressed herself against his back, her arms around him, one hand reaching for the joint.

'What did he say?'

'That he was going to bed,' Matthew said. 'Which he wasn't.'

She drew on the joint. Then she allowed her forehead to rest between his shoulder-blades.

'Shh.' Matthew heard footsteps in the courtyard. As he saw her father's head come into view he drew back from the window.

'Take care of me,' she whispered.

'Here?'

'Anywhere.'

13 ∫

My Stuff

Alison telephoned each of her pupils in Rome and explained that she would not be able to continue her classes. She missed the order and simplicity of teaching. She was eating more than she liked to, having lunch with Josephine, Edward, Tamsin, Bill and, once, with Constantine. She slept on the sofa in the afternoons, Matthew's puppy curled up on her feet. It was not the sort of summer she had imagined for herself. The peaches in England were useless. She thought about her apartment in Trastevere. Most of her clothes were there. She had painted the bedroom. She had watered the plants on the roof terrace. She had waited for her lover, often alone for whole evenings at a time, and then forgiven him when he telephoned her to explain that family commitments had kept him at home.

Matthew was out for much of the week, doing his market research work, he said. Every other Saturday, he drove to the country to visit his grandmother. Alison had no intention of telling Matthew about Sergio's visit to London, but he left a message on the machine and Matthew heard it.

'What did I do?'

'It's not you,' Alison said.

'You're going to see him.'

'He's brought all my stuff back from Rome.'

'What do you need?' Matthew asked. 'What do you want me to be?'

'I'm going to have dinner with him.' She wished Matthew could know what she wanted without her having to tell him. 'Everything's fine,' she said.

'You know something?' he asked.

'Matthew—'

But he went on. 'Say you love me.'

'You love me,' she said.

'Say, do you love me?' he said.

'Do you?'

'You do,' he said.

At the Connaught the doorman opened the door and helped her out of the taxi. She was escorted to Sergio's suite where a waiter was laying a table. She had anticipated the protection which being in a restaurant would have given her, a public place where any failure of intimacy might be mistaken for decorum.

She tried to emulate Sergio's pleasure, but her body resisted collaboration. She was dry. It hurt. He was not a cruel man. He stopped. He was confused. He opened a bottle of champagne. They smoked a joint. She waited for his perplexity to sour into anger. Then, determined not to allow Matthew to spoil her happiness, she went into the bathroom and lubricated herself. She gave an exemplary performance, until the end when she began to weep. She turned away, too late to hide her tears.

'It is too soon,' he said.

'It's not that.' Alison rolled away from him. She had not been thinking about her dead brother at all.

'Talk to me, *cara*.'

'There's nothing to say.'

'You have another.'

'There's always another,' Alison said.

Sergio got out of bed and put on a white towelling bathrobe. 'But you are in love.'

'No,' Alison said.

'Allow me to know what I know,' Sergio said. 'I should be happy for you.'

When she let herself into the flat, she found Matthew in bed, wrapped in two blankets, shivering. 'I thought you weren't coming back.'

'I was always coming back,' she said. 'It's hot in here.'

'What time is it?'

'Three? Four, maybe.' Alison sat down on the bed. 'You look terrible.'

'Touch of flu,' he said. 'Been coming on all week.'

'We're finished,' Alison said.

'No,' Matthew said. 'We can't be.'

'Sergio,' Alison said. 'I had to see him. To be sure.'

Matthew said nothing.

'He doesn't realise it's over.' She took Matthew's clammy hand in hers. 'He doesn't really know me.'

Matthew shuddered.

'I thought you'd stopped,' Alison said. 'You told me you'd stopped.'

'It's the flu,' Matthew said. 'Half the office is down with it.'

She bent down and kissed him on the mouth. His breath was rank with whisky fumes. Matthew was in withdrawals. She locked the knowledge of it away in a strong box under her heart where she kept her brother's ashes, her father's drinking, and her suspicions about what might have happened to the package she had hidden in the fuse-box. That way, Matthew had not lied to her and neither of them would have to bear the consequences either of his deceit or of her permitting it to pass unchallenged.

In the morning he cuddled her, half-awake. She could feel him hard against the small of her back. She turned and held him. Before she could caress him he came on to her wrist. She went to the bathroom and opened the medicine cabinet. She found old sunblock, an out-of-date prescription of erythromycin, a bottle of cough linctus with a pink crystallised crust around its top, and a tub of aqueous cream. The DF118s, the Valium, the Temgesic, the Ativan, even the Paramol, were missing.

Josephine had been attending a self-help group. Alison suggested to Matthew that he might accompany her.

'If Josephine's a junkie, I'm Captain Beefheart.'

'She says it helps when her stuff comes up.'

'I don't need help,' Matthew said. 'Josephine's stuff isn't my stuff.'

'Go for me,' Alison said. 'Go once, to prove that you don't need to go.'

A week later, Matthew went to a meeting. The week after that, he went three times. By August, he was attending meetings every night.

'What are you doing these days?' Alison asked him one evening. 'Should I look for a new boyfriend?'

'I'm learning to stay clean.'

'Aren't you over-reacting a little?' Alison asked. 'I never see you.'

Matthew smiled. 'I haven't had a drug or a drink for two months.'

'It seems longer.'

'That's normal, apparently.' Matthew went into the kitchen and returned with the dog lead. 'Happens to all the men at first.'

'How long does at first last?'

'I looked at that house today,' he said. 'It's perfect for us.'

'You're not hearing me.'

'It's only fifteen minutes walk.'

'This is home.'

'You'll love this house.'

'Come to bed.'

'I have to walk Char.'

'Matthew—'

'I won't be long.'

In the autumn, Alison took a job teaching English to foreign students at a language school in Kensington. In the evenings, she was home before Matthew. She paced around their new house, followed by Char, trying to find a room in which she wanted to sit. Matthew had persuaded her to move out of the flat in Hammersmith Grove, on the grounds that if they were to live together, it should be in a house which belonged to both of them equally. The sale of Hammersmith Grove released funds which belonged as much to David as to Alison. This Felshaw money, and the Kerrigan cash from the sale of Matthew's Earl's Court flat, allowed them to purchase a four bedroomed house. Char spent more time in the house than either of its owners. Alison accepted an unwanted kitten from one of their new neighbours thinking, at the time, that taking in a feline reject would diminish her own sense of unbelonging.

Matthew's evenings assumed a rigid pattern. He went to his meetings, had supper with other members of the group and did not return until after eleven. He took Char for a walk, returning a little before midnight. Alison was always between the sheets before him. After the walk, he would enter the bedroom. 'Are you coming to bed now?' she would ask. He would start to undress and, after hanging his jacket in the cupboard, walk through to the bathroom, run the hot tap and plug the bath. He returned to the bedroom, where she would be reading. Sometimes she watched him undress over the top of her book. He sensed her eyes on him but when he glanced her way – even through the mirror – her eyes had already swung back to the page. Often, she would wake in the middle of the night to find that she was alone in bed. He would be downstairs smoking and reading in the sitting room, Char curled up beside him on the sofa. One night she went down the stairs and heard his voice. She listened, trying to work out what he was saying, and to whom. She crouched and caught sight of him between the banisters. He was on his knees by the fireplace. He was praying. She crept back to bed and waited for sleep.

Communications Unlimited handled everything from media-buying and direct mail to whispering campaigns and disinformation drives. Communications Unlimited encouraged psychodrama and archetypal modelling. A glossy brochure on the coffee table in the reception area announced the arrival of 'Europe's First Holistic Marketing Consultancy' in embossed gold foil. Unlimited, as it was familiarly known by staff and clients, traded on the idea that anything – be it animal, vegetable, mineral, man-made or abstract – could be transformed into a product or a service with a brand.

Matthew's role, as a freelance researcher, was to collect data on people's susceptibilities: phobias and phantoms, paranoias and purchasing triggers, stimuli to envy and catalysts of greed. During the year after David's death, he refined his insights into human frailty. His reports and the data they summarised drew him to the attention of the account handlers whose role it was to pitch marketing plans to clients. One of them asked if he would role-play a pitch with her. Matthew sat in the boardroom, pretending to be the client, picking holes in the account handler's presentation. He was impressed by her control. She masked her irritation at his criticisms with charming ease, while still letting him know that she was irritated. She incorporated some of his points into her brief. He invoiced her for the role-play and was surprised, a month later, when a cheque arrived.

The account handler's name was Victoria. Matthew gathered from the gossip by the photocopier that she was one of the agency's hotshots, topping the commission chart for five months out of her first twelve. It was rumoured that she had gobbled her way to a modest eminence in another consultancy and while this transpired to be an untruth born of jealousy and lust, the notion still lingered that her oral acumen was other than verbal.

Her well-practised modesty helped to balance the unpopularity which taxed her rapid success. She understood the herd-responses and tribal superstitions of corporate life well enough to tread carefully over the brittle egos of the colleagues she had out-performed. Her role-plays with Matthew became a regular preparation for pitches.

'How about,' Matthew suggested one day over lunch, 'how about telling the absolute truth in the same tone that you use for smokescreen and bullshit?'

'Doesn't work.'

'Give them the shock of their lives. They'd be flattered.'

'You can't start with the truth,' Victoria said. 'If it doesn't work you've nothing to fall back on.'

'You should try it.' They ate in silence for some moments.

'What are you after?'

He thought for a moment. 'You think I'm selling myself.'

'Maybe you should be,' she said.

'Come on.'

'You're good at pretending,' Victoria said. 'You have an instinct for what you can get away with. You steer close to the unacceptable.'

He watched her face as she spoke. Whoever had fixed her nose had thumbed the clay too hard when remodelling it. Her dark hair was cut into a fringe and fell to the nape of her neck. He had once noticed a shadow over her upper lip which had disappeared by the following day. She must rise at dawn to carry out her waxing and tinting, her foundation-building and shadow-painting. He was yet to meet the Victoria who marketed the *Victoria* with whom he worked.

'Dealing with clients is like loveless sex. You bring in your wares and wow the bloke – the girl, in your case – for a night or two. He mistakes your heavings for devotion. Time passes and, depending on your shared capacity for deludedness, the arrangement lasts for weeks or months and sometimes coasts as far as an anniversary. At that point you either make a major declaration or the thread breaks and you take your promises, and the certainty that you will breach them, elsewhere. In communications consultancy you lose business as fast as you win it. If you don't go on seducing, you get lonely. The challenge is to maintain a passion for seduction long after the seduced has ceased to hold your interest.'

'A challenge you relish.'

'You, too,' she said. 'I can tell.'

One November night, Matthew returned from walking Char to find Alison sitting up in the bed, clutching her knees, wearing a T-shirt instead of her usual nakedness. She had not removed the lipstick from her mouth or the pins from her hair, as if she was in bed for effect rather than for sleep.

'Do you talk to the dog?'

'Shouldn't I?'

'I just wondered who you talk to these days.'

He took off his jacket and unbuckled his belt.

'Don't do that,' Alison said. 'Don't undress.'

He walked to the window and lit a cigarette.

'What aren't you telling me?' she asked. 'What do you have to say? There's something you're not saying.'

'I'm tired.' He sucked at smoke.

'That's it?' He returned to the bed and held her head between his hands. She shook her head from his grip. 'Don't pet me.' Strands of her dark hair fell loose, one of the pins hanging from a dangling lock. She plucked the cigarette from between his fingers and puffed. 'Why do I have to do all the talking? I don't know who you are. Who are you? What are you doing here? Why are you with me? Why did we buy this house? Why won't you make love to me? Why won't you talk to me?'

'You're untalkable to,' Matthew said.

'Do you know what that's called?'

'An accusation.'

'The experts call it transference.'

'And you're an expert.' He slipped his cigarette from between her fingers.

'Fuck off, Matt.' The filter tasted of her lipstick. He unlocked the sash window and heaved it open. He watched her reflection. She turned over and lay with her face pressed into a pillow.

'I'm going to undress now.'

She said nothing.

'And take a bath.'

She muttered something into the pillow. He unbuttoned his shirt and pulled it over his head. She leant on her elbows, talking to the pillow. 'I've wronged you.' He pulled off his socks and his underpants. 'Sergio was in London again last week,' she said. 'On business.' He walked across the threshold into the bathroom and turned on the hot tap. Holding his hand under the initially cold water made him want to pee. When the water was hot, he placed the chained plug in the hole. When he looked up she was standing in the doorway, in her long T-shirt. 'I went to his hotel,' she said. 'In the afternoon.' He turned off the hot water. They listened together until the tap ceased to drip. 'I wasn't going to tell you.' A spider had constructed a triangular web in a corner between ceiling and wall, a safety net strung from the cornice.

'I can't bear the silence.' She leant against the doorframe. Ash from his cigarette dropped into the shallow puddle of bathwater. He was trapped in the narrow room, his exit blocked by her expectant form. 'It was just once,' she said. Crouched beside the bath, naked, close to shivering but determined not to, he waited for her words as a man might kneel in the shallows, waiting for waves.

'I want to know all of it.'

'The more I tell you, the more you'll punish me,' Alison said. 'Can't I have a cigarette?'

'On the table.' He followed her out of the bathroom.

'My God.' She lit her cigarette. 'Look at you.'

'So?'

'It's not the usual reaction.'

'You know what the experts say.'

'You still like me?' She stood close to him.

'Take a guess.'

'Be cruel now if that's what you're going to be.' She touched him. 'Don't save it.'

'Did he do this?'

'Kind of.'

'Show me what he did.'

She indicated what Sergio had done to her. Matthew stepped back from her.

'And you liked that?'

'No.'

He stopped what he was doing to her.

'I mean, yes.'

'Did he hold your hair?' She nodded. 'One hand or two?' She raised two fingers. He gripped her hair as if it were the mane of an animal. 'Stop,' he said. 'Tell me what else he did.'

'You're angry.'

'Does that help?'

'I love you.'

'Tell me.'

'How much detail do you want?' Alison asked.

'How much have you got?'

'You can't let her run wild,' Josephine said.

'When did she ever run tame?'

'Did you threaten to leave?'

'We've bought a house together,' Matthew said. 'Why would I leave?'

'I wouldn't put up with it.'

'Oh yeah?'

'She's pressing your buttons.'

'That's what they're there for.'

'You're weird.' Josephine drained her coffee. 'When David had his flings, I couldn't go near him. Not for weeks.'

'It's nothing to do with David,' he said.

'Maybe you should be sharing this with someone else,' Josephine said. 'Denial is infectious and I'm prone.'

'I'm happy,' he said. 'Angry-happy.'

'I'm trying to live in the solution.'

'Maybe I've found the solution.'

'The road to relapse is paved with resentment.'

'It's not your problem,' Matthew said. 'Unless you'd like it to be.'

'I won't be coerced into celebrating your defects.'

'You don't get it, do you?' Matthew took her hand. 'It makes me feel like me. I'm having a rush of me-ness.'

'Have you looked at her pattern?' Josephine asked. 'Sex? Intimacy? Totally divorced. Gender slippage.'

'Stop,' Matthew said. 'I can't afford your rates.'

'What does he expect?' Alison said. 'It just happened.'

'That's what your brother always said.'

'To whom?'

'Can't you see what you're doing, Ali? Don't you think it's time you let go?'

'How's the training?'

'I should qualify next month,' Josephine said.

'Tell me what's going on with Matthew.'

'Ask him yourself,' Josephine said.

'What did he say to you?'

'Nothing.'

'You're supposed to be my friend,' Alison said. 'Tell me what he said.'

'If I tell you what he said you'll only think of me telling him what you've said. And then you'll stop telling me things.'

'Tell him I love him,' Alison said. 'Tell him I feel terrible.'

'Do you feel terrible?'

'Tell him whatever you like. Stop being so fucking pious.'

'I don't want to hurt you.'

'Please,' Alison said. 'Pretty please?'

'I'm not a bloke.'

'A bloke would have told me by now.'

'It's eerie sometimes,' Josephine said. 'You're so alike.'

'I don't want to talk about David.'

'One day you'll have to. You and Matthew.'

'Do you think he'll leave?'

'Do you want him to leave?' Josephine asked. 'Is that why you did it?'

'How should I know? I like Sergio. He's been good to me. Now, what did Matthew say?'

'You don't want me to tell you.'

'He hasn't started doing drugs again, has he?'

'Is that what you want him to do?'

'I got him clean, for God's sake.'

'The group got him clean.'

'Whatever,' Alison smiled. 'Now, tell me.'

'Say something,' Alison said.

'Anything?' Matthew asked.

'Lie to me.'

'It's not lying,' Matthew said. 'Unless the listener believes it to be true. You can't lie on demand.'

'Can't you?'

'Not in the way you're proposing.'

They lay still for some moments. She was comfortable under the weight of his body. His head was resting on her breasts. His hair tickled her face.

'Was it like this?' he asked her. 'Afterwards?'

'I went straight to the shower,' she said. 'I felt dirty.'

'You didn't want to get knocked up.'

'Why don't you knock me up?'

'Up? Or about?'

'When you take your revenge—'

'I just took a part of it.'

'Promise to take it all out on me,' Alison said.

'There's no one else.'

'There's always someone else.' She touched his face with her fingertips. 'Matthew?'

'Alison.'

'When?'

'I'll let you know.'

'What about just now?'

'That was an oversight,' he said. 'A mutiny of the flesh.'

14 ∫

Unique Selling Point

One morning, a year into full-time employment, Matthew paused between calls, lit a cigarette and wondered how on earth he had turned into a seal, balancing a bright-red ball on the end of his nose, mimicking belief until he believed, amusement until he laughed. He had become a provider of communications solutions. He and Victoria worked together to bring in new business. Matthew hooked a chain of restaurants which needed to redefine its customer profile and a What's On magazine launching in Brighton which had a small media spend it wanted to use creatively. Victoria ensnared a Turkish tour operator with a credibility problem. They won direct mail clients by using a variety of garishly coloured envelopes. Research proved that recipients were six per cent more likely to respond to lime-green than white or brown. Then they combined forces to win the account of a record label which required the full treatment from concept-refinement and logo design to sales promotion and retailer incentivising; a practice of architects which asked Unlimited to publicise their unique standards of accountability and time-keeping;

and a collect-and-deliver kennels which whisked the poodles of Knightsbridge to leafy Siddenham when the dogs' owners took flight for the Caribbean.

Matthew and Victoria surfed wave after wave, never getting wet. Posters above the fax and coffee machines commanded them to SERVICE THE CLIENT! HIT THE PHONE! DIAL YOUR FUTURE! LOVE THE CLIENT! CLOSE THE DEAL! Matthew accepted that he must be constantly available to the big cheeses whose money he was throwing around. He and Victoria were the favourite tarts in the bordello. They had to be washed and powdered at any hour of the day or night in case an exec. rang up to be comforted or appeased. Answering machines and mobiles proliferated in their homes and pockets to ensure that none of the clients suffered a moment of unstroked doubt. They started the day by dreaming up three pieces of good news to open any 'episode of client interaction' as they described the phone calls which they charged at three quid a minute on the billing sheets.

The expansion of Communications Unlimited restructured Matthew's life. His waking hours were spent almost exclusively in Victoria's company. He became familiar with her wardrobe as she shifted through the gears of her repertoire, week after week. She noticed that he had worn his red tie for the architect last time and should wear the green for the upcoming meeting. Living had to be squeezed into the slots between meetings. They snatched at opportunities to shop and collect dry-cleaning in their dashes from Soho to Notting Hill, Chelsea to Mayfair. The merging of domestic and professional lulled them into a sense of deeper partnership. The rhetoric of the pitch-to-clients became the ironic norm of their private exchanges. Matthew blushed when he contemplated the shite they talked. That they were parodying the rhetoric of their trade was the weakest of excuses for their abuse of euphemism and PR-babble.

'Ker?'

'Tell me.'

'You don't look branded this morning.' They were in his soft-top Saab, crawling down Park Lane. 'We need to upgrade your stall.'

'I'm short of sleep,' he said. 'I can't do four-colour.'

'You'll need to indulge in some load-sharing if you want to showcase the articles of faith.'

'My USP is looking like I don't know what I'm doing, but sounding like I do. I'm at the client-coalface, as long as you are by my side.'

'I get to be your product-enhancement?'

'You *are* the product,' he said. 'The airbrushed carrot I dangle in front of the client.'

'I could get you outplaced for saying that.'

'I'll swing in some technicolor,' Matthew said. 'Don't rollerball the human resource.'

'Make an effort, then,' Victoria said as Matthew pulled away from the lights at Hyde Park Corner and cut across an ant-trail of taxis coming up Constitution Hill. 'This lunch is important. Upsize your shopfront and download your life.'

'Talk English for a moment.'

'Not one of my languages,' Victoria said.

'When do I get to massage your figures?'

'When the action list is complete and the client renews.'

Matthew downloaded his life to upsize his shopfront. His sense of dispossession increased. With Alison, he wore a glove of indifference over a clenched fist of irritation. What did she want? Had he not pulled his life together? Did he not have a company car, health insurance and an embryonic pension scheme?

Alison withdrew, a meticulous draughtswoman erasing a lovingly composed drawing, section by section, until nothing was left but faint smudges on white paper. Rather than seek her out in the house on his return, he would more often walk through the kitchen to the scullery where the enthusiastic welcome of his black retriever neither understood nor judged the unshowered evidence of his whore's day. He left his phone and his briefcase in the hall. By the time he returned from his walk with Char these would have been stowed in their proper place in the study. His work offended her.

Matthew detested the parks of West London with their trampled dignity, their scattering of children and ball-players. They filled him with a sense of time wasted and windy afternoons of which he had been inexplicably cheated. A scarf of flesh tightened in his throat until he ached from groin to tonsils. He choked in silence. He preferred to take walks on roads and pavements where dogshit, haunted faces and stranded crisp packets had their rightful place. Char found plenty to sniff at.

Victoria's studio on Hammersmith Grove was fifteen minutes' walk from Matthew and Alison's house, a hundred yards north of the flat Alison had shared with David. Matthew maintained his habit of taking Char out for a walk before going to bed. It helped him to wind down from the day, his mute self uncurling and stretching as Matthew, the communicator, prepared for rest. Sometimes the midnight street-meandering stopped him from waking in the dead hour. He allowed himself to be led by the dog. One night Char's navigations took him past David's old flat and then, a hundred yards further on, past the place where he often dropped Victoria after work. He strode past, concerned that he should not be seen there under the trees, sober, insomniac, following a dog.

The next morning Matthew picked up Victoria and drove her to a meeting with the marketing director of the record label they were servicing. Matthew was just about done explaining to the marketing director how Unlimited was spending his money (and why they needed lots more of it to ratchet-up the label's visibility) when four young men lolloped into the boardroom.

'Hi guys,' said the marketing director. 'Ker' (– they were all picking up 'Ker' from Victoria –) 'have you met The Roadkills? They used to be The Stag Night but they just finished recording this, I mean, massively good disc and we want to remarket them as the – umm – The Roadkills.'

'Hello Roadkills,' Matthew said.

Then the marketing director introduced each Roadkill by name. Victoria nodded to each of them in turn. When it came to the last of them, Derry, she paused for a beat before responding.

'Fuck me,' Derry said. 'It's you, isn't it?'

'The Roadkills.' Victoria looked straight through Derry, nullifying him. 'Squashed in the road with no chance of resurrection. The name admits defeat before joining battle with the consumer. A stain on the hard shoulder you wish you hadn't seen. Little furry creatures, stupid enough to cross six lanes of traffic to reach a field to all intents and purposes the same as the field they just left. There's no progression in that, no upside, no selling catch.'

'Who's going to scrape you off the tarmac?' Matthew added, backing Victoria up out of habit. The Roadkills was as good a name for a band as any other. He and Victoria had become proficient in the art of creating vacuums which Unlimited's expertise was uniquely designed to fill. Once doubt about the name was established, the band started to eye the marketing director accusingly.

Victoria shifted gear to make an informal pitch for extra business. 'Let's take the music to the people and see what they come up with.' This meant Victoria and Matthew handing out demo tapes to the secretaries at work and teasing up their responses into what would pass – with the right typeface – for an exhaustive market survey (seven out of ten ABC1s found such and such to be the case). They would think up a new name in the car between meetings and then tweak the survey so that its findings justified their choice. 'We can offer this service at economical rates given the through-put of activity we already enjoy with your organisation.'

Derry left the room. Matthew excused himself and followed. Derry leant over the urinal in the mock-marble gents. Matthew lined up beside him.

'I couldn't almost recognise her,' Derry said. 'What with the hair and that.'

'I didn't realise she'd been in the music biz,' Matthew said.

'Music?' Derry turned to Matthew. 'Vicky? You doing her, or what?'

'What if I were?'

'That's all right, then.' Derry zipped up. 'Want some of this? Blinding stuff. Totally uncut.'

'I'm on duty,' Matthew said.

'Mental, man,' Derry said. 'Strictly mental. You mind if I take her to lunch after?'

'We have a full schedule,' he said. 'And a waiting list of meetings to go to if anyone cancels.'

'You got a number?'

Matthew finished washing his hands. Then he gave Derry a red-embossed business card on which a list of mobile and immobile telephone numbers was printed.

His glimpse over the perimeter fence of Victoria's past served more as a lure than a warning. He asked her about Derry in the car *en route* to the next meeting. 'Whatever you heard is not true.' She refused to elaborate on this phrase which had come to be a familiar refrain whenever he questioned her about her life outside work. In turn, she never asked him about Alison.

Once, he had invited Victoria to a supper party. She had

been strangely shy, hanging back in the kitchen, helping Alison and Josephine with the food, as if she had no personality available for such an occasion. Over the weeks after the supper party, Victoria received a blizzard of calls from Josephine. Matthew could find no easy way to discourage their intimacy.

Victoria and Matthew spent all day together, seducing whichever set of clients was scheduled for service. They had drained flirtation of all its charms. They used its ruses and reversals as tools with which to touch the client where he lived. If it came to a tryst between them there would be no rhetorical reserve games or set-pieces of foreplay. They would go straight to Wembley for the big match.

He tramped the night streets with his dog, the walks his equivalent of long dinners and thigh-stroking in taxis. The gradual tightening of his walks' circumference stood substitute for heavy-petting. He spent weeks circling closer and closer, accumulating the conviction that by the time he arrived he would be participating in an inevitability for which he could not be blamed.

He continued to visit his grandmother with painstaking regularity. She had no other grandchildren. Alison hardly saw him, what with work and meetings and the fortnightly visits to the old people's home. He eventually agreed to the idea that they could drive to Alison parents' house in Hampshire, stopping on the way in Sussex to see his grandmother.

Alison supposed he must be ashamed of his grandmother. Not so much of her senility, as of her revealing some aspect of him which, without her intervention, he could cloak until he chose to divulge it himself. Nurse Bradshaw greeted Matthew with a contrived mateyness which turned Alison's stomach. She looked capable of jabbing the old ladies' eyes out with knitting needles or torturing them with reports of the free world from which they had been exiled. Alison was introduced.

'How lovely you are, my dear.'

Alison smiled, wished she hadn't, and said nothing. Bradshaw told Matthew that his grandmother had been talking about the visit all week, looking forward to it. Once her back was turned, Matthew caught Alison's eye and shook his head.

'Come and sit down, Arthur,' his grandmother said to Matthew as they entered the room. 'Have a drink.' (This was her standard acknowledgement of his abstinence.)

'It's me, Gran,' Matthew said. 'I've brought a friend to see you.'

The old woman's cheeks were caved in. She wore a skim of white hair. When she looked at Alison, her expression changed. She turned away and stared out of the window.

'Gran?' Matthew approached her armchair. 'This is Ali. The friend I told you about?' The old woman shrugged and muttered something which Alison could not hear.

'Don't do this,' Matthew said. Again she spoke so that Alison could not hear. Her haughtiness was absurd, a bag-lady playing princess. Alison sat down in a chair and stood up again when she felt a cold dampness seeping through her skirt. The old woman's determination to give offence liberated her from taking it.

'Wait till you're left for dead,' she said. It was not clear whether this remark was intended for Alison or Matthew.

They were on the road for fifteen minutes before either of them spoke.

'HAZCHEM,' Matthew said, 'like the signs you see outside factories, etched against a vibrant orange background.'

'She's certainly a hard hat area.'

'I'm sorry,' he said. 'I warned you.'

'Who is Arthur?'

'Was,' Matthew said. 'My father.'

'You never speak about your parents.'

'Nothing to say.' Matthew's hand moved from the gear-stick to her knee.

'Do you mind me asking you?'

'Do you mind me touching you?' Matthew felt her muscles flinch under his hand.

'How many times do I have to repeat it?' Alison said.

'You'll have to talk about it soon.'

'Will I?'

'There's someone Josephine goes to,' Matthew said.

'No one's shrinking me.'

'This woman's cognitive,' Matthew said. 'It's different.'

They drove in silence as darkness fell.

'It's not about him any more,' Alison said, eventually.

'No,' Matthew said. 'Not any more.'

'It really isn't, is it?'

'It really isn't,' he repeated. The rain had stopped and as they drove away from the clouds, the moon washed fields and bridges in a haze of blue and silver. 'He would have loved this.'

'He would be hurrying somewhere,' Alison said. 'Too busy to notice anything.'

'We weren't wrong to love him, were we?'

'You talk too much,' Alison said.

'I like driving at night,' Matthew said.

'We could live in a car,' she said. 'A very long car with a bed and a fridge and an Aga. And a spare room so friends could come to stay.'

'Like who?'

'Choose a tape.'

Matthew changed down and moved into the outside lane to overtake.

After dinner, Matthew walked in the garden. The others watched television. He was huddled in his overcoat by the ha-ha at the far end of the lawn when he heard footsteps. Alison's father joined him. Together, they stared into the darkness where the river ran through the trees beyond the pasture. Matthew smoked a cigarette.

'Let me have one of those,' Frank Felshaw said.

'I thought you'd given up.' Matthew offered the packet.

'I have.' The father's face flared into view, illuminated from below by the match which Matthew held to his cigarette. There were strangely few lines and folds in the face. But the yellow light of the flame accentuated the wine-stained redness of his cheeks, and the web of broken veins, a darker red beneath the skin.

'Job all right?'

'—ish.'

'Can't talk about him in the house,' Frank Felshaw said. 'Women won't have it.'

'No.'

'As if talking made any difference.' Felshaw drew on the cigarette. 'Have a drink with me.'

'No thanks.'

'Go on.'

'I don't drink any more,' Matthew said. 'I can't.'

'He was a drinker.'

'Booze, drugs, pills,' Matthew said. 'It's the same.'

'We've agreed to disagree about that,' the father said. 'You can't equate claret and heroin.'

'Maybe.'

'Should I stop drinking?' Frank Felshaw placed a hand on Matthew's shoulder.

'It's up to you.'

Neither man spoke for some moments. Matthew heard water moving over stones in the river beyond the field.

'Nearly two years now,' Frank said.

'A day at a time.' Matthew supposed that Frank was referring to his period of abstinence. 'It gets easier.'

'When did you lose your father?'

'I was ten,' Matthew said.

'Miss him much?'

'Can't remember him well enough to be sure.' Matthew flicked his cigarette end into the darkness. 'And you?'

'David?' Frank Felshaw's hand squeezed Matthew's shoulder. 'Christ, it goes slowly.'

'What are you waiting for?'

The father dropped his cigarette, half-smoked, and stepped the butt into the lawn. 'Damned if I know.' Matthew turned to stand in front of the older man who was gazing into the darkness as if into a dream which he was being forced to abandon. Matthew put his arms around Alison's father and tried to hug him. The shoulder muscles under his hand were taut like ropes. Frank Felshaw pushed him away. Matthew heard his dog approaching across the lawn, running full tilt out of the night. Char streaked through the pool of light in the courtyard. 'Best go in,' the father said. 'Not a word, eh? Just between us.'

15

Close

On the night of the strange telephone call, Alison and Matthew had progressed from desultory bickering over supper to uneasy truce by half past midnight. They lay beside each other in bed, not touching. 'We should have a rule.' Matthew lit a cigarette.

'When else are we supposed to talk?' she asked him.

'Tell me a single time when we resolved an argument after midnight.' Matthew always wanted hard evidence and when she could not provide it, he considered himself victorious by default. He rolled on to his side, closed for business. She stared at a book for a while without being able to read. Then she must have slept.

She did not know for how long the phone had been ringing when she woke up. In her dream it was the sound of a blade cutting through wood in a sawmill. She sat up, stared at the ringing white telephone, thinking she should be answering the door until the phone ringing and the idea of the phone ringing dovetailed together and she picked up the receiver.

'Is that – who is that?'

'Who's this?' Alison asked.

'Oh, Ali, it's Josephine.' The green-glowing letters of the clock told Alison it was a quarter to four. 'Listen, Ali, this may seem – is Matthew there by any chance?' It should have told her something that she looked across at her sleeping partner before telling Josephine that he was.

'Can I speak to him?'

'He's asleep,' she said. 'So was I.'

Matthew groaned and elbowed himself off the pillow. 'What, for God's sake?'

'Josephine?' she asked him.

'No,' he said, still half-asleep. 'It's not Josephine.'

'Who, then?' She cupped her palm over the mouthpiece. Josephine shouted Matthew's name very loudly into Alison's ear.

'Alison.' His hands fumbled beside the bed. 'It's Alison. It's Ali.' He found his cigarettes and lit one. 'I can't.'

'Ali, I should go,' Josephine said down the phone. 'There's been a mix-up.'

'Josephine says there's been a mix-up.'

'Josephine?' Matthew woke up properly. 'Why are you talking to Josephine?'

'You tell me,' Alison said. 'Why would I phone her at four in the morning?' – and then, uncupping her hand from the receiver – 'Why would I phone you, Josephine?'

'I need a quick word with Matt,' she said. 'I'm sorry I woke you.'

Matthew took the phone from her. 'Josephine.' His ash dropped on the duvet. Alison rolled it off the white cover and into her palm, blowing on the deposit to avoid a smudge.

Matthew listened, grunted, yawned, dragged on his ciga-rette. 'I'll phone her.' Alison flinched as he turned on his bedside light and handed the receiver back to her. 'Someone thinks I'm wandering the streets, drunk, making despairing phone calls. In fact, there's someone out there, drunk, at this minute, in the rain, phoning people and begging for help or booze or something. Whoever it is is saying he's me or people think he's me. He sounds like me.'

'Would you phone Josephine if you were wandering the streets drunk?'

'It wasn't Josephine,' he said. 'Maybe she likes to think I would.'

'If it wasn't Josephine—'

'Tory phoned Josephine because she had this call half an hour ago and she thought it was me but she didn't have my number so she phoned Josephine and Josephine phoned me and talked to you.'

'When did you start calling her Tory?'

'Everyone calls her that.' Matthew put on his dressing-gown, scooped his cigarettes off the bed and left the room. Alison began to melt back to sleep. Images of Victoria – of Tory – distant, on a bank of television screens in a shop-front, slipped past her. She thought, vaguely, of the things she had pretended not to notice. And perhaps, being so good at it, training so hard, Alison had gone beyond choosing not to notice things, and was now incapable of seeing them. Matthew might think she was blind but she faked blindness. How much did anyone want to see, to hear? What good would it do to be conscious of all those signs and signals, writhing and tangling like maggots in a carcass?

She woke up with a start. The hair on her forehead was soaking, the pillow damp. Her body had overheated and grilled her awake. The air was dry and thin. Matthew must have left the central heating on constant. His side of the bed was empty. She tiptoed down the stairs and stood in the doorway just outside the drawing room. Her feet were cold on the stone floor of the hall. Matthew was sitting on the drawing-room carpet with the phone in his lap, staring out of the window into the dark garden, or perhaps at his own reflection. She listened.

'—of course not,' he said. Then he listened for half a minute. 'Maybe it means it's time,' he said. 'I don't want to wait any longer.'

In the silent pauses between his parts of the conversation she waited with him for the effect on him of whatever it was that whoever was saying.

'You're not forcing anything,' Matthew said. 'It's something we have to do anyway.'

Alison knew something was wrong. She knew exactly what was wrong but as soon as he wasn't speaking she could start to turn it into something else, saying to herself that he was talking about work, about his boss, about quitting and going into business with someone else, with Victoria.

'I think she'll be relieved,' he said. 'The atmosphere. You know.'

Matthew had balanced his finished cigarettes, still burning, on the flat end of their filters. They stood like bullets in a row on the low table.

'That would be much more hurtful.' He was wearing the dressing-gown that Alison's mother had given him, which he didn't like but used anyway. And she sometimes wore it too because she liked the cigarettey, Matthewy smell of it. 'I wish you were,' he said into the telephone. 'Or that I was.' He was definitely looking at his reflection in the window. He fiddled with the front of his hair. 'No, no, no, it's for you to decide. But I know it's right,' Matthew said. 'That comes afterwards. I mean I know it doesn't, but that's how it must seem.'

She should have made some movement, crept back upstairs and then come down noisily. With every word he spoke, every word she heard, Matthew took them closer to the place where there could be no reconciliations, no trading of her blindness for his diplomacy.

'I can't imagine,' Matthew said. 'I'll just have to think of it as going to the dentist – except I'm not the cavity.' He laughed. It was nerves, wasn't it? Apprehension. Like laughing at death.

Then she realised that, no, it wasn't Matthew talking who took them towards that place, but her listening. So the thing to do was to stop listening, to get away, go back to bed, to sleep. Ring a girlfriend in the morning, tell her what a strange dream she had dreamt – just as if she had been awake and it had really happened. Stick to her story and hope for the best.

'I know you will. I believe that,' he said. 'That's what makes it all right.'

She backed away from the door, from Matthew on the floor with the phone and the words he had spoken into it. Who was to say that she had heard him, or that the words meant any of the things she knew they meant? She was out of his line of sight before he called. 'Ali – is that you?' She stood stock still, fighting the urge to shiver, to breathe, her feet like ice on the hall floor. 'Hold on,' Matthew said into the phone. Alison closed her eyes. She sensed his approach. She did not believe that being still and having her eyes closed would stop him seeing her, but it would give him the option to pretend he hadn't. He touched her arm. She opened her eyes. He was standing in front of her. She closed her eyes. He was gone.

'It's all right,' he said. 'Don't – hang on just a minute.'

Then he went back into the drawing room, leaving Alison stranded in the hall, to finish his conversation.

'I have to go,' he said to the phone. 'Hello? Hello? Are you there?' And she heard him whisper a name.

'I have to say it is most bizarre. Almost unbelievable.' Matthew was back in bed beside her, employing a tone she had often heard him use when he was in a jam, the tone of the amazed enthusiast: you'll never guess what . . .

'She gets this call, she's fast asleep, the guy starts burbling at her, drunk out of his mind. He says he wants to come round. That he has to talk to her. He's been at a party and he's had an argument. He's in a phone box and he just needs to talk to her. He won't respond to any of her questions so she just kind of listens to him for a while, trying to work out who it might be. And the guy sounds a bit like me although she's not sure and she keeps saying to him, Kerrigan? Matthew? Is that you? But he keeps on about the party and how unhappy he is and how he just wants to come round for a cup of coffee.

'Tory tries to get him to say where he is and he says he's somewhere in Notting Hill but too drunk to read the street sign. Then, at last, he says yes, it's me, it's Kerrigan and she begs him to tell her where he is. She plans to find me – this other Matthew Kerrigan – and, I don't know, pour coffee down me, down him. Then he hangs up. She can't decide what to do. She's pretty sure it's me but not one hundred per cent and she doesn't know who to call or how to deal with it. She thinks maybe she should stay off the line in case I call again.

'Then she remembers the mobile, takes it off the recharger and rings Josephine, thinking, if Matthew's in trouble and phoning people, maybe he would call Josephine too. But I hadn't called Josephine and Josephine had some guy with her – or so she told Tory, but take that with a pinch of salt. It takes Tory a while to get Josephine to understand what's going on; what may be going on. Then Tory's other phone starts to ring—'

'I don't need to know all this.'

'But—'

'You're making it worse,' Alison said. 'Just stop and go to sleep.'

'I have to tell you this bit,' Matthew said, lighting a cigarette.

'No you don't.'

'Look, I don't know what you heard.' He blew smoke into the air above them. 'It's not what you think.'

'I don't think anything,' she said. 'I didn't hear anything.'

'Tory was talking to the other Matthew Kerrigan when Josephine phoned us. By the time he rang the second time he was much less drunk than before. He had become more rapidly less drunk than you would think possible in the thirty minute break between the two calls. He apologised to Tory for disturbing her, upsetting her. It was clear to her now that he wasn't me. He said his name was Max – which would plausibly explain why he might respond to being asked if his name was Matt. He told her he had mis-dialled by a single digit and was so drunk that he didn't realise, care or notice that Tory was not the girl he had been trying to talk to, a someone called Emma who had thrown him out earlier in the week.'

'It's a hoax,' Alison said.

'Tory doesn't think so,' Matthew said. 'There are too many random elements – Tory's response was affected by her worrying that it was me because—'

'Because she thinks you'll drink again.'

'She doesn't want to lose any of our new clients.' Matthew reached across to touch Alison's shoulder, a tentative are-we-touching-now? touch from which she forced herself not to shrink. It was a hoax. His fingers were cold through the thin T-shirt. Never mind that. It was a hoax.

'Then we talked about Terri, Tory's assistant,' Matthew said. 'I want her outplaced, but there are legal problems. Constructive dismissal.'

'The truth can be like that,' she said. 'It can feel like you've heard it before.'

'What are you saying?' Matthew lifted his hand away from her shoulder.

'I'm not saying anything,' she said. 'I'm glad it wasn't you.' She turned and moved closer to him, touching him. 'I'm glad you're sober Matt, in bed, not drink-sodden hoax-playing Max, pouring your heart out to Victoria – to Tory – in the middle of the night.' There, she had slipped the noose from his neck, but Matthew didn't seem pleased. His muscles were rigid, as if an electric charge were passing through him and he was determined to pretend that it wasn't bothering him. She imagined Matthew as a piece of Semtex waiting to be detonated. The others – Tory, Max, Josephine – were sappers, trying to pass the right current through him. They wanted flames and debris. They wanted crisis. Alison only wanted Matthew's happiness.

Victoria's studio flat was tiny. A feminine bachelor pad, policed by a Filipino maid. The bedroom was on the quiet side, away from the street, a room just big enough to contain her king-size bed, a chest of drawers and a chair upon which discarded clothes teetered in a flung pile. A tall sash window looked down on a constricted garden. On the wall opposite the bed hung three line-drawings in the manner of Matisse – a woman seen from behind, sitting naked at a dressing table brushing her hair; a young girl kneeling naked, in prayer perhaps; a muscled dancer reaching towards Heaven, his fingers splayed. The bedroom, less sanitised and lifeless than a hotel room, still lacked the intimacy of a room which is slept in every night. It possessed the latent quality of a spare flat.

The phone rang on the night-table. Beside it, the answering machine stood ready to receive messages. 'Let the machine take it,' Tory called from the bathroom. It was two in the morning. Matthew had not planned to answer her phone. 'Can you get me some mineral water from the fridge?' she said from behind the bathroom door. Matthew climbed out of her bed, resigned to not hearing the message she did not want him to hear.

The bedroom led on to a minuscule hall in which a slender couple might squeeze an embrace. On the wall opposite the front door Tory had driven nails into the plasterboard and perched a dozen hats. In the living room two sofas jostled shoulder to shoulder at right angles. A television stood on a chest of drawers. He walked through the hall and the corner of the living room. Char, curled up on one of the sofas, raised her head in expectation. He ruffled her ears and stroked her head, then stepped into the kitchen. The fridge contained four bottles of Evian, three half-bottles of Moët, a lemon, two eggs and a lump of celeriac. He opened pine cupboards and took down two long glasses. He filled them with Evian and hesitated before leaving the champagne where it was, laid horizontal on the bottom shelf. He looked down on the street from the first floor window.

It was early March. The trees which would make a shaded avenue of the street in summer were skeletons. He heard the creak of bicycle pedals, saw a cyclist labouring past in a heavy coat and a red woollen hat. He winced at the narrowness of the space between the lines of parked cars as a van overtook the bike, brakes wailing as it slowed at the junction of the Goldhawk Road. He returned to the bedroom. The answering machine was winding itself back in preparation for the next call. Tory was still in the bathroom. 'Where do you want it?'

'I'm just coming.' Her voice was muffled by the closed door.

The Entryphone buzzer sounded in the hall, super-loud in the confined space. As Tory opened the bathroom door, she was slipping her hand through the arm of her white dressing-gown, her nakedness exposed for a moment before she closed the flaps of the gown.

'It happens,' she said. 'Drunks pressing the wrong bell.'

'You've been crying.'

'I've learnt not to take any notice.' She turned back towards the bathroom.

'Did I make you sad?'

'You scare me,' she said. 'This scares me.'

'You want me to go.' Matthew was sitting on the bed, his legs crossed, holding the glasses of water.

'I don't think so.' She took one of the glasses and drank down half of its contents. 'Are you going to tell me you have to go?'

The buzzer sounded again in the hall. 'Perhaps I should.'

Victoria put the glass down beside the phone, her hand lingering for a moment beside the answering machine. 'I don't want you to. Trust me.'

'I'll have to, soon,' Matthew said.

'I hate it,' Tory said.

'You'll see me in the morning,' Matthew said.

'That's different,' she said. 'I wish we could wake up together.'

'Anything could happen.'

'People make things happen,' Victoria said. 'Nothing simply occurs.'

'Who made this happen?'

'Don't look at me.' She sat beside him, their bodies not touching. While Matthew knew the things he was not saying, he could only guess at her unspoken thoughts. He was accustomed to sharing a bedroom with someone whose unsaid words rang clearly in his ears.

'It was us,' he said.

'What about her?' Victoria said. 'Didn't she play a part?'

'It's not to do with her,' Matthew said. 'Let's not talk about her.'

'What if I like talking about her?' The flap of Tory's white dressing-gown had slipped from her knee. Her thigh was

revealed by the slowly parting folds of material. It would
be too obvious to touch her there. He stroked her face. She
inclined her head towards his knuckles and they pressed
into the flesh of her cheek. She allowed the inclining of
her head to tip her torso towards him. She fell against
him. The weight of her body keeled them over until they
lay awkwardly, he on his side, Tory across him. The entry
buzzer blasted again. Discomfort hummed off the surface
of his skin. Could she feel him twitch beside her? There
was a surrendering in his muscles as her body slid over
his, despite his suspicion that she was partly distracting him
from the entry buzzer. He found it impossible to believe in
her innocence. She slipped the cord of the dressing-gown.
As she lifted her weight off him, he opened the flaps of
towelling material.

There were so many foolish things he wanted to say to
her now that the moment of separateness was over, but he
did not speak. Through the window he saw the dull orange
glow of city sky. The moon was out of sight, but perhaps
moving through an arc which might bring it to shine on
them, if he were to stay long enough. He was caught under
her, solid but twisted flat against his own thigh. Again she
lifted herself and in a single graceful movement released
him, opened herself over him and subsided to recapture
him inside her with a steady, slow, downward pressure.
For a while there was no movement other than their lips
touching and her hand sweeping hair away from his face.
She began to rise over and fall on him in a long swell, her
arms straight so he could look at her, touch her. He pinched
her, a little harder each time, waiting for the moment when
she would show that he was hurting her. But she gave no
sign of pain. She could have cried out, but she was silent.
Instead, she sat harder upon him.

Suddenly, she flapped her hands above him, trying to
gain height. Wings began to beat at his face and under the

beating he squeezed her still as she made a deep hoarse noise which was not the sound of a bird, or a woman, but some ancient complaint he had conjured from her throat. She leapt from him and rolled away. He caught one of her legs and held on to her. He pinned her with the length of his body, hands over her wrists, knees opening to open her knees. She was silent and shaking her head from side to side. He paused. She smiled at what she could not help. Her mouth opened and closed. He leant down, his ear to her lips.

'Can't speak,' she whispered.

'Let's wait a while.'

She shook her head again. He could feel her cooling on him. A look of fractured distress flickered across her features. Her eyes smiled steadily at him. He guessed that he should continue. He wanted to speak but, once again, remained silent. The same hoarse exhalation sounded in her throat. She punched at his chest until he fell across her and rolled back. She whispered something, down by his stomach.

'What was that?'

'It happens,' she said. 'Not for a long time. But sometimes it happens.'

He did not understand. There was nothing to understand, surely. 'You can tell me,' he said.

'Are you going to go now?'

'I don't want to go.'

They were silent for some minutes.

'When I'm close,' she said.

'Yes.'

'Sometimes when I'm very close,' she said.

'But it was wonderful,' Matthew said.

'I can't speak. I stop because I'm afraid I won't be able to breathe.'

'I won't hurt you.' Matthew wondered if he had met a

twin who shared his moments of involuntary numbness, or whether he had somehow infected her with his malady. 'I'm sorry.'

'It's not you,' she said.

'I should have kept away.'

'It can be dangerous for me,' she said. 'I need water.' She separated from him, offering him the glass first. A sip. Then to her mouth. The glass moving between them from hand to hand.

'There's no hurry,' he said. 'We can talk of this another time.'

'It's not dangerous always,' she said. 'Just sometimes.'

'With some people.'

'Only one person before.'

'Who was that?'

'I meant it,' she said. 'When I said you scare me.'

'I meant it when I said I won't hurt you.'

'How long?' Victoria asked.

'What time is it?'

'Nearly three.' He sat up.

'Once I know you're waiting to go, I'd rather you went.'

'You want me to go.'

'I never want you to go.'

'But you accept that I must.'

'I accept,' Victoria said, 'that you think you must.'

Part Two

Fourteen Hours

16

Around Self-esteem

Every time Alison thought she was about to cry she took a very deep breath, as her mother had once taught her, and staved off the tears until she could pull over to the side of the road, apply the handbrake and reach for the box of tissues on the back seat.

Matthew had offered to drive her but that would have been absurd, like asking an undertaker to save your life. She had never been able to get used to his Saab. But as Alison was the one who was going, he could hardly expect her not to take the car. It smelt of him, or at least of his cigarette smoke which was part of him, part of the smell of his which Alison was supposed to be driving away from.

They had been together for almost two years. Their anniversary was the following week and she had not yet worked out how she was going to survive that. She thought she might book into one of those places where they put you to sleep with tranquillisers, but she would still have to wake up afterwards into whatever it was that Alison was supposed to do next.

There was bloke in a van in her rear-view mirror, probably trying to deliver something, honking and honking. She was frightened of speeding up in case she started crying and had a crash. She saw a place to pull over so she turned into it, put on the handbrake and reached back for the tissues.

The van stopped parallel to her. The bloke's head disappeared as he leant across the passenger seat to wind down the window nearest to her. She kept her electric windows up and pushed the button that centrally locked the doors. She was crying and blowing her nose and thinking about smoking one of Matthew's cigarettes which were in the slot above the new tape machine. The van driver's head popped up – 'What the fuck you doing on the road if you don't know how to drive? Put your window down. I'm talking to you.' She dropped her head on to the steering wheel. Her forehead pressed on to the central leather section and set the horn off. She jerked upright. 'They should tear up your licence and burn it.' He submerged again to wind up his window. Then he catapulted away.

What would Matthew have said? What difference did it make what Matthew Kerrigan would have said if he wasn't there to say it? A new surge of unbelief rolled over her: a net of electricity running down from the crown of her head, over her breasts, down her back, fading and dispersing at her knees. It was a sexual feeling, a great gush of incredulity about Matthew not being next to her, to say whatever he might have said. How could she imagine what he would have said, if he wasn't going be there to say it?

She had met Victoria in the gym, seen her body and noticed – the way one does – that she was vulnerable to all the corporeal shortcomings about which men are particularly unforgiving. How hard she must work to keep her belly flat, her bottom firm; to stop her breasts from sagging. How determined she must be, reforming her natural shape to please the eye of the beholder. Well, she didn't fool Alison.

Cancel Victoria's subscription to the gym and it wouldn't be long before she blobbed out. Alison felt compassion, for God's sake, for the Victoria who slaved away to keep her body in some semblance of the male-desired shape.

She depressed the lighter button and took a cigarette from Matthew's packet. Three left. Victoria was probably a better driver. Why had Alison bothered to pack things and stow them in the car and make such a business of it all? Because, she told herself, she didn't ever want to go back and have Matthew be gentle and polite, ushering her into a place that had been her home until fifteen minutes ago.

Perhaps he had placed that very cigarette in his mouth, thought better of it and put it back in the packet. At any rate, it would have touched his lips soon enough, had he kept the car instead of her taking it. He would have driven somewhere – to see Victoria, probably – and maybe he would have offered her a cigarette and she would have taken this very one and it would have been between her lips. Alison dropped the cigarette, unlit, out of the window. How can it be, she thought to herself as she reached for another cigarette, how can it be that you only realise how much you love someone when you can't be with them any more?

She lit the cigarette, started the engine and slowly (forward, reverse, forward, reverse) edged her way out of the parking space into the stream of traffic. She decided to survive the journey to Tamsin's. She focused on the fact that it was April and the days were beginning to stretch out. Now that the wiry man had gone, she could put the window down and feel the air nearly warm against her arm. At Shepherd's Bush, the traffic had come to a standstill. Ash from her cigarette fell on her skirt. She took the car out of gear, put on the handbrake and slipped her hand under the front of her skirt so she could flip the material up and make the ash jump off it and on to the floor. She didn't want one of those ashy smudges on her little black skirt. She let her hand glide under her skirt again, remembering how she battled to stop Matthew's endlessly dropped ash from making grey skids and blots on the duvet cover. Well, someone else could take care of that now, or love him skids, smudges and all. As she waited in the queue for the lights at the roundabout, she wanted to make love to him. More than that, she would have made love to anyone halfway attractive, if he were to present himself.

She didn't even realise she had been frozen – he never used the word frigid, and quite right too – until the day when he finally came clean and told her that he wanted to go, wanted to leave her, wanted it to end. Because that's what he wanted. He wanted to go. Whatever he said. She knew.

She had thawed so rapidly. She couldn't explain it. Not to him. Not to anyone. She was suddenly liquid. The blood moved in her and new nerves came to life so that she could feel its flowing. She was woozy and biddable. And wet. She put her hand under her skirt and touched herself with her knuckles. Not just for him. She honestly would not have taken much persuading. People pick that up. They notice it like a red lightbulb flashing on your head. That was probably what upset the wiry man in his angry van. His radar was telling him something, but he was too stupid to read the screen correctly.

Alison saw in her mirror that the man in the car behind had long black hair, held back by a dark-blue velvet Alice band. Must be gay, she thought. He was gorgeous. Indian or Moroccan. He sensed her look – she could see him sensing it – but he didn't know where it was coming from. He looked around behind him, then their stares connected via the mirror and she smiled. He nodded and raised his eyebrows, encouraging her to look forward, not back. The queue of traffic had moved forward in front of her. She yanked her hand out from under her skirt, put the car in gear and stalled as she released the clutch. She glanced in the mirror and the Indian man with the gorgeous hair was smiling to let her know he was happy to wait behind her. She started the engine but the car, still in gear, leapt forward like the tiger in the petrol ad, then stalled again.

Her unbelief in what had happened was so palpable, had such substance and mass, that it was like a body beside her. She could reach across and guide the hand of her unbelief – as if it were Matthew's – to the warm place under her skirt where her own hand could not be, because driving even two-handed, in the manifest presence of her unbelief, was difficult enough. She turned right into Kensington High Street. The beautiful Indian turned too. Maybe he happened to be going her way. Perhaps he was following her for the thrill of it, for the flirt.

She had not planned to make her grand exit on a Thursday evening, in rush-hour, on the eve of the Easter holiday weekend. But that was how it had turned out. She imagined Victoria making a similar but opposite journey across London, stuck in another jam, making her way from her office in Soho to their place – Matthew's place. She missed the house already and she'd only been away for twenty minutes. Victoria would be crawling along the Westway – on her hands and knees for all Alison cared, but more likely in her wide wheelbase Mercedes – on her way to Matthew, while Alison travelled east, with her unbelief and her Indian retinue.

It became more and more possible, then inevitable, that she would pass Victoria in the almost-warm April evening, the traffic trapped and lurching in both directions. They would take a good look at each other or, more likely, not look at all, each affecting not to have seen the other. Alison started to cry again, the tears coming without any throat-tightening vanguard, dripping freely off her cheeks on to her black skirt. When she shook her head and blinked, she showered her hands and the steering wheel, like a tree stirred by breeze after rain. She pulled over and bumped the front-left wheel against the pavement, too close to a group of passers-by who glared at her. Yes, Victoria was on her way, listening to soppy songs on her tape deck – Eternal, or Whitney Houston or Phil Collins. Alison was sure Victoria was privately soppy for all her cool-cat glibness. How else could she have fallen for Matthew? Her Matthew.

The tears stopped as suddenly as they started and only then did she bother with the tissues. More like having a pee than crying. She checked the mirror for the Indian but he had disappeared. She blew her nose. She dried her cheeks. She angled the rear-view mirror so she could put on fresh lipstick. She had one thing to hang on to and she didn't want to use it too much, like a vial of magic potion and she only had a few drops left: after he told her it was finished, that he was leaving, that it couldn't work; after he'd lied about there being no one else; after she had told him she knew who it was and he denied it; after she had told him to stop thinking he could fool her; after he told her he loved her – after all of that and after she thawed and went liquid (all of this in the hour preceding her halting departure) – they made love. Or fucked, rather. It was rough and exciting and it didn't last long, but it didn't need to. Both of them treated it like a piece of punctuation, or pretended to; a full stop between the sentences with which they had brought about the end of Matthew and Alison.

She had done something terrible. She had a horrible, half-glanced, picture of it. A girl sits in a glass bauble and a man tries to kiss her, but he bangs his nose against the glass. Like cats and flies and birds can't understand windows, and batter themselves again and again. Flies and birds kill themselves trying to get through glass which they just don't see as glass. People crash through plate glass because they don't realise it's there.

Then he told her he was in love with someone else and Alison didn't have a glass bauble round her any more – like when you open the window and try to persuade the bird or wasp to fly through it – and he leant towards her, expecting to bump his nose, but he fell into her arms and she was alive. She cried and laughed and fucked. So what could Matthew do then, after he had despaired of prising her out of her bauble? What was he to do with an unbaubled Alison?

Matthew had not taken a drink in twenty-two months. He had been having an affair with another woman for sixteen weeks, five days and nine hours. Alison had left at four o'clock in the afternoon on Maunday Thursday. It was now seven minutes to six. He was waiting for the sun to pass the yard-arm. He had not meant to tell her. He had not planned it. Why would she have asked unless she wanted to know? He had rebelled at the idea of spending a holiday weekend with her, the long silences in the car, remembering the things that could not be said and trying to intuit the right things to say. The weekend in Wales with James and Jennifer. Watching James and Jennifer smooching and sporting their complicity. For a moment, a stupid, regrettable moment, anything which might cancel the weekend had seemed preferable to the weekend itself. So when Alison had said, 'I don't think you like me very much,' as they brushed past each other on the stairs, he had not said (as was his custom) 'I love you', but instead, 'What do you mean by that?'

'You move around the house like someone who doesn't want to be here,' Alison said. 'You walk past me as if I need a bath.'

They stood on the stairs, awkward, neither of them wanting to be still.

'You smell fine,' Matthew said. 'I don't know what you mean.' Was she telling him he smelt? Did he smell of that?

'What is it?' she said. 'What is it that is going on?' Her question sounded ungrammatical and dangerous.

'I was about to pack some clothes for the weekend.'

'Why are we going?' Alison said. 'Wouldn't you rather be somewhere else?'

'It's what we planned to do,' he said. 'We're expected.'

'That tone of injured propriety reminds me of my father. In his more sober moments.'

'There's usually something ugly in the pipeline when you compare me to your father.'

Alison descended the rest of the stairs and turned to look at him. Matthew ascended to the half-landing and squatted on his haunches.

'Wouldn't you rather be playing tennis with Mike?' she asked. 'For example?'

'I am playing with Mike,' he said. 'Before we go to Wales.'

'That's what you said.'

'So?'

'Mike rang before you got home.'

'I should get ready,' Matthew said.

'From Paris. He wanted Patrice's number, which I gave him. He was surprised to hear that he was playing tennis with you in West London this evening. I told him he'd better hurry up and get himself to Charles de Gaulle. Matthew hates to miss his tennis.'

'I must have muddled up the dates,' Matthew said.

'You're not a muddler up of dates.'

He stood up. Anyone could see that he had been wronged, that he had only done a wrong thing because he had been wronged. At first, neither of them responded to the ringing of the telephone. After ten or a dozen peals, Matthew slipped past Alison – 'What?'

'Mr Kerrigan, it's Nurse Bradshaw speaking.'

'I can't speak to you.'

'Your grandmother's been asking for you,' Nurse Bradshaw said. 'Hourly. Since this morning.'

'I can't talk now,' he said. 'I'll come next weekend.' He put down the phone and switched on the answering machine. 'I haven't been entirely straight with you,' he told Alison.

'Who is it?'

'I didn't say it was anybody.'

'So it's somebody,' Alison said.

'I was going to tell you this weekend,' Matthew said. 'But I didn't want to do it here. Not at home.'

'You were going to tell me in the car,' Alison said. 'Where I couldn't get away.'

He had not planned to tell her anything.

'What have you done, Matthew?' Alison asked. 'What have you done to us?'

'It doesn't mean anything.'

'Who is she?'

He walked down the stairs with the idea that he might still be able to embrace her. But Alison backed away from him until she was standing by the front door. He affected not to notice her retreat and sat on the red sofa in the bay window.

'The phone call,' Alison said. 'It's her, isn't it?'

He had badly misjudged Alison's response. Outrage and humiliation, yes. Weeping and amazement, sure. But when he told her that it was over with Tory, that he wanted only her, only Alison, she was supposed to open her arms and welcome him home. That was to have been his reward for openness and honesty.

'Ali, I love you,' Matthew had said. 'Please don't go.'

'Was she good? Is she good, should I say?'

'We don't want to discuss it,' Matthew said. 'Let's not cheapen everything.'

'Oh, well.' Alison leant down and scooped the cat off the ground. 'It wasn't cheap.'

'It's over now.'

'If it's not cheap, you love her.' The cat struggled from her arms. 'Not just a lover but a beloved. My dearly beloved—. I won't say her name.'

'It's not her fault,' Matthew said. 'The feelings we have towards each other are completely separate.'

'What does she do?' Alison said. 'Have you sampled all of her body fluids? Have you come in her mouth?'

'Don't.'

'Did she call you darling? Did you call her Alison by mistake?' She looked up at him. 'Did she want to be fucked again straight away?'

'You don't want to know.'

'Of course I want to know,' she said. 'Otherwise I would have left by now. Did she lick your ear and say you were the only one? Did she wrap her legs around your neck to pull you deeper inside?'

'I'll tell you if you're not careful.'

'Tell me everything,' Alison said.

'It was always better with you.'

'Don't you dare.' Alison pulled away from him. 'Don't ever touch me again.'

'Not even like this?'

'No.'

'Or this?'

'Especially not that,' she said.

'Or this?'

'Please don't do that.'

Later, with the cat watching them from the window-sill, she asked 'Did she do this?'

'No,' Matthew said. 'Please don't stop.'

'Did she make you feel like this?'

'No.'

'Did it make her come just seeing you like this?'

'No,' Matthew said. 'Don't stop.'

'Did you use anything?'

'Always.'

'But not,' Alison said, 'when she was doing this.'

'Please,' Matthew said.

'I can't go on.'

'Please.'

'You're thinking about her,' Alison said.

'Come on,' Matthew said. 'You're thinking about her.'

'What have you done to us?' Alison wept, on her knees, still holding him. A tear dripped from her cheek and ran down his length. 'She's moved in, hasn't she? There's no getting away from her.'

'It's over,' Matthew said.

'No, Matthew. This is over. This is the end.'

The cat, a malign creature which betrayed signs of pleasure only when others were suffering, began to purr. Matthew promised the cat it would soon be homeless and have no bare ankles to wind itself around in its morning ponce for breakfast. With Alison gone, he could starve the cat with impunity. As far as he was concerned, she had done the leaving. After all, who had climbed into the car and driven away?

Who had said, rather formally, 'You have broken my heart but I bear you no malice'? Who had said, 'I love you as much as ever but I cannot live like this'? Who had said, 'I won't give you the satisfaction of leaving, of making me the one who was left'? He had followed her up the stairs to their bedroom and watched her open the tall cupboard, stretching up for the suitcases on the top shelf. She had been forced to ask him to get them down.

'You don't want to do this,' he said.

'You have lost the right to tell me what I do and do not want to do.' Alison spoke her words to the window, pointing them at the garden where they had knelt together the previous weekend, weeding the flower beds. 'I can ask someone else to get the suitcases down. Shall I get the fucking ladder from the fucking basement?'

'I didn't tell you to make you go.'

'Don't treat me like a puppet,' Alison said.

'Don't you see it would never have happened,' Matthew said, 'if you hadn't acted like a puppet?' He yanked the suitcases from the shelf, releasing them to arc over his head and land on the unmade bed. Then he went downstairs to the kitchen where he crouched and pulled from the back of a cupboard below the sink an unopened bottle of Laphroaig. He banged it down on the kitchen counter, like a gavel. His gesture was designed to bring the whole house to attention, to summon Alison from the bedroom. The cat brushed its tail along the back of his calf. He lashed out with his foot and missed. The catflap clattered as the blameless animal fled into the garden.

Matthew had not touched the bottle since he had placed it in the middle of the counter two hours before. Not once. He had walked past it any number of times. He had placed other objects beside it – keys, a cup of tea, a slice of toast on a plate. Matthew was not thinking about Alison. He was sure he had not thought about Alison in hours. Perhaps it was the effort of not thinking about her which made it so hard to engage in sensible thought about anything else. The bottle stood on the counter which divided the open space of the ground floor into kitchen and living room. He should return it to its proper place under the sink with the bleach and the scouring powder and the overlooked bag of green potatoes.

He pressed his cheek to the whisky bottle, rolling the green glass against his bristles. He pulled up a three-legged stool, forearms on the Formica. Sunlight fell through the glass, staining the white counter. He lit one of the stale cigarettes which he had found, after an extended search of his own drawers, in Alison's jewellery box. Why had she smoked in secret? His own cigarettes had been in the car when she left. As she pulled away and then stalled, he remembered the cigarettes on the dashboard. It was especially unfair that he should be denied his cigarettes now. Of course he wanted Alison to stay. Of course, if she insisted on going, then go she must and that was a separate fact from him wanting to claim his cigarettes. How could she slope off with the Miles Davis compilation? *And* his tennis racket. He could hear Alison telling him how indicative it was that he should be thinking of Miles Davis and cigarettes and tennis when she was leaving him because he was in love with another woman. Was it because he was in shock, Matthew wondered, that Alison seemed more present now than when she had been upstairs packing or on the sofa weeping? For how long would he be having conversations in his head with an absent Alison?

Josephine, who had recently qualified as a psycho-therapist despite the history of manic episodes revealed by her medical records, had told Matthew that it was important to keep separate facts separate. Matthew and Josephine had sat in the 'safe environment' of her sitting room with the blinds down like co-conspirators. They had discussed Alison issues and Matthew issues. Josephine had demonstrated – with blue and red Lego blocks, for God's sake – how Alison's and Matthew's thoughts and feelings had become interlocked into 'problematic stuff', 'areas of profound interpersonal stress'. Then she had lobbed in the old chestnut about blame: blame, would you believe?, was not an efficient structure and could lead to emotional confusion. Matthew must learn to take responsibility for his actions and own his feelings, but not Alison's. He must understand that he had no proprietorial rights over Alison's feelings. And Alison, Josephine added, must look at the issues she had around compassion and enabling.

It was obvious, to anyone who thought about it, that Josephine was to blame for the whole sorry game of soldiers. Who was she to determine that honesty and openness – the qualities with which Matthew had ambushed their relationship – were self-evident goods? He should have kept quiet. He should have stuck to dissimulation. In the openness-and-honesty game, he was a cripple who didn't know the rules. A sustained, bald-faced denial would have done the trick. He would only have been telling Alison what she wanted to hear. They had kept each other in the dark to good effect for two years. But thanks to Josephine he had gone against his instinct and shed light where darkness would have served a better purpose. He did not believe that Alison wanted to leave. She was behaving as an independent entity, a separate fact, because she thought she was supposed to.

'You love that fat tart.'

'It's not simple,' he said. 'I love you too.'

'Alison Felshaw also ran,' she said. 'No thanks.'

'I haven't been able to see that you love me,' Matthew said. 'Not until now.' Was that one of the things upon which light had usefully been shed? What was the use if the condition of Alison making plain her love for him was that she packed two suitcases and left in his car? The car which she would probably crash, which was not insured for her to drive?

Alison had left at four o'clock. It was now six o'clock. Matthew had actively avoided taking a drink for two hours.

He was due to meet Tory for dinner at eight. Dinner with Tory which had been advertised, in discussion with Alison, as tennis with Mike. And then an Indian with Mike and, well, we got held up at the Indian and then I went back to his place to see his new computer and I didn't want to ring you darling because I thought you'd be asleep. We can go down to Wales tomorrow.

Perhaps he had wanted to be found out. What had Josephine meant when she suggested that he try to like himself? He was perfectly fond of himself, he had told her. It was Alison who had the problems around self-esteem. WITH self-esteem, he corrected himself out of the infectious jargon. Alison's problems WITH self-esteem.

'Alison is not your problem, Matthew,' Josephine had said. 'Alison's problems are not your problem.'

'What am I doing here, then?'

'I think you should try to answer that question for yourself.'

'I know what you want me to say,' Matthew said.

'What do I want you to say?' Josephine asked.

'That I don't value myself so how can I value Alison. And conversely, because I don't value myself I deposit all my sense of value in her. But because I resent her holding all the value, I abuse the trust I have placed in her and her in me. In doing so, I only punish myself. And so on.'

'I want you to listen carefully to the feelings you have just expressed,' Josephine said. 'Listen with your heart.' She edged the box of man-sized tissues across the floor.

He was not going to think about Josephine. He was not going to think about Alison. The bitch had taken his car and his tennis racket *and* his Miles Davis tape. Who wouldn't have had an affair if he was with a woman who forced him to play hunt-the-feeling, who couldn't even smoke openly? What difference would one drink make? And when had he last had just the one? When had he last had less than a number of drinks over which he had failed to keep count? What would a single drink taste like? Or, let's say, one double? Just one. Without ice, because often it was the ice which caused the problem. Would it taste different to six drinks or a bottle of drink? He had tried to explain to Alison that Tory was beside the point, but it was hard to find a set of words in which to persuade her that his infidelity was about wanting Alison, not about the other woman, not really about Tory at all. This had sounded true to him when he said it. But with Alison gone and the evening with Tory approaching, he told himself that it was only out of kindness to Alison that he had tried to make the separate facts separate. Tory was the green Lego which could be unpicked from their life, but he was no longer sure if he wanted it removed. His intention, in confessing to Alison, had been to bring things to a close with Tory. Yes, it had been a confession. Under duress, certainly, but he could have faced it out. He could have told her something she would have preferred to hear. Matthew curled his fingers around the neck of the bottle and resolved to behave towards Tory as though nothing had changed. He did not know how to tell Tory he was in a position to fulfil the fantasy in which they would be free to wake up together in the same bed. Josephine liked to say that one person's sin can be another's redemption.

The phone rang. The answering machine responded before he could pick up the receiver. 'I'm here, I'm here.' His own words sounded savage, absurd, desperate. 'Let the machine finish.'

'Is that you?' He spoke over Alison's recorded voice telling him that they were out but not to waste the call and please to leave a message or send a fax. 'Is that you?' Knowing that Tory would not risk leaving a message, surprising himself by wanting it to be Alison phoning with an accusation or a change of heart. 'I'm hoping to speak to Matthew.' The voice sounded familiar, but he could not place it.

'It's me,' Matthew said. 'That's me.'

Hearing the voice which sounded like Alison's (but could not be, because the voice did not seem to know his voice) he was sorry. He wanted her to come back. He would do whatever he needed to do to cancel his confession. He would promise never to see Tory again. But it was Terri, Tory's assistant, briefed to be discreet. Tory would be late for dinner, he was told. Perhaps it might be better to have dinner on another evening. 'She's been in meetings all day.'

'Tell her I can't make any other evening.' Matthew lit one of the stale cigarettes from Alison's hidden packet. 'I'll meet her at Brutino at nine instead of eight.'

'I'll certainly pass that on,' Terri said.

'Come on. I must talk to her.'

'I can't reach her at the moment. I'll ask her to ring you as soon as she contacts me.'

'It's an emergency,' Matthew said.

'I'll try to get a message to her,' Terri said. 'Should she use this number?' What, Matthew wondered, had Tory told her assistant?

'She can call here,' Matthew said. 'It's fine.'

'She asked me to remind you of the last thing she said to you.'

'And what was that?'

'She said you would remember,' Terri said. He could discount goodbye. But was the penultimate thing she said 'This will never work,' or 'I want you inside me again,' or 'I wish you didn't have to go'?

'Terri, darling?'

'Mmm?'

'Could you change the booking for me?'

'Have you forgotten how to dial?'

'It's not personal,' Matthew said. As he replaced the receiver the answering machine beeped, whirred and clicked to signify the end of the message. He pressed 'play'. The way the machine worked a message had to be played through before it could be stored or erased. He listened to himself and the way he had said 'Is that you?', thinking of Alison. And then, only moments later, 'I must speak to her', thinking of Tory.

17

Displacement Theory

In Tamsin's fringe district – which was Earl's Court, but she called it South Kensington – there was nowhere to park. After ten minutes of cruising, Alison found a space two streets away from Tamsin's flat. The newsagent would not give her any twenty pence pieces, so she bought some cigarettes but only got two twenties in the change. While she was trying to tear the cellophane off the cigarette packet, she started to cry again and the man in the newsagent, who was Australian, offered her first a light, then a tissue, which he pulled from a five-pack by the till. She received the tissue and offered him her pound coin again. He was swift to produce five twenty pences but she became muddled, thinking that six twenties go into a pound. He took offence at the idea that she thought he was charging her twenty pence for a tissue which he had been happy to give her.

She stood on the pavement outside the shop with her hands full, suddenly affronted by the complexity of what were, after all, simple movements. She had to slow down and concentrate before she could get one cigarette into her mouth, the packet into her purse, drop the cellophane to the pavement, put the change which was not twenties into her purse and keep the twenties together in one hand while dangling the car keys from the fingers of the other. She returned to the street where she had parked the car, imitating a habit Matthew had of wandering around with an unlit cigarette in his mouth.

The meter jammed after she inserted the first coin. It flashed at her, still sufficiently operational to declare itself out of order. She kicked the tyre of the Saab, the pressurised rubber bouncing her foot back. A woman dressed from top to toe in brown leather watched her from the doorway of a pub across the street. She went on kicking the tyre, performing for the leather woman in the movie in which Alison Felshaw now starred. She previewed it as moody and noir, with an ambivalent ending from which, it was possible to conclude, the characters might progress if not towards happiness, then at least towards less suffering. It was a French film because she was wearing not much make-up and her hair wasn't perfect and she looked, she supposed, like someone who was having a life-crisis rather than someone pretending to.

Alison opened the boot of the car. Because she had forgotten to de-set the alarm, the siren went off and the indicator lights flashed. More women emerged from the doorway of the pub as she fiddled with the little black box attached to the keys. They were bottle-blondes, some semi-leathered, others in jeans and T-shirts, one in cowboy garb. They did not look like the sort of women to sympathise with another of their gender who could not de-set a car alarm.

The siren stopped wailing and she inspected the two suitcases of clothes, the box of books, the Sainsbury's bag with decaff and Marmite in it. She rummaged in one of the suitcases for a nightie and some knickers and her bathroom and face things. She emptied the Sainsbury's bag of its sensible provisions and replaced them with her overnight essentials. The filter of the cigarette had stuck to her lips. She could not open her mouth properly without the risk of tearing the tender flesh. She climbed into the front seat of the car, licking around the filter to try to loosen its grip. She lit the cigarette and prised the filter away from her mouth. Despite the care she took, the separation pulled skin from her lower lip. She ran her tongue across the raw flesh, sipping blood. When she put down the window to let out the smoke, the woman in brown leather crossed the street towards her.

'Do you realise,' she said, 'that your boot is open?' She used a tone in which she might more appropriately have said that Alison's stocking tops were showing.

'Well, thank you.' Alison blushed.

'Come and have a drink.'

'I can't,' she said. 'I'm late.' Alison opened the door and closed the window with the busy determination of someone trying to make up time, to limit the effects of having arrived too late, understood too late, made the decision to see clearly far, far too late. Except with Matthew, who always retreated when she started crying, her weeping in the hope that people would go away had the opposite effect to that which she desired. As she wept in the car, she decided that it was Matthew's reaction which was unnatural, not everyone else's.

'Let me help you with those bags,' Brown Leather said. At the doorway of the mansion block which contained Tamsin's flat, she parted from Brown Leather with the promise that she would join her in the pub some, carefully unspecified, time later. Alison rang the bell of flat two, as instructed, and was handed the keys to Tamsin's flat by a silent Iranian man. Tamsin's telephone was ringing as Alison unlocked the front door to the flat. She didn't rush, assuming that the call would be for Tamsin, from someone who didn't realise that she was away. Her friend Tamsin was a journalist which sometimes entailed her rushing off to different parts of the world. Tamsin had left for New York an hour before Alison's arrival.

It had been easier to talk to Tamsin because she was going away. Alison knew she would not have to sit in the same room with her, with Tamsin knowing what had happened, with her own knowledge that Tamsin had always disapproved of Matthew, hoping that Tamsin would curb her desire to celebrate the separation. Tamsin had rung to say goodbye in the middle of Alison's last hour with Matthew. She had offered her the flat to stay in and Alison had immediately accepted, imagining that her own company would be easier to control than that of other people. But as she stepped into the shadowy hall, bumping into the bicycle which leant against the bookshelf, she did not in the least want to be on her own.

The phone stopped ringing. Alison stood in the hall, her Sainsbury's bag hanging from the handlebars of Tamsin's mountain bike, staring at the bookshelves, feeling like a trespasser despite Tamsin's invitation to trespass – 'Make the place your own, rummage around, discover my secrets'. Tamsin's flat was clean and neat. It was a place where possessions were stored. She half-expected to see a mini-bar in the corner of the bedroom. The duvet cover was impossibly white. It could not have been slept under since it was last changed. The kitchen was blonde and spacious and full of light.

There were definite signs of a human presence on the desk around the telephone – an unemptied ashtray, loose change, names and numbers jotted on a pad, some carefully folded white knickers which Tamsin must have planned, and then forgotten, to pack. The window by the desk looked down on a communal yard. A row of six industrial-size metal dustbins were backed against a wall. She pledged to do her best to start distrusting things and the first thing she was inclined to distrust was her desire to run out of Tamsin's flat in search of company, any company. She phoned Bill's number. She decided not to speak to his answering machine. She phoned Natasha, but when she heard a man's voice she cut the connection. She opened her address book and tried to think of who she could phone, people she could talk to who would not enquire too assiduously after her well-being. She would have to tell her mother something. If Mum rang the house and heard Matthew's version – she lay down on the chilly duvet cover, the light starting to fade in the window on the other side of the room, through which she could see a section of wall, a budding branch and grey sky. She wanted to know in advance whether she had the courage to sleep on her own in Tamsin's flat. When she laid her head on the pillow and began to relax the muscles of her neck, an energy like electricity, but more human, ran around her body. Soon it was as if she were inside a net of all-too-human energy which she recognised as generically related to the undirected, sexual urge she had experienced in the car. She sat up on the bed. The phone rang and she ran into the next room to answer it.

She was too late to stop the machine answering before her and shouted hello, hello, hello, over Tamsin's voice to tell the caller to hang on.

'Darling, is that you?'

'Hold on, Mummy.'

'—any messages after the tone,' Tamsin's recorded voice said, as Alison found the right button and switched her off.

'Where are you, Ali?'

'A friend's flat,' she said. Knowing her mother would find it reassuring, she added, 'In South Ken.'

'Matthew was mysterious on the phone. He's reverted to calling me Mrs Felshaw.' Alison visualised her mother and father sitting either side of the grate, a fire burning despite the mild weather, everything polished, the first drinks of the evening on little tables beside them. Her father was listening to one side of the conversation and guessing Alison's words from her mother's expression, adding his comments which her mother would have to decide whether or not to relay.

'He was probably in the bath,' Alison said, 'and felt he had to be formal.'

'Are you all right, darling?'

'I'm fine.'

'You've usually phoned by this point in the week.' It was Thursday. 'Your father and I were beginning to wonder about you.' Which meant that Dad was fretting and had ordered Mum to phone her.

'Matthew and I had a bit of an argument.' Why did she so rapidly tell her mother more than she wanted her to know, more than she wanted to burden her with? 'It's nothing. It'll pass.'

'Matthew said that you and he needed some space,' her mother said. 'I'm not sure what space means in that context.'

'Let's not talk about Matthew.' There was silence on her mother's end of the line. Alison knew that she had cupped her hand over the mouthpiece to take in one of Frank's interjections.

'Your father says that you should come and stay.' Joan Felshaw spoke these words evenly, so that Frank would not later accuse her of cancelling the invitation in the tone with which she issued it.

'Mummy, I can't talk to you like this,' she said, knowing that her mother would understand that by 'like this' she meant, while her father was watching over the conversation, directing it. 'I promise you, I'm fine. Tamsin will be back later and we'll eat and talk and it'll be like a girl's dormitory and then at the weekend I have plans with friends.'

Her mother said, 'Is there someone else?' and Alison sensed from her tone that the question was her father's, relayed through her mother. The net of human electric energy which had surged around her when she lay on Tamsin's bed was surrounding her again. She was close to putting the phone down as facts which had been submerged broke on to the surface, like sleek black submarines: neither of them had ever liked Matthew; both of them were struggling to conceal their enthusiasm about the rift. She knew these things to be true but had contrived not to notice them before. They were like the detailed features of a much-repeated car journey which, because she had learnt to take them for granted, she had never really seen. But that day, for some reason, she could not help seeing everything with an unwelcome clarity.

'Ali?' her mother said. 'Are you there still? Hello?' How long had it been since her mother had asked her if there was someone else?

'I don't have anyone else,' she said. 'It's not like that. I really am fine and I'm going to ring you tomorrow and we'll talk for longer. For the moment, please trust me when I say that I'm fine and nothing's going to happen and you don't have to worry.'

'Come at the weekend, darling.' By which she meant – you are frightening me, Ali, and you know why I am frightened and my fear trumps any inconvenience you might suffer in coming to visit me. 'Your father says it's four weeks since we last saw you.'

'Things have been a bit frantic.' Inside the net of electricity, her words sounded hollow. She had to find a quick exit from the conversation, a shorthand notation which would reassure them because – and this was another submarine breaking the surface – their anxieties were harder to bear than her own and she could manage all right, she was fine in fact, as long as she didn't have to think about them fretting and about the fact that always attended their fretting. She would not, she decided, allow them to goad her into thinking about her brother because what had happened to David—. Already she was failing, thinking about his death. Another submarine came to the surface. A flag went up and on the flag were the words, THEY'VE GOT YOU WHERE THEY WANT YOU, HAVEN'T THEY?

'It was much worse with the two of us in the same house,' she said to her mother. 'Matthew and I need a little time apart and then we'll meet and talk and things will be fine again. It's happened before,' she said. 'We always find a way to work it out.'

'When did it happen before, darling?'

'Oh, I don't know.' How could she light a cigarette without her mother hearing the lighter's flint scratching, the rhythm of the puffing? 'Last year? Stop worrying, Mummy, please. There really is nothing to worry about. I'm fine.'

'Do you want to talk to your father?'

'I'm supposed to be going over to see Josephine,' Alison said. 'I should have been there ten minutes ago.'

'Well, darling, do please take care.' There was another pause.

'What, Mum?'

'Your father sends his love.'

'Lots of love to you both,' she said.

As soon as she heard her mother break the line she dialled Josephine's number. After she had arranged to visit Josephine, Alison worked out how to change the answering machine message and included herself in it. Then she left a message at Tamsin's hotel in New York and another on Bill's machine in Notting Hill. She peed in Tamsin's sparsely decorated bathroom and when she was wiping herself she experienced again the ridiculous oversensitivity which made her want to be touched, smothered, ravished by someone – not just Matthew but anyone, the more anonymous the better. She didn't know whether the oversensitivity was part of the net which surrounded her more tightly as the minutes wore on, or whether it was some separate oddness or awakening. The tingling between her legs was a place into which she wanted to climb, a sleeping bag into which she wished she could snuggle.

Alison had a poor sense of direction. After a few minutes walking through the streets near Tamsin's flat, she became convinced that she would not find the car. Which meant she could give up on going to see Josephine and climb into that sleeping bag. It started to rain. She turned a corner and recognised the pub from which the brown-leather woman had paid her unwanted attention. There was a large white van double-parked in the street near her car. Men in blue jumpers and silver epaulettes were striding briskly between the parked cars. She ran as best she could in her mid-heeled shoes and reached the car as a man placed on the windscreen a large sticker which told her not to panic. It was an order which provoked exactly the response which it was designed to staunch.

'Can I pay you now?' she asked.

'What you saying?' The man squatted out of sight, perhaps to check that the padlock on the yellow clamp was secured. 'You saying something?'

'This hasn't happened to me before,' she said. 'I want to know if I can pay you now and have you take the clamp off.'

'I've been punched and threatened with a knife. I've had people trying to bribe me and people trying to take the shoe off with pliers. I've had people yell and scream and cry,' the man said. 'So don't start, all right?'

'The meter broke after I fed the money—'

'Tell it to the office down Warwick Road.'

If she hadn't lied to her mother, she would not have been

clamped. Or: if her mother hadn't kept her on the phone for so long, she would have been back in time to avoid being clamped. Or: if Matthew hadn't made her feel she had to leave her own home—.

'You bastards, you fucking love it, don't you?' Brown Leather leant out of the window of a car which she was moving off a yellow line just outside the pub. 'Why don't you go and do something useful like jump off a bridge and drown. Dickheads! Fuckbreaths!' Two of the blue-jerseyed men moved through the drizzle in the half-light, bearing down on Brown Leather. She accelerated away before they could reach her.

It was rush-hour and big lorries crawled past Alison as she walked along Warwick Road. The pavements were crowded with people making their way home from the Tube with carrier bags and brief-cases, umbrellas and intentions. As Alison approached the pedestrian traffic lights by Earl's Court Tube station, she made a mental calculation. She was ten days late, a lot for her, when she was usually like clockwork.

Matthew knew he should not have allowed his control to slip, should not have touched her; should not have let her turn the touching into another reason why she had to leave. 'Why did you start this?' he had asked.

'I'm not like you.' Alison knelt before him and hugged his legs, performing a tender rugby tackle, her head turned to one side. 'I don't live to a schedule.'

He tried to imagine what the two of them might look like to someone bursting through the front door, someone like Tory. He levered himself into his trousers and zipped up. 'I'm not trying to hurt you.'

'You never had to try,' she had said. The cat was back again, winding itself around his legs. He saw Alison reach out her hand to the animal but it sidled away from her touch. He felt the convulsion of her sob through the conductor of his legs.

'There's no reason for you to go,' he said. 'Please don't go.'

'You can't tell me you don't love her,' Alison said. 'And don't say it without meaning it because I'll know. I know you too well.'

'Maybe I'm not the person you think you know.'

'Obviously,' Alison said.

'I don't know if I love her,' he said. 'I know that I've wanted you to be alive with me for so long and been disappointed each time you weren't—'

'For God's sake—'

'You haven't been here,' he said.

'Where the hell have you been?' Alison stood up and pushed against his chest with the palms of her hands. They fell away from one another and Matthew turned back to the bottle on the counter. 'Have a drink, get stoned, fuck everything up. I'd rather you did that.'

'I will never see her again,' he said.

'Sure.'

'I'll make a decision not to see her and stick to it.'

'That's not the same,' Alison said.

'It's more,' Matthew said. 'Isn't it?'

'How can you love me and love that tart?' Alison said. 'How do you think that makes me feel? Am I supposed to feel good about myself?'

'You don't want me to be the guardian of your self-esteem,' Matthew said. 'I don't think I'd be very good at that.'

'There's nothing you'd like better,' Alison said.

'You didn't realise what you were in for,' he said finally. 'When you helped me to clean up.'

'I preferred you all fuzzy and emotional and hopeless.'

'You don't want to say that.'

'There you go again,' Alison said. 'You really think we'd be better off if you stage-managed all our conversations.'

'Piss off, then,' Matthew said. 'Just piss off, if that's what you've decided to do.'

'You made all the decisions,' Alison said. 'Don't turn them into wounds I've inflicted on you.'

'You're not like this,' Matthew said, surprised to realise it was true. 'You don't talk like this.'

'Don't I?' Alison said. 'Well, maybe I should.'

Matthew stood by the counter, within reach of the bottle. Alison crouched on the floor in the middle of the living room. Both were waiting for something.

'Have you got somewhere to go?'

'Tamsin offered—' she said. 'I don't know.'

'I should go.' He stood against the window facing the room. His shadow fell across the counter.

'I'll go,' Alison had said, standing up. 'Even if you go. I don't want to be here.'

He rose from the stool to fetch a glass from the kitchen cupboard. A small glass would do. Just a small one. The emptiness in the house was not simply the palpable absence of Alison but a reprise of a sensation from two years before. To be always confronted with the cause of his salvation had become intolerable. And now she was gone. So why not take a drink? He had not been able to imagine what her absence would feel like before she left, had given no consideration to the idea that he might be lonely. If Tory were to walk through the door all that might be gone.

But Tory did not walk through the door. The phone rang. 'Hello? Hello?' he said. 'Is that you?' The line went dead. Alison's mother again? If Tory arrived now, would he forget the image of Alison looking back over her shoulder at him as she opened the front door to carry her suitcases out to the car? A look of childish amazement at the injustice he had committed, which modified to an expression of jaded familiarity at the hurt he was capable of causing her. 'To fall in love with a woman like that,' Alison had said, 'is like drowning in a puddle.'

He had not been able to answer her out of the paralysis which beset him in the stretched moments of her departure. He had waited for the tension to transform into a sensation of liberation, or relief that the confession and its consequences were over. But he was left with nothing more than the leaden banality of what he had done.

He should call Jim and Jenny. A four day weekend had opened up before him. Surely Tory would make herself available to him, change her plans so that they could spend the weekend together. He had made no claims upon her beyond the brief periods which they spent together outside the office. Could their simple arrangement be sustained over four uninterrupted days without becoming – or failing to become – something else?

He gazed at the bottle. Surely he had now satisfied the jury in his head that a drink was something he might reasonably take. A drink might be a good thing. It might help him to think a little less clearly. So why not get on and take it? He picked up the phone on the first ring.

'Mr Kerrigan?'

'Speaking.'

'Desmond Largesse from Longacres,' said the voice. 'I hope I find you well.'

'Has she gone?'

'Mercifully, she's with us still.' Desmond Largesse spoke with a sigh. 'Your grandmother says she needs to see you.'

'Is she about to go?'

'That I can't say.'

Thousands of people gave up alcohol for Lent. They would be taking their first drinks together on Sunday, in an attitude of celebration. Perhaps he should wait until then. He wanted all the momentousness of the day to be over, for things to be safe; for a game of tennis with Mike and a predictable weekend with Jim and Jenny. But what he had to look forward to instead was the wait beside the bottle for the phone call from Tory which he no longer believed would come.

He had sat in meetings where reformed drinkers described fellow alcoholics who had fallen off the wagon. From time to time, there would be talk of a dry alcoholic who had suddenly become so wet as to drown altogether. The terminally lapsed were proclaimed as the fellowship's martyrs. There, but for the Grace of God, go I. In the displacement theory championed by the long-term sober, one alcoholic took a drink to spare another from the same fate. Matthew's lapse would permit another alcoholic to remain sober.

The sacrifice model gave a specious purpose to an action which was otherwise futile. What, after all, could be gained from witnessing a person allergic to intoxication whirl back into self-destruction after a hard-won period of abstinence? And yet there were others who drank again and suffered no loss of control, no plunge down the spiritual vortex, no agonies of remorse. Who could know what reaction he might have to the first drink? He might sip in a measured fashion, rounding the jagged edges of a splintered day, softening the impact of Alison's departure. And if he lost control with the first or second glass, he could be the sacrificial lamb of bevy, weeping Jesus on a bar stool, Christ surveying Creation through the bottom of a glass. They would talk of him in the church halls and cafés where reformed alcoholics gather: Matthew's gone on the piss; there, but for the (capital G) Grace of (capital G) God, go I. From this new perspective, picking up a drink was an act of selfless heroism, a contribution to the greater good, an act of transcendent generosity. He wouldn't touch gear.

He knew what was good for him. Or pills. He would stick to the sauce. He picked up the phone on the first ring.

'Mr Kerrigan?' It was Largesse again.

'Yup,' Matthew said. 'It's still me.'

'Forgive me.'

'What for?'

'I think you should try to come down today.'

'Are you telling me it's the end?'

'One can't say that,' Largesse said. 'She asks for you hourly.'

'I'll come when I can.' It was just as well that Alison had taken the car. Driving would certainly interrupt the drinking he had planned and vice versa. Those pious old cunts. If he wanted a drink he'd have a fucking drink. He'd have ten drinks. He'd drink any of them under the table and live to tell the tale. But half the point of taking the drink had been Alison's reaction. Now that the threat of it no longer constituted a device for claiming her attention, why bother? Melodrama needs an audience.

It had all been self-sacrifice on his part: beginning the affair with Tory as a means of releasing Alison from an arrangement he knew deep down she no longer wanted. Yes, he had spread himself supine (with Tory, admittedly) on the altar of Alison's freedom. He was proud of his self-lessness. But was anyone showering him with gratitude?

Matthew floated, dragged by a current towards Alison, then nudged by a breeze in the direction of Tory. The bottle on the counter was the anchor which held him. Only by raising it could he hope to move further than the length of the tether which tightened as he reached the peripheries of sober thought – find Alison and win her back, tell Tory everything, go to bed, go to Wales, go to a meeting—.

The chop and swell of colliding impulses induced a physical discomfort on the backs of his arms. The skin over his triceps became chilly and raw as if scraped by a frozen knife. He shivered, releasing a charge of sensation which ran from his hips to his shoulders. He poured a centimetre of whisky into the small glass.

18

Healing

Alison dialled and listened to the ringing tone.

'Yup?' Matthew. Matthew? She looked at the display on the phone and saw that, instead of Josephine's number, she had dialled her own. The series of digits was close enough to muddle up.

'Hello? Hello? Is that you?' Matthew asked. She replaced the receiver, leaving both of them with a residue of uncertainty. Was you Alison or Victoria? She dialled Josephine's number and told her she was going to be late.

'You just have to tell yourself,' Josephine said, 'that all of this has a meaning, even if you can't see it right now. It's like an opportunity, an opportunity—'

'Josephine, I have to go.' Alison avoided telling her what she had been telling everyone else – that she was late – because Josephine was the thing, one of the things, for which she was late. 'This isn't my phone, OK?'

'I'll be here,' Josephine said. 'When I woke up today something told me it was one of those days when I have a higher purpose.' Alison began to regret the plan to visit

Josephine, unsure whether she wished to be anyone's higher purpose.

She could not cut her body off from her head in the old familiar way – making the neck a no-man's land dividing the city of the head from the provinces of the body. The guardposts in her throat had been knocked out by weeping over Matthew, by making love to Matthew despite his loving Tory. She decided that if she was borrowing Tamsin's flat, it would be all right to borrow her bike as well. It didn't fit in the lift so she hauled it down the two flights of stairs and left it in the hall while she checked the street. The coast being clear, she set off, wobbly at first, then with growing confidence.

Josephine cooked a supper of rice and vegetables, healthy and tasteless, for which Alison had little appetite. At Josephine's encouragement, she forced herself to eat and then cried into a mug of camomile and spearmint tea, while Josephine talked. 'I believe these experiences are given to us for a purpose. I mean, for example, when Giles and I split up—' There were a lot of comparisons with Josephine's Giles relationship. In fact, they seemed to talk much more about Josephine and Giles than about Matthew and Alison – 'Of course, it was terrible and, of course, the bruises took ages to stop aching, but there was something extraordinary, too. I mean, you know, in the end it was a healing experience and I look back on it now, and so does Giles, as a thing which helped us both deal with lots of important issues—'

Josephine's sentence failed to complete her thought, but came to an end none the less. Perhaps, hitting the buzzword – issues – she had lost her capacity for independent thought. Despite the rice and vegetables and her talk of issues, Josephine did not wear a uniform to match, but rather the court shoes and tailored jacket of a Cadogan shopper.

'—it was so beautiful. And so healing.'

'Yes,' Alison said, wanting to believe it, searching herself for any glimmer of being healed or made more beautiful by the loss of Matthew. 'I'm glad you feel that.'

Josephine was weeping and Alison could not help being infected, even though she only half-believed in Josephine's tears. Josephine's crises had a greater claim on their attention and sympathy than anything which had happened to her. She considered trying to shock Josephine – as she passed her the box of recycled tissues – by describing her encounter with Brown Leather. But what was the point? Josephine would find a card to trump it, a near-death experience with a psychotic ultra-dyke and throw in an exotic location (Goa, the Galapagos isles, Guatemala), forcing Alison to respond to Josephine, rather than Josephine to Alison. If Alison had arrived with a broken finger, she was sure that Josephine would have had a story about how she broke her leg (in three places, no doubt). But she had arrived with a broken heart and could only feign interest in Josephine's amorous débâcles.

'When this is over,' Josephine said, 'I am sure you will thank Matthew for the learning experience. It will become part of your process.'

'I don't want it to be over,' Alison said. 'Can't you understand? I love him and I want to be in our house with him loving only me. I cannot accept that it's over. I can't live without him. I don't want to. What's the point?' Josephine moved across the room to the sofa on which Alison was sitting, placed her hands on Alison's shoulders and pulled her close. Alison's head came to rest on Josephine's breasts, her ear against the pumphouse of Josephine's heart. Josephine stroked her hair. Alison noted just what it took to silence Josephine, to staunch her tide of appropriating empathy and solicit a simple gesture of comfort.

It was hard to breathe. Josephine's perfume, which Alison could not identify, was powerful without being enticing. Alison breathed more deeply, and as she began to bring her sobbing under control, Josephine touched her neck with a motion which Matthew always used – a gentle circling massage of the vertebrae just below the medulla. Her chance imitation of this tender and particular touch set Alison off again. She pulled away from Josephine and assessed the significance of the caress. 'What do you think about Matthew's behaviour?' Suddenly Alison could breathe again. She slapped tears from her cheeks. 'What do you think about Matthew? Mmm?'

Josephine said nothing for a full minute. They stared at each other. Alison wondered whether she should pinch Josephine and then repeat the question. As she waited for Josephine to speak, she was piecing it together, reconceiving the dynamics of the triangular friendship between herself, Josephine and Matthew. 'Where did you learn that thing you were doing to my neck?'

More silence. Then – 'What I'm struggling with, Ali, is whether to tell what I think is really going on between you and Matthew,' Josephine said, 'rather than just putting it all at his door and trying to comfort you.'

'I should know what's going on,' she said. 'I think that would be a great help.'

'We could meet up next week,' Josephine said. 'And talk about it then.' There was something hooded about Josephine, even though Alison knew she was doing her best to look open and unguarded. Alison's back was aching. Did that mean she was pregnant? Or that all the excitement she'd been exposed to had hardened into a fist at the bottom of her spine, a fist that wanted to open and close, clenching.

'I'm totally available to you,' Josephine said. 'If you need to talk or anything, all you have to do is pick up the phone.

I mean, this is what friends are for.' There was a tingling sensation in Alison's abdomen, unlike anything she had felt for years. Yes, and a slight itching at the back of her knees. Different bits of her body seemed to be waking up after a long hibernation. Not just her erogenous zones, but all the other parts, thawing out, stirring. 'And if you want to sleep here tonight,' Josephine said, 'we can make up the sofa. Or you can share my bed.'

'You still haven't told me where you learnt that thing you were doing to my neck.' Alison walked across the carpet to her handbag and dug out her cigarettes. 'Or about what you think of Matthew's behaviour.'

'I can't speak for Matthew,' Josephine said. 'I think we should stick to your feelings. I mean, you're just so extraordinary and beautiful and in a few months all this will look so different and you'll feel excited by the change and kind of liberated. Pain really does teach us something, the wound contains a sort of accompanying—'

'Shut up.' Alison lit her cigarette.

Josephine immediately lit a candle – her silent protest to the smoke. Alison waved the cigarette close to her friend.

'You need to talk about this,' Josephine coughed. 'When I left Giles I had to go to people – and so did he – and just pour it all out and not take any notice of what other people said. Just talk it all out, listen to yourself, hear your own truth and, you know, get in touch with it all.'

'What if you don't like what I'm going to say?' Alison blew the smoke towards Josephine. 'Have you got an ashtray?'

When Josephine came back, Alison said, 'I think I'm pregnant.'

'That must be what it is,' Josephine said.

'What what is?'

'The spiky feeling you're giving me,' Josephine said. 'The feeling that I've become the enemy.'

'Have you?'

'Matthew used to talk about the way you go cold, disappearing out of a conversation, leaving an odour of disapproval behind you. He said it made him feel condemned – as if you'd decided that he'd done something wrong and you weren't going to discuss it or say what it was. So he had to live with a sense of having failed you and with the punishment you were giving him for a crime which he wasn't aware he'd committed.'

'When did he tell you all this?' Alison puffed smoke into the air above them. 'Was it while he massaged your neck? Or was that another time?'

'You see?' Josephine had her opening now. 'You turn people into the enemy and they don't know what they've done wrong. You're doing it to me.'

'Who started it?' Alison put her cigarette down in the ashtray where it smouldered noxiously.

'Started what?'

'I thought he was happy with me.' She was crying again. 'We argued, of course, and things went up and down and there were difficult times. But I always thought that he loved me.' Josephine stubbed Alison's cigarette out on her way across the sofa. Alison put her hand on Josephine's shoulder to hold her back. 'So some of those times when he said he was going to meetings and I sat stoically in front of the telly, waiting for him to come home, he was with you.'

'No, Ali,' Josephine said. 'No.'

'Was this before or at the same time as Victoria?' Alison had her attention now.

'You've got it wrong.'

'You didn't know about Tory,' Alison said.

'You're in a state of grief.' Josephine offered a tissue, her hand shaking slightly at the end of her extended arm. 'You've got this all muddled up.'

Alison waited until Josephine put down the box of recycled tissues. Then she plucked one. 'Did he promise to run off into the sunset with you, too?' The tingling in her abdomen had turned into an itching deep in her guts. Alison wanted to scratch, but she would have to tear through the skin and the muscle wall to get to the part that tickled.

'I want to be your friend,' Josephine said. 'I want to help you.'

'I want a drink,' Alison said.

'I'll make some more tea.'

'A drink drink.'

'You know I don't keep alcohol in the house,' Josephine said.

'I don't know anything about you,' Alison said.

'It wasn't what you think,' Josephine said. Alison had been about to give up, to write it off as a phantom, as paranoia. All Josephine would have needed to do was wait a minute or two longer. Alison would have believed her. 'Matthew was desperate. I thought he was going to drink again.' The card they loved to play – the higher evil of the first drink, which trumped all other sins.

'Well, that's all right,' Alison said. 'As long as he didn't have a drink.' Alison hadn't even known that Matthew was attracted to Josephine. He looked at women the way all men do, assessing them in the abstract for fuckability, but Alison couldn't remember him giving Josephine the second, more serious look. There was nothing wrong with Josephine's body. Her legs and her tits were the prescribed shape. Josephine explained that she had resisted for months. Surely she realised that this only made it worse from Alison's point of view. The idea of Matthew laying siege to Josephine's virtue was deeply offensive.

'You took pity on him.'

'He was desperate to be close to someone,' Josephine said.

'As close as possible.' Alison lit another cigarette.

Josephine left the room and returned with an asthma inhaler. 'I'm sorry, Ali. It just happened.'

Alison was in danger of being understanding because, of course, she understood.

'You closed him out.' Josephine drew deeply on the inhaler. 'He told me you disappeared and whatever he said, whatever he tried to do to get your attention, you stayed blanketed in the place you had gone to, wherever that was.' Alison knew this to be true. 'He tried everything, but whatever he did, you just weren't there.' Josephine drew on the inhaler again. She reminded Alison of a baby with a comforter. 'You said you loved him. But all the evidence suggested the opposite.'

'Why—' Alison put her cigarette out, losing courage.

'What?'

'Why didn't you tell me this before?' she asked. 'Before it became an excuse for sleeping with him?'

'You can be hard to talk to,' Josephine said.

'How many more are there, behind my back, queuing for confession?'

'I was trying to be good,' Josephine said. 'To look beyond my own feelings and offer you some comfort. I owe you amends.' Alison recognised in this statement the militant naïvety which Matthew and the other non-drinking drunks of their acquaintance were swift to adopt in crisis. They expected to be excused for their behaviour, because they didn't mean it, because their intentions were good: Special-pleaders Anonymous.

'Was it good?'

Josephine took a drag on her inhaler. 'Not as good as David.'

Damp with sweat from carrying the bike up the stairs, Alison played back the messages on Tamsin's machine –

a man offering financial services; a man with a voice like David's who didn't leave his name and said 'You never call me. I never see you. This must change—' and then a number. Should she have a bath? Wash her hair? What would she do in the morning? Would she put on clean underwear and pretend everything was all right? She felt a movement in her stomach, air or food working its way down, but she imagined it as the frantic multiplication of cells in her womb, the first hints of a form, a torso, a jellybaby. She dialled home and heard her own voice on the answering machine, a voice she hardly recognised, recorded some weeks ago – jolly, welcoming, established; a voice which knew where it was coming from and encouraged people not to waste their calls, to leave their messages for 'Matthew or Alison', spoken as if the three words were one – Mattheworalison. 'I didn't think you'd be there,' Alison said to the machine. 'Why would you be there?'

She was failing to keep the promise of bravery and steadfastness with which her leaving home had begun. She had been trying not to smoke since she got back from Josephine's. The cigarettes reminded her of Matthew. She could still unknow what Josephine had told her. Come to think of it, she could unknow the fact of Tory and Matthew. Unknowing was a device she had always used, and she had better not abandon it now. She had unknown David's death. She'd better not know all the things she knew because the pressure would crush her, like water around a diver, plunging deeper than she should. She put the phone down and ran a bath. She undressed in Tamsin's bedroom, catching sight of herself in the long mirror by the door. She placed her palm on her flat stomach, imagining it swollen and curved. She could not get into the bath. It wasn't the temperature of the water but the idea of such an absolute submission to her circumstances, accepting the new arrangements without question.

'It's Ali.' She had been keeping Bill up her sleeve, just in case she needed him, since the time when Matthew had been in Paris (in retrospect, doing God knows what) and Bill had taken her out to dinner and made a fat juicy pass at her, his hands sweeping all over her as they stood on the street outside the restaurant, supposedly saying goodbye. Goodbye, then, she had said and he had kissed her again. She had allowed it because she knew she wasn't going home with him. She only went home with Matthew. Apart from Sergio. But that was different, and besides, she had never actually gone home with Sergio.

She was sitting naked at Tamsin's desk, hoping that Bill would ask her over. She listened to him telling her how he was in the middle of moving flats. He was always moving, moving on. She knew that she could not be on her own in Tamsin's neat, unlived-in flat, which was worse than a hotel, almost a home but not quite, whereas a hotel was just impersonal and nothing to be done about it.

Bill asked her what she was doing. She said she was at a loose end. Absurd! Why couldn't she say that she wanted to see him, that she wanted him to kiss her, that she wanted to close her eyes and have him take advantage of her with the lights off and loud music and drugs?

'Why don't you come over?'

'I haven't got any clothes on.' She did not mean it to sound provocative. It was just a fact. It was, as Matthew liked to say, the case.

'Well, put some on.'

'I can't come and see you on that basis,' Alison said.

'You can hardly come as you are,' Bill said.

'I mean—'

'Hush,' Bill said. 'Don't be too long.' Then he put the phone down.

The bath was tepid. Alison smelt strange to herself. Two soapings under her arm-pits would not take away the unfamiliar scent which was not fear or nerves – she knew how those smelt. She washed some more but she could not sluice the smell away. Perhaps she should just go to bed. Her little black skirt and her mid-heeled pumps were not right for bicycling at night. She had already received some strange looks on her way back from Josephine's. The thing she liked about Bill – apart from the fact that she liked him liking her – was that he acted as if everything was simple. He assumed that everyone saw things exactly as he did. So he was direct and didn't get bogged down in other people's uncertainties as she did in Matthew's, and Matthew in hers. Bill didn't think she was inaccessible or remote. He didn't weigh his words against a dictionary full of other words which he and Alison had already said to one another. He didn't need to gain or regain her regard. He adored himself and assumed that everyone else would adore him too.

She cycled through West London, constructing the state of mind in which she would allow Bill to seduce her. She rode on the pavement to avoid the cars and buses swishing past. She thought about the future, about the vastness of the future which she would have to endure. A future in a pushchair, with tiddly shoes and a dirty nappy.

Bill was direct, oh so very direct, and thank God, because she didn't want to talk. She was deep in the day-dream place, mixing and muddling things, far away from her body, in the fishbowl of her head, high above the things which Bill would do to her body and she to his. The chances were that she wouldn't weep, at least not too soon, not before they reached the point where it wouldn't matter.

Bill didn't ask any questions. Although she was relieved that she didn't have to talk, apart from the occasional yes, yes to encourage him, the occasional no, no, no, to let him know that she was enjoying what he was doing, she could not help being affronted that whatever she was apart from the body he was handling, was of no consequence to him. Affronted, even as she was glad that he was behaving like that.

When she touched him, he flinched and flickered in response, stretching and hardening in her fist. She undid his trousers and belt while he pulled down her tights and knickers. She hoped they could get past the clumsy bit quickly. At least she was not wearing a bra – her tits weren't that big and supported themselves without straps. But that would change with babies, wouldn't it? And of course, now she came to think of it, with Bill's fingers inside her, pointing to the place where the baby was coming into being, there was no one to say who the father was; no one but her. It could be Bill.

19

Ice

It was bollocks about the first drink. Same with the first fuck, the first cigarette or the first anything. One thing did not necessarily lead to another. The down-escalator of inevitability was really an elevator out of which Matthew could step at his chosen floor. Back in the lift, he was going up. Up and up. Up to town to find Victoria. He poured another centimetre of Scotch into the small glass and carried it upstairs. He found his wallet, his keys and his mobile. He put on his black overcoat. He let Char out of the back-kitchen and attached the lead to her collar. He drained the Scotch into his mouth, squirted it through the gaps between his teeth, gargled and swallowed. He slammed and double-locked the front door.

There was an orderliness in the unfolding of events now, the yellow light on a taxi appearing just as he rounded the corner on to the Uxbridge Road. He waved, then spoke through the open window to the driver, telling him the Soho address of Communications Unlimited, opening the back door for Char to leap in. He sat back and realised, from the matted feel of his groin, that he should have washed.

He was waiting for the lift to carry him up to the offices on the sixth floor when the doors slid back to reveal Terri. They stood together in the marble lobby. The night security guards watched television behind the reception desk.

'Tell me where she is.'

'I honestly don't know. Everyone's been trying to reach her,' Terri said. 'You should call The Roadkills' manager. He's going up the wall about the poster campaign.'

'I take one day off and she disappears.'

'You were going to Wales.'

'Terri, I need your help here,' Matthew said. 'You know—'

'What do I know, Ker?' He had not paid enough attention to Terri. Now that he needed a lever with her, he had none. 'Have a good weekend.'

'You're her secretary—'

'Personal assistant,' Terri said.

'Even more so, then,' Matthew said. 'You should know where she is.'

'I have to go, Ker,' Terri said. 'I'll miss my train.'

'Thanks for everything.'

'You're welcome.' Terri turned her back on him and made for the revolving door. Perhaps he had paid her too much attention, then not enough.

Out in the street, his conviction returned. An accordance had been established between the pulses of the city and the rhythm of his decisions. He saw a pattern in the strides of the passers-by, heard a music of accelerating footsteps as the office world retreated towards a four day weekend. Victoria would be at Brutino's on time.

The third drink presented no more problem than the first or the second. He stayed with whisky, not wanting to shock his metabolism by switching. In the office, The Lucky Sinners were still referred to as The Roadkills. He called their manager, dredging the number out of the mobile's memory. The pub was crowded and it was hard to hear what Trevor was saying. He took his drink into a dim passage which led to the lavatories, and continued the call.

'The poster's crap,' Trevor said. 'The name's crap. Nobody's buying the single.'

'This is transitional,' Matthew said. 'Whenever we re-position an entity in the market we expect a swirl of indecision. The consumer has to adjust and re-tune. I can show you statistics. You get a lull for a week or two. Then the public locks on to the new concept and sales go ballistic.'

'The band are pissed off,' Trevor said.

'The *Guardian* piece comes out next week,' Matthew said. 'Then the tour starts. Tell them to be patient.' Matthew returned to the bar and gestured for the same again as he listened to Trevor relaying the band's carping. 'They know it. You know it. We all know it. The first single was weaker. Like a loss leader,' Matthew said. 'When "Broken Swing" comes out mid-way through the tour I tell you this band are going to be very hot indeed. Trevor?'

'What?'

'Relax. Enjoy your weekend. Tell them to call me if they want to. Tell them, any time.'

Outside the pub, half an hour later, his feet were mushy and half-numb. A sharp pain winked in his solar plexus. He fingered his liver. After leaving another message on Victoria's voice-mail, he dialled Josephine.

'Josephine, it's me,' he said into the mobile. 'Pick up the phone.'

He heard a clatter behind Josephine's recorded voice explaining that she could not come to the phone right now. 'Ali was here,' Josephine said over the bleep. For a moment, Matthew flipped to the other side of the street and saw himself, alone on the pavement with his phone, neck drawn in under the collar of his black coat, an anyone, a stranger, a nobody.

'I'm sitting here trying very hard to contain my feelings,' Josephine said.

'Was she in a bad way?'

'I have a lot of stuff coming up,' Josephine said. 'This speaks to my deepest insecurities.'

'What did she say about me?'

'Abandonment, first of all,' Josephine said. 'I have to try to own that, otherwise I'm going to end up rejecting myself.'

'Can I come round later?' Victoria might not turn up at the restaurant.

'I need a meeting,' Josephine said. 'I need to see my sponsor. I can't share about this with you.'

'She told you.'

'I thought we had an understanding,' Josephine said. 'But it's my pattern all over again. I swore I would never do this. Being someone's well-kept secret.'

'What do you mean?'

'What was I supposed to say?' Josephine said. 'Did you want me to lie?'

'What is there to lie about?'

'I'm getting a hostile vibe from you,' Josephine said. 'I don't have to sit down and take this. I'm learning to assert myself.'

'I took a drink.'

'You what?'

'Nothing happened,' he said. 'I feel good.'

'And I thought I was in trouble,' Josephine said. 'Can you get to a meeting? I don't want you on my conscience—'

'It's nothing to do with you or your conscience.'

'What about yours?' Josephine wailed.

'It's fully-booked.'

'—and you don't want me there.'

'What did you tell Alison?'

'About us.'

'What sort of Us?'

'The you-and-me sort,' Josephine said. 'A man and a woman.'

'What the fuck did you tell her?'

'She was obsessing about Victoria.'

'That's different.'

'Good different or bad different?'

Matthew was silent. Char pulled on the lead, dragged by the lure of a fresh scent. 'You told her we were having an affair.'

'Get to a meeting,' Josephine said.

'You lied to her.'

'She thinks she's pregnant,' Josephine said.

'When did she tell you that?'

'I want a child. I thought I could have yours and not tell anyone who the father was. But now you're drinking. It affects the sperm, and anyway I would never let a drinker near any child of mine. I have to have boundaries. We need to talk.'

'How late is she?'

'I mean talk talk,' she said. 'I'm confused about the messages you're giving me.'

'How late did she say she was?'

'You can't come here if you're drunk,' Josephine said. 'I'm trying to live in the solution. I have to protect myself. Are you going to deny that you feel anger towards me?'

'I can explain about Victoria,' he said. 'It's not what you think.'

'I have a pattern,' Josephine said, 'of choosing to be second choice.'

'Did she say how late she was?'

'Don't have more to regret than you can handle,' Josephine said.

Alison was regular. Her period started on the anticipated day of every month, a lunar snub to his fertility. She had been trying to get pregnant since David died. He had *not* been not trying to impregnate her.

Losing the insurance of Josephine was manageable, like losing a waistcoat rather than one's trousers or jacket. But a waistcoat would still be something worth having if his jacket didn't show up for dinner and his trousers were holed up at Tamsin's. He called Tamsin's number and was surprised by Alison's voice on the machine. How distraught could she be if she'd found the composure to change the message? He pressed *end* and broke the connection. Alison was glad of the chance to leave. Now that she had his seed. She was off – with his car and his tennis racquet and his Miles Davis compilation – to the land of single motherhood.

He had supposed that the fifth drink might be the problem, but the cold air on the street encouraged him to reconsider. The sixth was more likely to be the drink which would present genuine difficulties. The fifth was the one after the fourth and, with no ice and plenty of water – still water, mind you, no bubbles – he was confident that he was still some way short of his limit. Sobriety had taught him a new dexterity in pressing back the frontier of the problematic by careful management of his intake. The nips at home were more like an experiment, a practice round to establish pole position. So it was five, in fact. And five was no problem. You have to have boundaries, just like Josephine said. But how absurd to end up being the one who was going to be late. He had imagined himself alone at Brutino's, not taking the sixth drink, grazing on breadsticks. Now he was ten minutes late and by the time he arrived it might be as much as half an hour. His taxi crawled along Oxford Street.

The Maitre d' told him Victoria had arrived only five minutes before him. 'We were on the point of giving your table away.' He was asked to hand over his mobile phone with his coat.

'When did all this start?'

'We had complaints, sir,' the Maitre d' said. 'We still allow them at lunch-time.' Before crossing the room to his table, he asked the waiter to bring him a vodka and tonic. He did not realise, until he was separated from the phone, how certain he had been that Alison would call him.

Victoria pretended that she had been at the table for half an hour. He did not bother to challenge her deceit. His lateness was a useful decoy from the live targets of his drinking and Alison's departure.

'Can I have a sip of your water?'

'Let me get you some.' He summoned the waiter.

'You left about a hundred messages,' she said. 'What's up?'

'Trevor,' Matthew said. 'Freaking about the poster campaign.'

'Did you stroke him?'

'He nearly came.'

'Please.'

'He's right, though,' Matthew said. 'The poster is crap. Terri doesn't know what she's doing.'

'It's the name,' Victoria said. 'Who thought up the name?'

'Don't look at me.'

'I like to look at you,' Victoria said.

'Where were you all afternoon?'

'Shopping.'

'Sure.'

'I could show you what I bought,' Victoria said. 'If you weren't going to Wales.'

'You tried to cancel me,' he said.

There was a long silence while she looked down into her lap.

'It's hard for me, too.'

'You're not the one on her own,' she said.

Why could he not simply tell her? The waiter asked them

if they would like to order; there was a second sitting at eleven.

'Do you get the impression,' Matthew said, 'that your employer is becoming a tad greedy?'

'The proprietor is in New York this week.'

'Why should I give a fuck where he is?'

The waiter had no answer for this remark. He stood holding his pad like a prayer book, awaiting their imprecations. Victoria ordered a salad, followed by ravioli of langoustine in lobster sauce. Matthew asked for mussels cooked in Chardonnay, followed by breast of duck over fruit salad.

Victoria left the table. Matthew ordered another vodka and tonic. Six drinks was the limit up to dinner time, but once he was eating – he tore a piece of olive-laced ciabatta bread in two and chewed the smaller piece – he could ease off on the counting. Then again, a little coke and he wouldn't have to count at all. He was pretty sure he had a couple of numbers in the mobile's memory. He had been a fool to tell Victoria about the Illness-of-Mind-Body-and-Spirit. He was suddenly jealous of the woman to whom he was now at liberty to give his full attention. There should be shopping bags at her flat. He would check. Except she was expecting him to leave for Wales after dinner.

'What was this week's excuse?' she asked as she returned to the table.

'Tennis with Mike.'

'You're becoming regular partners.'

'Yes,' Matthew said. 'We are, aren't we?' He sipped at his new drink. 'I think I might be free this weekend.'

'And what of Wales?' If Victoria felt any enthusiasm for his change of plan she kept it well concealed. 'And her indoors?'

'Her father's ill,' he said. 'She's gone to Hampshire.'

'When you're busy, which you usually are,' she said, 'I

rely on friends who are reliable when I can't rely on you. If I become unreliable – you know what I mean.'

'I'm not asking you to do that.'

'Not asking is another way of asking,' Victoria said. 'Just like me not asking you to be unfaithful to her indoors.'

'Stop calling her that.'

'I had a message on my voice-mail,' Victoria said. 'From Josephine.'

It was not the alcohol in his blood which confused Matthew. Rather, he was finding it increasingly difficult to remember who was supposed to know what, which pieces of previously concealed information had recently been imparted, and to whom. 'Josephine can be strange.'

'Have you forgotten what I told you when I gave you your break at Unlimited?'

'About the universality of marketing paradigms? Pu-lease.'

'I issued a caveat.' He remembered her warning well enough: when you lie for a living, beware the tendency to live a lie. Determined to take her advice lightly, he had asked whether, if you lie down for a living, you can live down your lies. 'Did you take heed?'

'Josephine has this thing,' he said. 'This obsession.'

'You must enjoy that.'

'With unavailable men.'

'And you're unavailable,' Victoria said. 'Is that the idea?'

Matthew left the table, telling her he needed to check on his dog. At the bar, he ordered another vodka and tonic. On the other side of the window-pane, Char slept on the pavement. Sitting down to rejoin Victoria, he banged his foot against the table leg, unbalancing her glass. It toppled, throwing a gash of red wine across the yellow table cloth. They sat in silence while two waiters took a millennium to clear the cutlery, spread a new cloth and re-lay the place settings.

'You can make a fresh start,' Victoria said.

He lit a cigarette. 'I had a drink or two.'

'Didn't I teach you never to state the obvious, unless you have no other option?'

'I know you're smart,' Matthew said. 'You don't have to prove it all the time.'

'*Moi?*' Victoria said. 'You told me you were allergic to alcohol.'

'Propaganda,' he said.

'You and I see through each other,' Victoria said. 'That's the point of us. That's why we're here.'

'I don't mind,' Victoria said. 'Don't worry about it.'

'Be all right in a minute.' Weren't the drinks supposed to immunise him against numbness? Perhaps vodka had been a mistake. Or the ice in the vodka. He had forgotten to tell the waiter no ice. His cock was a piece of unfeeling hose. He sat up to stop the bedroom whirling, slowing it like a carousel, until the window stayed in one place. He heard his mobile phone ringing, somewhere in the darkness.

She began to laugh. Drunk as he was, he could tell that she was also drunk, although less drunk than he. Ready to be infected by it, he smiled. The trapped bird of her laughter banged against the walls. She pressed her palms to her mouth, trying to cage it. She shook her head, attempting to deny with her eyes the hilarity which rose in her throat. She ran naked to the bathroom and slammed the door.

Matthew fell backwards, his sense of balance gone. Char moaned and scratched at the door between the bedroom and the hall. His mobile phone was still ringing. The bottom sheet had come adrift of the mattress, entwining his feet. He leant forward to release his legs, breathing against the queasiness in his stomach. As her hysteria filled the bathroom, he crawled to the floor and gathered his clothes, searching pockets until he found the phone.

'Yes.'
'Harry?'
'No.'
'Tim.'
'Wrong again.'

By the time he had won the struggle to guide his stubborn limbs into the correct portals of trouser and shirt, her laughter was fluttering to an exhausted conclusion. He heard her whimper and sniff. The bathroom door opened. He levered himself on to the far side of the bed, facing away from her. 'I haven't laughed like that for years.' She climbed on to the bed behind him. 'It's better than sex.' She ran her fingers through his hair. 'Maybe you really are allergic to alcohol.' He could hear the laughter gathering strength inside her, ready to burst out again and take wing. 'It's not the first time.' She gulped back the words as she said them. 'It was me the first time.'

As he stood, her hands slid down the length of his back and gripped his belt. He succeeded in maintaining his balance. 'Don't you see that it's funny?' she said. He did not see it. He wanted to find his other sock. And his cigarettes. Then he remembered that he had smoked them all. 'Darling?'

He opened the door to the hall, slumped on the floor beside Char and pulled at the laces of his shoes. Tory followed him on to the shared landing outside the front door to her flat, her hands on his left arm, tugging. He gripped the banister with his right hand and half-slid, half-stumbled, to the next landing. She stood above him. 'Come back,' she said. 'I mean it.' The frantic wings beat in her again, belying her words. 'You can't be serious.' He made a success of the next four steps. Then his knees and his ankles betrayed him. At the bottom of the stairs, nose against the carpet, he smelt dogshit, walked into the hall carpet on someone's shoe. Char leapt down the stairs behind him and snuffled at his neck. He heard Victoria's footsteps. 'Slipped.' He struggled to his feet. 'Not a problem.'

'You'll get run over.' He opened the door to the street, catching Char by her collar to hold her back. He tottered down more steps – so many fucking steps, think of the disabled and the blind, never mind the drunk – on to gravel, losing his grip on Char, who rushed past him towards the pavement. He followed, hands searching his coat pockets in the hope of finding a forgotten packet of cigarettes, his right ankle unsocked and cold. Streetlight filtered through a thin canopy of early leaves. It started to rain.

He leant against a tree and gazed down Hammersmith Grove. Some distance away, riding on the pavement, a cyclist approached. He lost his balance and fell, jarring his wrists as his palms slammed against the curbstone. He was on all fours, swaying like a tree in a big wind. He heard the creak of pedals, the click and clatter of the chain as the cyclist changed gear. Char stood beside him, his twin-on-all-fours. Together, they sniffed the night.

From somewhere behind him he heard the shriek of tyres, a surge of rising noise as an engine revved to a note of high excess. Then, much closer, an explosion, the wrenching yelp of metal sliding on metal, the crack and crash of glass breaking. Char barged past him and rushed into the road. He wished he had waited until he had found his sock. Through a gap between two parked cars, he saw the bicycle flash past. Pulling himself up by the bark of the tree beside him, he heard a scream which did not sound human. His eyes refused to focus. He saw two cars careering out of control, two bicycles swept under two front bumpers, two riders thump on to two bonnets, then somersault up into the air, gymnasts completing their syncopated act with an aerial flourish.

Two cars accelerated away, neck and neck, down Hammersmith Grove. He failed to make out the number plate. Car alarms whooped and bleeped, an audience applauding the gymnasts. The road was decorated with a confetti of red, white and orange glass. He listened to the car alarms, a symphony lit by the Christmas-tree profusion of hazard lights, flashing orange, flashing white through broken amber casings.

Char lay inert in a puddle, nuzzling her snout against the front wheel of a parked car. When he knelt beside her, the puddle was warm through his trousers. A black wreck in a black pool, collar torn half-off, trapping an ear against her skull, pinning it back to reveal a coral-tinted inner delicacy. He crouched on the tarmac and fingered her neck for a pulse. It might not have happened at all. It might not have happened here, beneath Victoria's flat. He unbuckled her collar, checked for the identification tag, then ran into a side-street. He did not stop running until he approached the Goldhawk Road, close to Shepherd's Bush Green. He slowed to a walk, his unsocked foot chafed by his shoe. He could have been any out-of-breath, worse-for-wear punter struggling home at four in the morning. He could have been anyone.

20

Otherness

Bill was tearing open a condom packet with one hand and his teeth. The fingers of his other hand moved in and out of her, trousers round his ankles, cock sticking out between his shirt-tails. She could hear Capital radio in the background. 'You don't need that.' She might as well not have spoken. He had the condom in his hand. The spermicidal lubricant smelt like stale urine. Despite being in a state of readiness to come all day she somehow knew that whatever Bill did to her would not push her over the edge. She noticed the packing cases and the inanities of the disc jockey.

She wanted the lights out and she wanted to be in a bed. She would have liked to talk for a while – talk dirty, or tell jokes, not meaningful talk – before they went any further. And she wanted the radio off because it was only a matter of time before it played a soppy song which would make her cry. But how could she interrupt him and not ruin whatever momentum they had built up? He had turned her around and was holding her by the hips, pulling up her skirt. She was holding on to the arm of a brown velvet sofa which smelt of pets or drunken sweat, sour and rank. She submitted to Bill's weight pushing her face flat against the arm of the velvet sofa. She smelt the strange scent, the smell she had failed to wash away in Tamsin's bath. Why couldn't she tell Bill she wanted to go to bed? How could she eject the clot of wool which sat in her throat and silenced her? The electricated sensation was returning and the voltage increased as her new smell curdled the air. She did not want Bill to smell the deserted stink over the spermicidal fetor. She uttered rising sighs. If he thought she had come, he would feel gratified and powerful and stop. They could go to bed, turn the lights out, the radio off and talk.

'I often think about this,' Bill said. 'Doing this to you.'

Was there something she should do? or say? She should tell him she had been thinking about it, too. But she persisted with her rising scale of moans and sighs, her narrow vocabulary of pretended pleasure. With her cheek squashed into the arm of the sofa, she saw something jammed down between the cushions, in the tight lips of the angle between cushions and sofa-back.

She heard feet passing on the pavement above them and wished it were summer, not this gusty impossible spring. The minutes had slowed to torture. The squish-squish of blood through her heart was a prophecy of hospitals and parturition. Not next summer, when she might be swollen with child, but last summer or the summer before when – french windows thrown open to the garden at the back of his basement flat – she could have been fucked by Bill in a midnight breeze, crossed London to her cuckolded Matthew, smoking in the car, showering off one man before lying down beside another.

Bill should not have turned her around. She had allowed herself to pretend that it was Matthew behind her, pushing her down, easing himself in and out. Her heaving breath and liquid sighs became less contrived. She pulled the slip of material from between the lips of the sofa. White knickers

– creased but clean. Bill stopped moving. He grabbed at the knickers. She clung on to them. His strength dragged her across him and his cock brushed against her hand in its slimy stocking.

'Who wears these?'

He yanked at them, losing his balance, ankles shackled by his downed trousers, toppling backwards. She held on to him, hanging him in the balance until he reached back and found support for his hand on the edge of the table.

Her skirt had dropped back over her thighs so she could pretend that none of this had happened. Bill let go of the knickers at last, needing his hand to right himself, to untrouser his penguined feet. She unfolded the white knickers. He didn't try to stop her. Perhaps, as she was, he was imagining the owner of the knickers into whose most private place Alison now stepped. They were tight, but she didn't mind that. She pulled them up, snug, and her skirt dropped back to cover them. She turned off the radio and the lights. She pushed clothes and books off the unmade bed.

Now that Bill was confusing her with someone else it was all right to confuse him with Matthew. Wearing another girl's knickers made her feel like someone else. Matthew was no longer so achingly real and predominant. The anonymous underwear made her, if not invisible, then unrecognisable, both to Bill and to herself. She didn't let him take them off her, for fear the spell would be broken. He either understood what was going on or wasn't bothered by not understanding. She came quickly when he slid his hand inside and fingered her, the movements stretching the material over her behind, the narrow ribboned sides cutting into her hips.

She woke in darkness and made out the mess on the floor where she had thrown Bill's books and clothes off the bed. She had been dreaming about a telephone ringing perpetually but, search as she might, she could not find the instrument, could not answer the call. The dream receded, but the sound of the ringing telephone became louder instead of fading away. She climbed off the bed, the tight knickers cutting into her flesh. She walked towards the sound of the ringing, but could not seem to draw nearer to it, wherever she went in the flat. At last, on the wall above the counter in the kitchen, she saw a phone and picked up the receiver. The ringing didn't stop. She listened to the dialling tone, her feet cold, something sticky under the toes of her left foot. She put the phone down and the ringing, which must have been in one of the basement flats either side of Bill's, stopped. Then it started again. She tiptoed back to Bill's bed and lay down beside him. Who could be trying to reach whom at – she glance at her watch – three-fifteen in the morning; a Friday morning in April? She did not want to be conscious for a minute longer in the half-abandoned basement, in someone else's knickers (which she still didn't want to take off, because taking them off would turn her back into Alison).

She curled herself up, wanting so much to be asleep. The phone stopped ringing, then started again. She surrendered to the temptation of wondering what there was above or below, in the ether or the grinding configuration of the stars, which could have consigned her to be lying there, unable even to answer the phone, which mocked her with its every ring. A gust of wind rattled the door which led from Bill's bedroom on to the terrace outside. A potted plant toppled over and rolled from side to side on the flagstones. A cat yowled. The phone rang on. She could not understand what she had done to deserve this, to be treated like this. Was it some special test which she was being asked to undergo? And if she could survive, what would be her reward, she wondered? A two-bedroomed flat? Chats on the Habitat sofa with girlfriends who turned out to have slept with Matthew because they felt sorry for him, yoga classes and sensible bedtimes and adventure holidays with people who went on holiday together because they were lonely, and desperate to forget their aloneness? Her flat would be a monument, complete with houseplants and distracting bric-à-brac, to an independence which she might mime, but could never inhabit.

The phone rang and rang. She curled up tighter, knees to her forehead, arms wrapped around her shins, ankles pressed tight to the backs of her thighs. Bill turned in his sleep. His insensible hand dropped on her side, knuckles knocking at her ribs. The phone stopped ringing. She breathed deep into the shrinking curl of herself and then, as she let the air out of her lungs, as Bill's hand slid off her, as the phone purred into life again, she gripped herself as hard as she could, squeezing herself into a smaller bundle, squashing her nose between her knees.

She retrieved her clothes from the front room, from among the rolled rugs and boxed books. Her tights had a long ladder from the front of the left knee to the top of her thigh. She lit a cigarette and pulled on her coat. She had half a mind to leave the bicycle in the hall and find a cab, but the thought of returning in daylight to collect the bike dissuaded her. The phone rang on.

Holding the bike upright, while trying to open the door, proved complicated. She clanged one of the pedals against a radiator as she manoeuvred the machine out of the narrow hallway and through the door. She threw the half-smoked cigarette out of the open door. It landed on a black dustbin-liner through which it burnt and sank. A cat squatted by the railings, watching her struggles. Her armpits were tingling from the exertion of moving the bike. The peculiar smell rose once again to her nostrils.

When she had edged the stupid machine out of the door and was standing in the little yard outside the door to Bill's basement, she realised that she was still wearing the white knickers she had found in the mouth of the brown sofa. Their capacity to confer otherness upon her seemed to have faded. She could not face going back. She began to cry again at the thought of some other girl finding her knickers and wondering who they belonged to or, worse, Bill finding them between boxes as he loaded his stuff into a van and, not knowing what to do with them, either throwing them away or tossing them into a bag with his own clothes where they might nestle, unwashed, for ever. Or, worst of all, he would not even notice her knickers. They would lie on the floorboards with dustballs and pieces of old newspaper and an empty cigarette packet, until the next tenant arrived to wonder about them.

Bill came to the door naked. 'Come inside.' He reached over the bike and hugged her clumsily, his big arms around her neck, his collarbone against her chin. 'I do breakfast, you know.'

'It's too late,' she said, unable to think clearly. He wouldn't let go. His penis touched the crossbar of the bike and the sight of his sensitive flesh on cold metal made her shudder. 'Come back to bed.' He loosened his grip and looked at her. She couldn't. When he fell asleep again she would be all alone and the phone might ring all night. 'I left my knickers somewhere.'

He grinned at her. 'You should stay,' he said. 'You can't leave in tears. I'll feel guilty.'

She decided that if he pleaded with her, if he asked one more time, she would submit. 'It's not your fault,' she said.

'Come to Italy with me,' he said. 'For the summer. Run away with me.'

'I'm not running away.'

'Jesus.'

'I'm sorry,' Alison said. 'Just don't tell me I'm running away.'

'Stay, then.' She could not remember why it was so important to be blind and absent but she knew it was and she knew that being sighted and present for Bill could not change anything between her and Matthew. Being with Bill in Italy would mock her for each day she had hidden herself from Matthew. Bill would taste her bitterness like unripe olives. At least she was being unblind about running away with Bill. Or maybe she was being blind in another way, pretending to herself that the finality of Matthew's choice could be undone by her hanging around, waiting for him to realise his mistake and take her back. And yet she had gone. She could no longer remember what imperative had forced her to leave.

The skittering of these thoughts exhausted her. She didn't trust Bill to help her separate the facts from the hopes. She didn't understand why he would want her to go to Italy with him. Who did he think she was? The girl whose knickers she was wearing? 'I'm not kinky,' she said. Bill stared at her, perplexed. She struggled with the bike, pulling it up the steps from the basement yard to the street. Then she mounted, bumped down from pavement to road and began to pedal. Some minutes passed in a sanctuary of blankness as she rode down half-familiar streets, taking turnings by instinct, approximating the direction of Tamsin's flat because she only half-wanted to go there. Alison had nothing before her but the end that she dreaded, the terminus which her visits to Josephine and Bill had been designed to avoid. She didn't understand why the avoiding had been worse than the unavoidable which approached her now. She pedalled faster towards the picture of her head asleep on Tamsin's pillow. She was tired enough to have run down the net of electrification which had trailed her all night. She surrendered, after a long and futile struggle, to the truth that staying awake or being with someone else would make no difference to Matthew. However much she bicycled around town, she was shackled by the brute fact that it was over over over, just as the car was shackled in its yellow clamp.

Her sense of direction failed her. She ended up on the wrong side of the Shepherd's Bush roundabout, coming on to Wood Lane north of the A40 flyover. She had drifted off the most direct route to Tamsin's flat in Earl's Court. She turned down a street she didn't know and passed a little park. She crossed the Uxbridge Road. As she emerged on to the Goldhawk Road, she recovered her bearings and turned down Hammersmith Grove. The nearer she got to the old flat – passing Tory's flat, just there, on the right – the more convinced she became that she would bump into someone who would change everything, a messenger who would explain that things were not as they seemed, that she had no cause for unhappiness. Like going on believing in Father Christmas after your friends at school have told you he's only your Mum and Dad.

The trees along Hammersmith Grove were in bud. The light from the streetlamps filtered through the first pale leaves, speckling the tightly-parked cars on both sides of the street. A spray of water, rain held by the branches and shifted by a wheeze of wind, fell on her face. She turned off the road and rode on the pavement: the space between the lines of parked cars seemed too narrow for two lanes of traffic.

The Father Christmas principle led her to the old flat. She wanted so badly to talk to David, to see his face. She would have told him about being pregnant, asked him to talk to Matthew, get Matthew to see sense. 'Bastard,' she said out loud. She stopped the bike. She was warm from pedalling. She smelt the fear which was not fear. She dismounted and let the bike drop to the pavement with a crash. She had passed up opportunities to shout at people all day. Now that she was ready to do so, she had no audience. She kicked a beer can across the pavement. It banged against the hub-cap of a parked car. She ran her hands through her hair and gripped a ponytail tight at the back of her head, until it hurt. She had brought David into it. It wasn't his fault. She should have left him in peace.

It started to rain. She picked up the bike, turned it around, remounted, and headed back in the direction from which she had just come, up Hammersmith Grove towards the Goldhawk Road. She had pedalled all that way, pretending not to be heading for Victoria's flat. She stopped fooling herself. She planned to ring Victoria's bell and see what happened. See if Matthew was up there in the pocket-sized boudoir.

Thirty yards ahead, a silhouette staggered out on to the pavement from one of the forecourts. A black retriever shot out on to the pavement, ran, checked, tore back to the man, circled his feet and jumped up. The drunk leant against one of the trees, knees buckling, and dropped to all fours on the pavement. As she approached, she confirmed that it was Matthew, kneeling on the pavement, blocking the path between her and Victoria. She thought about turning round, but then she was damned if she would and she pedalled harder towards him, wondering if he would scuttle out of the way. The closer she got the more pathetic he looked, trying to lever himself off the ground and collapsing again. She turned off the pavement in a gap between the parked cars. She thought about stopping, lifting him to his feet and helping him home. But he didn't want her help any more. She was looking to the left, trying to see him between the parked cars, to see if he was all right. A screeching of tyres, metal shrieking on metal, pulled her attention back to the road. A car weaved towards her. The driver looked beyond her, as if she wasn't there at all. In the oasis of seconds which opened before her, she saw the bicycle lamps on the bookshelf in Tamsin's flat; she saw

Char leaping out between parked cars; she saw the top of Matthew's head; she saw the light from Tory's kitchen window slicing through the new leaves. The driver rammed into another car and bounced into her path again. She had time to count down the split seconds of his approach, to curse the Father Christmas principle, to curse David and Tory and Josephine and Bill. She cursed herself for not changing out of the other girl's knickers. She made time to curse clamps and telephones, to curse answering machines and marketing, to curse the clean and the sober. But she could not persuade herself to curse Matthew.

She tumbled up into air.

Part Three

Fourteen Days

21

Non-returner

The cat stood on his stomach, clenching its paws and then plunging them into his stomach. Seeing that it had succeeded in waking him, the animal miaowed and then cowered. He swiped at it with the back of his hand. The quantity and brightness of light was unspeakable. Inside his mouth someone had rearranged consistencies: his tongue was spasmed and solid, his teeth mushy and woollen. He scratched at a sharp prickling beneath his skin. His hands were coated in a flaky, sticky substance. He curled his toes and confirmed the embrace of unshucked shoes. He was lying on the sofa in the living room at home. He called for Char but the only response was another miaow from the cat. He was still wearing his black overcoat.

He remembered a telephone conversation with Josephine. He had gone to the restaurant to meet Victoria. He had changed his mind about stopping at Tamsin's to see if Alison was there. Was he supposed to be at Victoria's, or searching for Alison? Or at work? The phone rang. A needle pierced the top of his head as he sat up, its tip lodging behind his left eye. 'Mmm?'

'Mr Kerrigan, this is Desmond Largesse.'

'Who?'

'From Longacres, about your grandmother.' She had been crying out all night. Not for Arthur, but for Matthew.

He sniffed his fingers and smelt an iron tang. The stuff on his hands must be rust. He climbed the stairs to inspect himself in the bathroom mirror. He searched for cuts. He blew his nose, hoping the tissue might contain the black crust of dried blood. He turned on the taps above the basin. A twist of rose-tinted water curled from his cupped hands on to white porcelain. When his face was safely over the toilet bowl his stomach refused to offer up what, a moment before, it had promised to eject.

He assembled the coffee machine. The smell of the catfood which he lowered to the floor produced in him an involuntary heave. The animal purred and hogged. Alison's hidden supply of stale cigarettes lay on the counter, by the winking answering machine. He closed his eyes, listening out for the boiling water forcing itself through the pod of coffee. The messages – the machine told him there were six – might fill the gap between the meal at Brutino's and waking to the cat's attempts to eviscerate him. He lit a cigarette and poured coffee. As he sipped and inhaled, a gust of panic rippled the surface of his exhaustion. He ran out into the street. He could not see the car. Then he remembered that Alison had taken it. He returned to the house and called a cab. He pressed the play button on the answering machine.

'I didn't think you'd be there.' Alison. 'Why would you be there?'

'Matthew, this is Joan Felshaw ringing. Call me back, please.'

'Matthew?' Victoria. 'Pick up, if you're there. Are you all right? Call me.'

'Matthew, I need to talk to you.' Josephine. 'Call me when you wake up.' The last two messages were blank.

The blood on his hands must have been his own. Innocent blood. Or menstrual blood. Whatever he had done was not yet his responsibility. He had no knowledge of it, no memory. The incubus, born in the attic bedroom of his grandmother's cottage, had acted while his back was turned. Last night, in some unremembered place – a damp basement? a darkened street? – he had become what he had always known himself to be.

He dreaded his encounters with Nurse Bradshaw. It was with relief that he shook the hand of an agency nurse. 'Oh, Mr Kerrigan, it's a terrible thing. I've been up and down in that lift a dozen times if I've been once.' They walked through the television lounge. Kerrigan nodded to two old ladies who claimed his grandmother's friendship. 'She's up there on her own, off in her head all day. And she barely sleeps.'

'You must have her on some form of medication.'

'She refuses,' the nurse said. 'She'd be better off in the old country, but.'

'Matthew, my Matthew,' his grandmother greeted him. 'Sit down, quick. Off you go now, Rosie.'

'I'm Siobhan, Mrs Kerrigan.'

Disregarding the correction, his grandmother smiled at Matthew. 'You've come. You didn't want to, but you came. It won't be long now. Ah, Matthew.'

'Gran?'

'You can smoke.' Her body sagged at an angle in the armchair. Her eyes and her mouth twitched with impatience. 'You're no more than a child, but you smoke.' She nudged an ashtray across the low table between them. 'Thank God you stopped the drink.'

'They say you can't sleep.'

'What do I need with sleep? No time, no need, no sleep.' She paused. 'I loved him well enough, poor lamb. There was no lack of love. The look of him and the lovely smile of his eyes. You remember? You were too young to remember?' There was a murky stillness in Kerrigan where his father's face might have been. 'You have it too, Matthew. But not today, not for me.'

'Alison—'

'Smile for me, Matthew.' His grandmother stared at him. 'Smile for your old grandmother.' He lit a cigarette. 'No, no, with the eyes, the eyes. There. That's it, now. That's the smile.' On her television a couple sat together on a pastel sofa, taking turns to chat to the camera. 'I don't intend to be forgiven.' She breathed through her mouth. He saw her tongue nudge her lower dentures, tipping them forward. 'That's not what you're here for.' The row of teeth settled back behind the cracked mound of her lower lip. 'He speaks to me now. He has forgiveness enough for both of us. He speaks to me because you won't listen. So I promised.' On the television, a sportscaster gave way to a goals package. 'I've made my promise.' Matthew stood up and leant across the table to switch the television off.

'There was so much rain, the sky tipping it down like a provocation, jeering at us. When he arrived, it was sleek in his hair, trickling off his chin. I took his coat and hung it by the airing cupboard, as I did when he came home from school. On a wooden hanger, so the warm could reach it.

'He came straight from his office. I was so alone. Once he was there with me, I asked him to stay. Just for supper. So he phoned her – your mother. She was difficult about him visiting me. I could tell from his face when he finished the call. I should have sent him down the hill, but I couldn't. I couldn't do it. You don't see that?

'We had a couple of drinks. I put on the food. What devil in me pushed him, I'll never know. He loved your mother. One child is too few. Have more if you have them at all. Have two, have four. Not just one.' Matthew remembered the first drink. The first, the second and the fourth. 'Arthur heard him. Drank to close him out. Not drinking at the devil's bidding but to be rid of the voice muttering, questioning, tempting. Men drink against the devil while women shun him, sober.

'By the time the food was ready, he was cut. Not falling down drunk but so the muscles of his face relaxed and his skin hung by the bones. All the sense was washed out of him. The phone was ringing, the food burnt. He shouted at me for the love I'd drowned him in.

'Then he was suddenly asleep. Just like his father. Sitting stiff and upright, chin dropped on his chest, across from me in the other armchair with the picture window between us and the rain beyond it. I loosened his tie and his shoes. I threw a blanket over him.

'I invited her? No harm would have come to him, sleeping in my chair, sleeping it off. I woke to a banging on the window at the other end of the sitting room. She was holding an umbrella and knocking on the glass. I feigned sleep, hoping she might leave. But he woke and saw her there, stood up, tripped and fell hard across the carpet, raised himself and stumbled to the door.' His grandmother had exhausted herself. She was panting, hands held before her, gazing at her yellow, shrunken palms. 'I hated him to drink. But not as she hated it.'

'That's enough,' Kerrigan said.

'I went to the hall to see what the trouble was. When they saw me they fell silent. She asked me to fetch his coat. Like a servant. I stood in the porch while they walked down the path into darkness and rain. I heard their footfalls on the steps to the road. I heard him say, "Of course I'll drive. What do you mean? No one tells me what to do." She asked him why he was always like that after visiting me. It was no business of hers, he said, and he was right.'

'I won't hear this.'

'The times I've tried to tell you. You always ran off. As if they'd never existed.' She was panting hard, a runner or a lover, straining to the finish. Matthew gripped the arms of his chair, cigarette burnt down between his fingers, ash tottering. 'I was in bed when they came. I never knew why they turned up at the cottage. Perhaps out of kindness. They could have phoned. I thought they were there to take me away. Uniformed men, dripping in my hall. He was almost home, almost safe. They skidded off the lane. The car rolled. The stream was deep enough to take them. What with the rain.' She panted, trying to catch her breath. 'A farm-hand. Up early for the milking. He found the car. Ran back to the village. Called for an ambulance. But they were gone.'

What she had told him was absurd, impossible. His parents had died on their way to visit him at school. Her gush of apparent lucidity was nothing more than an extreme example of the free-form synchrony which had typified her ramblings for years. 'The accident happened the following day,' he said. 'You're confused.'

'If only she'd let him be. Let him stay with me.' His grandmother was panting hard. A rasping in her throat accompanied each exhalation. 'Just once. Just for one night.'

'Don't you dare blame her,' he whispered.

'I blame only myself,' the grandmother said. 'But she was driving.'

His hands still clenched the arms of the chair, sweat slick on the varnished wood. 'What time did they leave your cottage?'

'I need the nurse.'

'The time,' he said. 'I have to know the time.'

'Between three and four,' she rasped. 'Nearer four.'

He watched her fighting for breath, her dugs rising and

falling as her lungs begged air. He watched the blue seeping on to her lips. Matthew and his grandmother stared into one another's eyes, waiting.

'I had only you,' she gasped. 'You don't see?'

'Be quiet.'

'And that dog.' Her last word had opened a well in him at the bottom of which he could see, distant, but clearly reflected, the events of the night before. He saw the flash of lights reflected on the bicycle spokes. He saw Char, bleeding on to the tarmac. His grandmother stretched for the button beside the bed, but it was beyond her reach. 'You're no better than me?' she whispered.

He stood at last and pressed his palm flat against the wall, holding down the button until he heard footsteps approaching in the corridor. Once out of the room, away from her centrally-heated aroma, he gulped air. He had been clenching his jaw. He forced himself to loosen the clutch, stretching his mouth open until he yawned. He lit a cigarette. A tingling in the tips of his fingers heralded a numbness that threatened to engulf him.

Desmond Largesse approached him in the corridor. Matthew put his hands in his pockets as Largesse prepared to greet him. 'It distressed you to see her.'

'Not at all,' Matthew said.

'She's been asking for a priest,' Largesse said.

'Do whatever you see fit.'

'Whatever?'

'Certainly,' Matthew said.

'It's rare to speak to someone who understands our difficulties.'

'Is it?'

The train passed through woods of evergreen and oak, accelerating on to a viaduct across a wide valley of ploughed fields. The turned earth shone slick in the silver light. He sat alone in the smoking compartment, gazing through the grimy window.

He remembered a June day when he was six. He was at a school in the nearby village from which the children were sent home for lunch. Five mothers shared collecting and feeding their children. Matthew went to a different house each weekday. On Fridays it was the Landrys. They were farmers. The five boys played in the yard while Mrs Landry prepared lunch. They climbed the gate which divided the yard from high green corn. As the others dropped down into the field, Matthew hung back. He warned the others it was wrong. Their feet would crush the corn. He climbed down on the yard-side of the gate and squatted by an old plough which lay rusting in the shade of the barn. Matthew's friends, shorter than the stalks, disappeared into the labyrinth of corn.

A few minutes later, Mr Landry pulled into the yard in his Land Rover. He switched the engine off and sat at the wheel. He had not seen Matthew. For a moment, the world balanced on a point of absolute stillness. Matthew tried to draw down the silence, like a blind between the yard and the cornfield. Then the lazy buzzing of an aeroplane high overhead merged with the drumming of a tractor passing behind the barn. The machines broke the shared silence, as a plough breaks the crust of hard ground, furling it over on itself. Matthew heard a shout from inside the forest of corn. Another shout and then an eruption of laughter. Farmer Landry strode to the gate and yelled at the boys. His rage was like fire. But the corn was still green and his anger could not ignite it.

At lunch, he watched his friends mimic repentance as they forked their food. Matthew felt queasy – a sort of travel sickness. He had departed from himself and was travelling back too quickly. The smell of the food – it was cottage pie – was intolerable. Mrs Landry tried to persuade him to eat. He could not answer her. Eventually she phoned his mother. You did nothing wrong, Mrs Landry told him. It was the others. No one's blaming you. When his mother arrived, she neither questioned nor scolded him. She drove him home, lifted him out of the car and carried him into the house.

As the train slowed, Matthew saw a clear picture of his mother's face, close to his own. He felt her breath move his hair as her hand stroked his cheek.

He took a taxi home. He found the bloodstained dog-collar in the rubbish-bin and buried it in the garden. He phoned Tamsin's flat and heard Alison's voice on the machine. When it was his turn to speak, he could think of nothing to say. He phoned the number a second time, to hear her voice saying – 'Alison Felshaw can't take your call. Wait for the beeps.' He dialled a third time, but left no message. He ordered a mini-cab to take him to Tamsin's flat. He asked the driver to wait while he rang the bell. Receiving no reply, he instructed the driver to take him to Hammersmith Grove.

The broken glass had been swept from the street. A number of dented cars were parked under the trees. A narrow beach stranded the gutter outside Victoria's flat. The emergency services must have first covered Char's blood with sand, then hosed down the tarmac. He rang Victoria's bell. He crossed the street and looked up at her windows.

Outside Josephine's flat, he paid the mini-cab driver. He entered the mansion-block as one of the residents was leaving. After he knocked, he heard her footsteps behind the door.

'Go away.'

'Please,' Matthew said. 'I have to talk to you.'

'What about me?'

'I'm not going to infect you.' Matthew remembered Base, outside the door to David's flat. 'Let me in.'

'I'm not comfortable about this,' she said. 'I need to protect my space. Are you smoking?'

'Are you my friend?'

'This is not a friendship issue,' she said. 'This is a life-and-death issue. I have to stick with the winners.' He heard the locks turning. She opened the door. She had kept the chain on. He saw a slice of her, legs naked below tight shorts. 'I have someone here,' she said. 'I didn't think you'd come.'

'Josephine.' Matthew held the cigarette behind his back. 'I need your help.'

'It's very inconvenient,' she said.

'Who's in there with you?'

'I said there was someone here,' Josephine said eventually, 'because I don't know if I want you to come in.'

'So, there's no one else?'

'He left earlier.' She stood back from the door, concealing her face. 'I've had very little sleep. I get into a bad space when I'm tired.' She closed the door, slipped the chain and opened it again. Matthew followed her along the corridor and made the familiar right turn into her living room, knocking over – as he invariably did – the blue umbrella leaning against the wall by the door. He had forgotten to take his shoes off, as was the custom in her flat.

'Who was here, then?'

'I can't discuss it,' she said.

'So be it.'

'Do you have any idea how this makes me feel?' she asked. Through the open window Matthew heard rain, hushing in the air, spitting on the glass. 'If you were feeling even a small portion of what I am feeling right now—' Josephine paused. 'Well, I think you might explode. Literally.'

'Do you believe in curses?'

'I've been under a curse since the lifetime before last.'
She led him into her kitchen and filled the kettle. 'I was an
untouchable.' He listened to the rain and then to the sound
of an aircraft passing overhead, swallowing the sound of
the rain. 'Next time I'm supposed to be a dancer. Put that
cigarette out. A Russian, they said. And then, if I keep my
karma clean, I have a seventy per cent chance of becoming
a non-returner.'

'I've had a weird morning.'

'Out of the cycle. Fully evolved.' She opened a cupboard.
'Camomile, Rosehip or Roibos?'

'Coffee?'

'Decaff?'

'Two spoons.'

'Pure awareness.' She poured water into the cups. 'No
more vale of tears. No more soul-making.'

Matthew stood by the window, trying to see the aeroplane.

'I have a fantasy,' Josephine said. 'About the way you
use silence. You and Alison.' Her phone began to ring in
another room. He heard a mechanical click as the answering
machine intercepted the call.

'You have a lot of fantasies.'

'You came here to tell me something.'

'I went to see my old Gran—' Matthew stopped. 'Ah,
fuck it.'

'And?' She handed him his coffee.

'I'm going to smoke a cigarette,' Matthew said.

'Are you asking permission to abuse my air?'

'I can open another window.'

'Oh, Matt.' Josephine saw the look on his face. 'What
happened?' She took his hands in hers. Then she stared
at him with an unblinking gaze. After a few moments, he
looked down at his hands, breaking the eye contact.

'Char was run over.'

'God, that's extraordinary – I'm so sorry – I lost my cat only last week.'

'When I woke up this morning there was blood on my hands,' Matthew said.

'What have you done?' Josephine moved away from him and fiddled with a bowl of pot-pourri on the counter by the fridge. Matthew sat down at the kitchen table. 'It's not me,' he said. 'I don't make all the bad things happen in my life.' He placed his hands over his eyes and cheeks, the tips of his middle fingers touching his hairline.

'When David died,' Josephine said, 'I felt like it was my fault. I still believe it was my fault.'

'Is there anything you can't find a way of appropriating?'

'Alison didn't tell you,' Josephine said. The phone rang and, once again, the answering machine snapped up the call.

'David died of an overdose,' Matthew said.

'She didn't want to freak you.'

'David told me it was only the one time,' Matthew said. 'One fuck does not a relationship make.'

'I'm not going to argue,' Josephine said. 'I'm just telling you he didn't die of an overdose.'

'Yeah?'

'I can't even make amends properly.'

'David was ready to die,' Matthew said. 'It was an aesthetic thing. It's got nothing to do with you.'

'You force your way in here.' Josephine dug in a handbag and produced an inhaler. 'You start smoking. Then you accuse me of lying. It's pretty rich, don't you think?'

'The hell with it.'

'The dead can't die until we release them,' she said. 'They might seem to hold on to us, but it's the other way round. We cling to the wreckage, to save ourselves from drowning.'

'What the fuck's that supposed to mean?'

'Please,' Josephine said. 'Please don't be angry with me.'

'Stop talking shit for two minutes.'

Josephine dragged on her inhaler. Matthew closed his eyes and let his head rest on his folded arms. He felt the touch of Josephine's hand on the back of his neck. There were some moments of quiet in which he allowed her to stroke him, thinking of nothing at all, listening to the rain.

'They killed him, Matt. Ask her if you don't believe me.'

The phone rang. Josephine slipped into another room to answer it. He waited in the kitchen. Josephine returned, holding in her hand a portable phone, palm jammed over the mouthpiece.

'It's Victoria,' she said. 'She won't tell me what it's about. She won't even talk to me.'

He took the offered phone.

'Where were you?' he said.

Josephine strode away down the corridor.

'Matthew,' Victoria said. 'I don't know how to tell you this.'

'It's not like you to be lost for words.'

'Please. Don't.'

'Christ, are you all right?'

'Something bad has happened,' Victoria said. 'Something terrible.'

22

Medication

She approached a curtain of pain on the bright edge of blackness. She retreated into the darkness, but it was neither safe nor warm. It was just very black. She moved towards its perimeter once more, drifting closer to the tasselled fringe of hurt. She scanned her body, searching for a place where there were no stings, no aches, no throbbing or jabbing. Her arms and legs were itching. She couldn't feel her feet, perhaps because they were so far away, perhaps because they didn't hurt. Then she was scared and wanted to know if they were still there.

A voice spoke a name. 'Alison.' She wanted to know who was being addressed. 'Alley, Alley.' She fell towards the blackness, towards the empty vastness which was different from the fleshly container of sleep. As she dragged herself back, a gymnast doing the final pull-up, chin drawing level with the rail as her arms gave out, she heard other voices around her. She opened her mouth and touched her tongue to a brail of cracked skin along her upper lip.

'She moved.' The words were accompanied by a kiss of warm breath on her cheek. If they expected words they were going to be disappointed. She didn't much care where she was or who the others were. She had nowhere to go, no resting place between the unknowable blackness and the taunting pain. Had she been able to speak she would have told them to leave her be. Bugger off, she thought. Bugger off, the lot of you. She wobbled on the fence between blackness and pain, thinking Bugger off. Then she must have fallen off on the black side.

The next time she climbed the fence, she opened her eyes to whiteness. She moved her jaw. The pain in her nose brought tears to her eyes. 'Welcome back,' said a female voice. 'Don't try to move.' The whiteness retreated. She had seen a nurse's uniform, very close up. She tried to speak but her tongue was asleep.

'Blink once if you can hear me.' She obeyed. 'Good girl,' the nurse said. Who did they think she was? A child? A pet? 'Blink once if you can feel your finger-tips.' She wasn't having any more of that. She closed her eyes. She dropped back from the pain and fell, not into blackness but on to the soft pillow of sleep.

Later, when she opened her eyes again, everything was sharp and clear. Why had they allowed her mouth to become so dry? She could see the bed on which she lay and that her legs were in plaster. The itching under the plaster was as bad as the pain. There was a tube stuck up her nostril. Her throat hurt. Something moved at the periphery of her vision. She turned her head a fraction. A girl sat beside the bed, sleeping on a grey plastic chair.

Alison made a humming noise in her throat. The sleeping girl's chin rose, then dropped towards her breasts as she settled back into slumber. Alison continued to hum in her throat, with her mouth shut. Her lips were stuck together. She took deeper breaths, which made her ribcage hurt, and hummed more loudly. The sleeping girl stirred.

'Ali,' she said. 'You're back.' Her tone claimed an intimacy which Alison found offensive. She glared at her visitor and emitted a short, throaty hum. The visitor stood and leant over her with a saccharine look of adoration. Alison risked tearing her lips, forcing them open to croak 'Go away.'

'It's me, Ali,' the visitor said. 'Josephine. Your friend?'

Alison had never seen the woman before. She wanted water.

'Let me fetch the doctor.' As Josephine left the room, Alison experienced two powerful and contradictory impressions. The first was a conviction that someone who should have been present was absent, as if she had lost a limb or two, which she hadn't; she'd checked. The second was a certainty that someone who was not supposed to be there was hiding under the bed or had wormed his way under her skin while she had been – well, wherever she had been. A small, subtle thing, like a scorpion or an anemone.

Josephine returned with a woman doctor and an old couple. The doctor strode up to the bed and adjusted the flow on Alison's drip. Then the old people approached the bed, holding hands. The woman touched her cheek. The doctor shone a bright pang of light into one of Alison's eyes, then the other. Who were these people?

The woman reached into her handbag and her hand emerged clutching a tissue with which she dabbed at her cheeks. 'My darling,' she said. 'Thank heavens.' The doctor offered a straw to Alison's lips. She sucked water. It was sweet and so cold that it made her tongue ache. As she began to draw deep, the doctor pulled the straw away, ushered the others out of the room and returned to the bedside.

She was a senior registrar. Her name was Heather Freestone. She explained that Alison had been in an accident, that she was going to be all right. 'Did you recognise any of those people?' she asked. Alison inspected the room. White walls, a window through which she saw a trapezoid of grey sky. 'Can you tell me your name?' Two more grey plastic chairs stood together under the window. It was right there, close enough to touch. Everything was hurting and the questions annoyed her. She offered the name the others had used. 'Alison?'

Later, after the doctor had explained that her legs and her nose were broken, that she was lucky to be alive and even luckier that her face was so little damaged, the old couple returned with the one called Josephine.

'I'm your mother,' the woman said. 'And this is your father.'

'Someone's missing,' Alison said. 'Who's missing?' The woman glanced at the man. 'What are you frightened of?'

'Nothing, darling.'

'You're lying.'

'Why would we lie, Alison?' The old man grinned at her.

'How should I know?'

'It's the shock,' the old woman said. 'You're not yourself.'

'Do I like you?' Alison asked. 'I mean, did I like you? Did we get on?'

'You were always good,' the woman said. 'Kind and good. You never complained about anything. Always sunny and easy and sweet. It worried me sometimes.' When Alison said nothing, the woman continued. 'Do you remember the Wendy house your father made out of old doors? You used to sit in it, down at the bottom of the garden, giving tea-parties for your dolls.'

'Who do you think I am?' Alison asked. 'Some kind of retard?'

'We never had to tell you what to do,' the old man said. 'We never had to punish you. Not once.'

'Your favourite doll was called Hilda. She had lemon-yellow hair and a light blue dress which you asked me to iron. She always looked clean and smart.'

'Who's missing?'

'What do you mean, darling?'

'I don't want you here,' Alison said to them. 'Go away.'

When Alison woke again there were flowers and plants on the window-sill and on a trolley which over-arched her like a giant staple. Cellophane girdled the brick-coloured plastic pots. A nurse was watering the plants. When she saw that Alison was awake she left the room and returned with another nurse. They changed Alison's pan and gave her a bed-bath, which was humiliating. She could smell herself without being able to do anything about it.

The girl – Josephine – came in as they were finishing.

'They say you're getting better.'

'Why does everyone patronise me?'

'You're still quite fragile,' Josephine said. 'No one wants to upset you.'

'Can I trust you?'

'How do you mean?'

'Not to patronise me?'

'Sure.' Josephine sat on the chair beside the bed. Alison told her to sit under the window where she could see her more easily.

'Are you my friend?'

'Of course I'm your friend.'

'Tell me who's missing, then. Are they trying to protect me by lying to me? Did someone die in the accident?'

'Do you mean the driver?'

'What driver?' Alison began to weep. 'I don't even know why I'm crying. Do I look very ugly?'

'There's some bruising around your eyes from the broken nose,' Josephine said. 'But that's all. You're beautiful. In your spirit. You're very grounded and real and – well – beautiful.'

'You know who's missing, don't you?'

'Ali.' Josephine offered her a tissue. 'Please.'

'What's wrong with you?'

'I'm fine,' Josephine said.

'Why say that when you're not?'

'Someone has to be fine,' she said, looking away. 'Otherwise everything falls apart.'

'Oh dear.'

'You not knowing who I am,' Josephine said. 'I can't get used to it.'

'That's your problem,' Alison said. 'Wipe my face, please.'

'You're different.'

'Tell me.'

'You used to be – I don't know—'

'And now?' Alison asked.

'You're different,' she said.

There was an emptiness under her lungs, where the missing one should have been; and a fullness lower down.

'Is there someone else in the room?' Alison asked. 'Is someone listening?'

'Just us,' Josephine said.

'What have you done to me?' Alison asked.

'I have gentle feelings towards you. Gentle feelings and healing thoughts.'

'Go away,' Alison said.

'I was only trying to help,' Josephine snivelled. 'Don't reject me.'

'Off you go,' Alison said. 'You don't fool me.'

'I know who you remind me of—'

'Who's that?'

'I don't feel safe now,' Josephine said.

'You're enjoying this,' she told her. 'Holding all the cards.'

'I'm shame-spiralling.'

'What on earth is that?'

'When you get your memory back, you'll know.' Josephine

approached the end of the bed. 'Enjoy yourself while you can.'

Spinning off the curve of sleep, Matthew was grabbed awake and slammed against the wall of night. He fingered a damp patch of sheet where toxins had wept through his sleeping skin. Memory, a bibulous incontinent, had drenched the bed. The wings of bats stretched tight across struts of cartilage. His grandmother swung above him upside down, eyes small and lava-red. The river in which he swam was filling with a tide of memories. Riding the precarious current he swerved out of dream, flailing for purchase, hauling himself to the bank by sodden branches. But he was weak and the bullying tide dragged him back and drew him on.

He struggled from the bed and stood at the window, looking down at rain shining on the street and fallen cherry blossom patterning the cracked pavements. No moon. A pressing flatness of orange-stained cloud was wrapped around the city, secured by canvas straps. Which no one could unbuckle. Unless prayer would unstrap the strait-jacket.

He dressed in a hiatus of resolve, teasing cufflinks into cotton slits, knotting himself into a tie. By the time he had thumbed on his shoes he changed his mind. He pulled off his socks, unleashed himself from his tie and lay down. From under the bed he pulled a folded square of tin-foil. He placed a rolled tube of foil between his lips and opened out the square. He fumbled for a lighter and ignited it below the foil square so that the brown smudge at its centre liquefied to a puddle. He tipped the square of foil and, as a brown stream ran off the puddle, trailed it with the tube between his lips, slurping at the wisps of rising smoke. Before the rivulet could reach the edge of the foil, he levelled it and then tipped it back, trailing the smouldering stream to its origin.

He did not wake until the refuse lorry roared on the street below. He wished he had clung to the idea of rising before light and walking the streets. Later still, he woke to the ringing of the telephone downstairs. He awaited the crawling of lizards through his intestines, which would force him out of bed. As soon as he remembered to wait for them the lizards arrived, romping and tumbling in his belly.

Rage walked him for hours – until he sat in a church on a chill brown pew, waiting for dark. In the early evening, he saw Terri, Victoria's assistant, approaching him in the street. He was unshaven and in anticipation of her proximity smelt the sour cloud around his body. He backed away. Suddenly he was sandwiched between a taxi and a Range Rover, both drivers with their windows down, shouting at him – dickbrain, half-wit, cunt. In the middle of the road, swinging bags of shopping. He stood there, remembering how, when she arrived at Unlimited, Terri used to put a circle instead of a dot above the 'i' of her name. She was making her way towards him, drawn by the shouting. He dropped his shopping and ran.

After the close encounter with Terri, he drank two capfuls of cough mixture and three fingers of whisky. He lay on the bed, Char's lead twisted like a bandage around his knuckles, pinching flesh. The phone rang. He reached under the bed for the foil.

He woke as cerebral singing leaked from his ears. It sounded like the high pitch of an electrical device inserted between the hemispheres of his brain or an alarm ringing miles away, carrying through the streets. A quarter to four in the morning. He tracked along the ceiling with his eyes, looking for clues. Streetlamp glow pressed against the curtains. He lay with his coat open, cooling down, limbs loose and glowing. A flashing blue light washed intermittently across the ceiling, but he heard neither siren nor engine.

He splashed and thrashed, beating his way to the shore. He would not surrender to the belief that above the ceiling, behind the walls and under the floorboards were worms, carpets of worms, oceans of worms writhing and turning and hungry. Beyond the worms, deep in the fibre of the dawn, was the person who chose this hour of each day to cuff him into consciousness.

A bird cheated the dawn with a tentative announcement of the coming light. An apologetic warble: sorry to interrupt and everything. I shouldn't think you even want to know but pretty soon, in fact just about any minute now, it's sun-up and the whole fiasco of feeding, fucking and surviving is going to start all over again.

The sheet of muscle across his abdomen warped and tightened. He tussled in half-light. No urge to breathe, but breathe he must. He heard banging on the front door. Alison visited in dawn chimera, painted in eggwhite brushstrokes, furled in the billowing silk of his agon. He teased himself with her nakedness, pumped and spilled as he watched the shimmering forms flicker across the walls. A brief span of thudding repose. Then cooling shame. Endorphined and languid, he asked forgiveness. The phone rang. He slept.

Afternoon sunshine filtered through the trees. He drifted down the gutter of tin-foil, following the smoking streak of brown liquid. He sucked on the foil tube, drawing down the bitter smoke. Lungs bursting, Matthew held on to the smoke until he reached the surface and exhaled. Salt water flowed over his body in tepid shallows where sunlight wobbled through water to warm his skin. Waves embraced him, each surging into the ruins of the last. A gash of spittle widened at the lip as the wave stooped, tumbled, then slushed out flat, spilling lemonade on rock and sand.

He woke to banging on the door. He heard keys turning in locks. A swishing rumble of street-noise entered the house as the door opened, then was muffled again as it closed. Footsteps creaked the loose board at the bottom of the stairs. The banister squealed as it bore the pressure of a hand. The cat scampered into the room and disappeared under his bed.

'Matthew?' He lay still. 'Can I come up?'

He slipped the foil under the pillow and closed his eyes. He heard her enter the room, and felt the mattress slope away from him as she sat on Alison's side of the bed. Her hand touched his shoulder. He opened his eyes.

'You're pinned.'

'I just woke up,' he said. 'Little lie-in.'

'You're pinned to fuck,' she said. 'I know when someone's stoned.'

'Whatever.' He rolled away from her.

'Matthew?' Josephine pulled at his shoulder until she had forced him flat on to his back. He stared past her, at the ceiling.

'You should stay away from me,' he said. 'Bad influence.'

'I told her,' Josephine said. 'I told Alison about us.'

'Again?' Matthew leant up on an elbow.

'It's better she knows.'

'Better than what?' Matthew sat up. He was recalling a conversation with Josephine, from deep in the night of the first drink.

'She doesn't remember anything,' Josephine said.

'Is her face all right?'

'I told her about you and me. I had to start somewhere. And about Victoria. I'm sure she'd be pleased to see you. She keeps on about someone who's missing.'

'It wasn't you,' Matthew said. 'It was never going to be you.'

'You can't undo the past,' she said. 'I told Victoria too. I don't mind what you do.'

'You're losing it, Josephine.'

'Actually, Matthew, I've found it. It's hexagonal, crystalline and multicoloured.'

'You stopped your medication.'

'I don't take mood-altering substances.' Josephine wriggled free of his grip. 'It's against the principles. As you may recall.'

'Lithium isn't against any principles.' Matthew sat up. 'When did you stop?'

'I'm better than ever,' she said. 'Aren't you going to kiss me? You didn't kiss me. You always used to kiss me. Whenever you had the chance.' Josephine strode back and forth in the narrow run between the bed and Alison's dressing table. 'I don't suppose you planned it. But when you saw her coming along the pavement on the bike you thought, here's my chance. You forced her into the path of the car. Then you ran away. That's her done with, you thought. That's her turned to strawberry jam. And when you had your first moment of doubt you thought of me – I could sense it, I was awake – and you knew that I was there for you, that I was your alibi, that I would understand. And I waited for you. I waited.'

23

Qualified

When Alison was asleep, she forgot that she couldn't remember anything. Her dreams were full of daylight, sharp and clear, more vivid than waking time. This was, as she intuited, exactly the wrong way round. She was the conduit of dreams which seemed to belong more to other people than to her. One night she awoke to the touch of a hand on her cheek. She knew it was his. She recognised his smell. 'Where did you go?' she said out loud. 'I was asking for you.' When she opened her eyes there was nobody.

The day before he came to the hospital, Alison dreamt that she was a man. She was walking along beside the Alison she had been before the accident. They were returning from a public event – a fireworks or a picnic. It was night-time but daylight too, a deep blue light. Others were walking beside and behind them, a big crowd returning to town. They passed drunks collapsed on the pavements and surly people who scurried in the wake of some outrage which had just been perpetrated or exposed. She noticed two men and a girl walking, as she was, in the direction of the accommodation blocks. The girl was plain but shapely.

Dressed in student uniform – blue jeans, a shirt. The men wore jeans shiny with old dirt and stained anoraks. Their hair was thick and curled over their collars. They had the hunched anonymity of extremists or the terminally unemployed.

The dream jumped to morning: Alison saw the group of three again. One of the men punched the girl hard in the face. She keeled over stiffly, as if she had suffered instant rigor mortis. The aggressor followed the girl to the ground and raped her. Alison backed away. He had a knife. He cut the plain girl's throat. Alison (who had stopped being a man and was now Alison again) did not want to bear witness. She backed away, then started to run. She was half a mile away, retreating across a lawn, then up some stone steps. She turned and saw her own footprints written in blood on the steps she had just climbed. Perhaps she was not the witness at all, but the killer, the rapist.

She decided to go back. She sat in a room with a dozen other students who had volunteered to give their accounts of the incident. There was no one to take her statement. Perhaps, she thought, I am going to make a confession. She learnt that each student who gave evidence triggered a sum of money which the police would donate to the university accommodation budget. As the dream ended, she realised she had known all along that something terrible would happen to the girl, and that she might have been able to prevent it.

By her third day in the hospital she had begun – formally at least – to accept the strange couple as her parents. They talked at her bedside, hour after hour, telling her about Alison – her dresses, her friends, their house in Hampshire, Sergio. She was growing fond of them: the mother with her habit of reaching out to Alison's hair and playing with it; the father, whose formality was quick to dissolve into the expression of thrilled sorrow which he wore when he thought she wasn't looking. Alison knew all about her pony, her wardrobe, her good reports from school, the holiday they took in Australia, her year as a model, her time in Rome. Together, they composed a life into which they hoped she might suddenly slip. It was useless, of course. No one would tell her anything which accounted for the twinkling presence in her abdomen or the aching emptiness above it.

Josephine lied to her, little flecks of truth on a tissue of fibs. And yet it was obvious that Josephine had been a close friend. What could Alison have been thinking? Had she been blind to Josephine's faults, or drawn to them? Josephine alleged that she and Alison had slept together. Alison laughed out loud. Josephine stood over her, ranting. Alison flinched. Josephine saw her fear and smiled. Then she started to describe their sexual congress in the hackneyed rhetoric of a wank mag. A nurse came in to change Alison's pan and the fantasy-coitus was interrupted. Alison pleaded tiredness and the nurse sent Josephine away. Alison asked the nursing staff to ban Josephine from the ward.

The day when he arrived, her mother was telling her about a holiday in Scotland where it rained and rained and there were cattle wandering about on the beach and they all fished for mackerel. It was news to her. Alison was bored with these daytrips to the past. She couldn't remember anything.

The door opened slowly and he walked into the room. He would have to step further forward to allow the door to close behind him. He was doing it deliberately, hanging in the doorway to heighten her response to his entrance. Her father looked at him in angry amazement. The mother lowered her eyes to the floor, as if ashamed. There he was, the first person she recognised. 'David,' she shouted, overwhelmed that he had come, suddenly recalling a thousand things in a great rushing flood. He was deathly pale. He began to back through the doorway. The others were silent and still. 'Come back. David, come back.'

'Fetch the doctor,' her mother said to her father.

'Come in,' her father said to David. He entered the room and stood to one side of the doorway so that her father could leave. Alison wanted to leap up and hug him, but she could barely move.

'Aren't you going to say hello?' she asked him. He was stoned, taking his time about everything. His hair was all wonky, rubbed and scrubbed about. He looked like he'd been living rough. He pulled a packet of cigarettes from his coat pocket. 'You can't do that here,' the mother said. He lit up anyway, just as she knew he would.

'Give me a puff.' He shuffled over and placed the filter of the cigarette between her lips. She sucked the smoke into her mouth and drew it down into her lungs. A few seconds later she puffed again, as the lovely dizzy feeling wavered through her.

'Put that out immediately.' The doctor strode into the room.

'Where?' he said.

'Basin.' The doctor indicated. 'Quick. And then out. All of you. I need to talk to Alison alone.'

'Don't send him away,' she yelled. She was fighting to move her legs, which were entombed in plaster. The mother ushered him out. 'Come back. Please, come back. Bring him back.'

The doctor stood at the end of her bed. 'They're only doing what's best for you.'

'I remember them now,' Alison said. 'That's just the sort of thing they do. Tell you everything except what matters. How could they sit with me for two days and never once mention my brother?'

The doctor was silent, struggling for words. A little bubble burst inside Alison as she recognised what the carers and healers must go through when, if only for a moment, they allow themselves to engage with their charges. 'You must be tired,' Alison said. 'You've been on duty for ages.' The doctor's eyes glazed. They looked like the windscreen at the end of the carwash cycle – a sheet of clear water breaking up into runnels. The doctor turned away and dug in the overloaded pockets of her white coat, dropping her stethoscope, hunting for tissues. When she had composed herself, she turned to face Alison again.

'You said before that there was someone missing. Is that David?'

'Of course.'

'And a presence you can't account for.'

Suddenly it was obvious. 'I'm pregnant.' Alison felt sick. Sick with excitement.

'We thought you would miscarry,' the doctor said. 'But with every hour you keep it, the chances of its survival improve.'

David's inside me, Alison said to herself and wondered what she meant.

'Do you want to carry the baby to term?'

'Why on earth not?'

'Josephine told you one or two things about the more recent past,' the doctor said. 'In a misguided attempt to trigger your memory.'

'She said I'd been to bed with her.'

'Have you?'

'What are you frightened of?' Alison asked, watching the doctor hesitate at the brink of openness.

'You've suffered enough,' she said. 'I don't want to hurt you.'

'Bring David back,' Alison said. 'He'll know what to do.'

'I can't,' she said. 'No one can.' As the doctor outlined the circumstances of her brother's death, the sensation of absence returned to Alison's midriff, particularly when she filled her lungs with air. The foetus was dancing in her blood, a busy pulse beeping and shushing.

'The father?'

'We don't know,' Dr Freestone said. 'Perhaps the man you mistook for David.'

'So I wasn't seeing a ghost,' Alison said.

'There's no physiological reason why you shouldn't experience a normal pregnancy. We've been trying to protect you—'

'I need to be by myself now,' Alison said. 'Would that be all right?'

During the course of the next hour, Alison fought alone. She knew he was giving up – she chose to think of him as a he. Conditions, he seemed to have decided, were not propitious. Alison whispered to him and by concentrating on the little pulse in her belly she found that she could make it stronger. She tried blanking the empty place just above her womb, but that seemed to upset him, so she let it be as it was.

She asked him to stay. She told him how happy she was that he had come and to please, please, not give up. She forced herself to stay awake, pressing the nail of her thumb into the flesh of her forefinger, until she was quite sure that he was going to stay. Then she carried him into her dreams.

Matthew stood in the hospital corridor. Alison's parents sat together a few yards away, close to the nurses' station. He could hear snatches of their muttered conversation.

'Took him long enough to get here,' Alison's father said.

'He's not well.'

'Thought I'd heard the last of David.'

'Won't you ever forgive him?'

'Not this again.'

'He's gone,' the mother said. 'Make peace with him.'

'That wretched boy with some other woman,' the father said. 'While Ali's laid up, helpless.'

'She left him.'

'You can see why,' the father said. 'And that other oddball. Where do these people come from?'

The father's torso was convulsed by what looked like a spasm of laughter. As Alison's mother put her arm around her husband's shoulder, Matthew approached the couple. He squatted beside them. The father glanced at him and then lowered his head. 'I love your daughter,' Matthew said. 'I loved your son.'

Alison's father let out a roar of pain and indignation. He stood up, knocking Matthew backwards. He stalked away down the corridor, shoulders shaking.

'I'm sorry,' Matthew said.

'He can't forgive himself. He wakes in the night and paces by the window. He won't forgive anyone else either.'

'I've made it worse,' Matthew said.

'Yes,' Joan Felshaw said. 'You probably have.'

'I'll look after her,' Matthew said.

'Your can barely look after yourself,' Joan Felshaw said.

'I'm changing,' Matthew said.

'I've heard that statement too many times, from too many intractable people, to be reassured by it.'

'Please don't equate me with him.'

'I wouldn't dream of it,' she said. 'Have you any idea what it is like to lose a son? A child you have made, out of love? He was more to me than anything you can imagine.'

'I'm sorry.'

'You're going to find out what it's like.'

'How do you mean?'

'They haven't told you?'

'I stopped answering the phone.'

Joan Felshaw slapped his face. Her knuckles struck his cheek-bone, making his ears ring. 'You're going to be a father.'

'My God.' Matthew stood up. 'You must hate me.'

'Feeling guilty's a bad habit, like smoking or chewing your nails. When you get sick of it, you'll give it up.'

While Matthew was absorbing the implications of this statement, they were joined by Dr Freestone who explained what she had told Alison. 'We'd better get you sorted out,' the doctor said to him. 'When did you last eat?' Matthew could not remember. 'Come with me.' In the canteen, the doctor forced him to select a number of dishes. They sat together while she watched Matthew struggle to swallow mouthfuls of food. 'You'll have to use your instincts,' she said to Matthew. 'You're her link to the world now. The world after David.'

'What about the child?'

'I don't know,' the doctor said. 'It depends on how much Alison wants to be pregnant. We're assuming you're the father.'

'That's what I'm assuming.'

'Do you look like her brother?' the doctor asked.

Matthew described the circumstances in which he and Alison had met.

'You've been her David,' she said. 'And she yours.'

'It's more than that,' he said. 'She's my everything.'

'That must have been tough.'

'She managed to bear it.'

'I meant for both of you,' the doctor said.

'I love her,' Matthew said.

'Then you must be strong.' Matthew could not look at Dr Freestone. 'The first time I lost a patient, I wanted to give up doctoring,' she said. 'The consultant on the ward – he's retired now – told me that everyone loses a patient sooner or later. A patient she believed she might have saved, if only she had marshalled more foresight, more vigilance, more skill.'

'But—'

'No. Listen to me. None of us has as much control as we would like. Doctors don't have nearly as much power as our training leads us to believe. One day we work a miracle and the next we lose a child under anaesthetic during a routine operation. You've qualified now, the consultant told me. You know you're not God. He handed me back my letter of resignation and asked me to think about it overnight. The next morning I was back on the ward, saving lives and making mistakes.'

'I don't know how to begin,' Matthew said.

24

Possessed

He sat beside Alison's bed, waiting for her to wake. He noticed a geranium plant on the window-sill and plucked away the browning leaves. The scent on his hands reminded him of David's flat, of his first days in Alison's care.

'I'm supposed to know you, aren't I?'

He turned to the bed. Her eyes were still shut. 'Yes.'

'I was dreaming about David,' she said. 'He sent someone with a note for me. One of his cronies. The note was written on a torn-off piece of plastic fertiliser bag. I don't remember what it said. It certainly wasn't reassuring. The gist was that the duty, along with the fault, was his. It ended with an instruction to give the messenger five pounds. The crony stood there while I puzzled over the note, waiting for his money. I knew David was hiding round the corner, that the note was an elaborate way of scamming a fiver.'

'That's David.'

'Come here,' she said. Matthew stood beside the bed, level with her hips. 'Are you any good with children?'

'I don't know.'

'Are you prepared to hang around and find out?'

'I'm not going anywhere,' he said.

'You look as if you might.'

'I've wronged you,' Matthew said.

'And what about me?' she asked. 'Have I wronged you?'

'Perhaps,' he said. 'But not on purpose.' He told her how she had found him in her brother's bed. 'I wasn't used to being looked after. I distrusted it.'

'I've muddled the two of you up before.'

'We tried to hang on to him,' Matthew said. 'As best we could.'

'Say that again?'

'He was catalytic. He wanted to be indispensable.'

'Why are you talking that way?'

'Which way?'

'Trying to tell me something without saying it.'

'That's what English people do when they have emotions.' Matthew walked over to the window. 'They smuggle them out under cover of night.'

'Like they're at war with themselves,' Alison said. 'Tell me more.' Her eyes were closed. 'Tell me other things.'

Matthew stared out of the window at the trees of Hammersmith Cemetery. 'My parents died when I was young. David helped me to survive their loss. Which made his death doubly devastating. I became kind of choked up. Cleaning up from drugs increased my reticence. You and I were like two swimmers out at sea with a third – David – we were trying to bring back to shore. We struggled to hold up his dead weight and kicked each other by mistake. He held us together, but he kept us apart too. He threatened to drown us.'

'You really aren't him, are you?' Alison said.

Matthew was silent.

'It's all right,' she said. 'It's fine. Tell me some more.'

'As you started to disappear, I supposed that you were disappearing from me in particular. But you were only struggling with David's loss, as I was. I thought you were keeping yourself back from me, deliberately depriving me. And you probably felt the same. The more you backed away, the more I closed up.'

'Did I throw the first stone?' Alison asked.

'You slept with an old boyfriend,' Matthew said. 'Used him like a telephone, trying to get through to me.'

'And you took your revenge.'

'Kind of.' Matthew spoke at the window, not looking at Alison.

'Are you with me?' she asked. 'Because if this is going to end with a sorry-babe, I'd much rather know.'

'I'm not going anywhere,' he said.

'Come back, then,' she said. Matthew returned to the bedside. 'You know when you're about to sneeze and that itchy feeling builds towards an explosion in your nose? I'm about to remember all this stuff and then it fades.'

Matthew was silent.

'Put your hand on my tummy.' Matthew rested his hand on the blanket. 'No, properly.' She pushed down the covers and pulled up her nightie.

'You're all warm,' he said.

'There's something growing in there,' Alison said. 'Somebody we made.'

Matthew's proximity filled the empty place in her. As his narrative hurtled towards the present, she sensed him applying the brakes. The pre-sneeze itchiness and the backdrop of half-felt pain made her impatient.

'What have they got you on?' he asked.

'Pethidine,' she said. 'And a few other things.'

'Nice?'

'Mmm.'

'You're different.'

'Stop stalling.'

'I was going to say that I like it,' he said.

'It scares you,' she said.

'No it doesn't,' he said. She looked up at him. 'Really.'

'Why do people lie to me?' she asked. 'Do they think that's what I want?'

'Who do you mean?'

'Josephine. My Mum and Dad. You.'

'All right, it scares me.'

'I'm immobilised and amnesiac,' she said. 'There's nothing to be scared of.'

'It's not you I'm frightened of,' he said. 'I love you being different.'

'What, then?'

'It's hard to talk about.'

'Your revenge,' Alison said. 'You're in love with her.'

'Not any more.'

'Don't do this,' she said.

'Look at me,' he said. 'If you're suddenly so acute, you must have noticed something.'

'But you're in love with her as well.'

'I'm here.'

'Are you sure you want to be here?' Alison asked. 'Will you still be here after you've made your confession and been absolved?'

'You have to understand the context,' Matthew said.

'I'd much rather not,' Alison said. 'If it's all the same to you.' She watched Matthew cross the room. He stood by the window, looking out.

'I need to explain something,' he said. 'Something which may not seem relevant.'

'Come back.' She had not meant to drive him away. 'Come closer.'

'I need a cigarette,' he said. 'I'd better go outside.'

'No,' she said, surprised by her own firmness. 'I want to hear about the irrelevant thing.'

Matthew returned to her side and sat down. 'We're well matched in our reticence, if in nothing else. While you never discussed David, I refused to talk about the death of my parents. I preferred to believe that they'd never existed than that I'd lost them. They died on my tenth birthday, in a car crash. I had waited at school for my mother. When she didn't come, I was bitterly angry. An hour later I was told they were dead. I was convinced that my childish rage had run them off the road. I clung to that idea, never questioning my culpability, refusing to listen to anything which contradicted it. I suppose it was my way of hanging on to them. They were always by my side, accusing. But at least they were there.'

'Did you tell me this?' Alison took his hand. 'Before?'

'Only that they were dead.' Matthew lowered his head, concealing his face. 'I didn't understand the rest of it.'

'But that's awful,' Alison said.

'A few days ago I was summoned to see my grandmother. She's getting ready to die, putting her affairs in order. She told me what really happened. Mostly to get it off her chest. They died on their way home from her house, after an argument, in the very early morning. It makes sense. I remember waking up that night at school and looking at my watch. It was raining hard, the gutter was overflowing outside the window. It was four in the morning. The time they died.'

'My poor darling,' Alison said. 'She left you to shoulder the blame.'

'I wanted it,' Matthew said. 'It was all I had of them. I'm a bit lost without it.'

'And when David died?'

'Exactly.'

'You can't kill people like that,' Alison said. 'We'd all be dead. Well, most of us.'

'The alternative is more frightening,' Matthew said. 'To

me, at least. If bad stuff just happens to people, what chance do we have of protecting those we love?'

'I'd like to kill your grandmother,' Alison said.

'She's damaged enough already,' Matthew said.

'Think of what she did to you.'

'I know,' Matthew said. 'I know.'

'And I'd like to kill your revengette.'

'I haven't seen her,' Matthew said. 'Not since the accident.'

'You didn't go to bed with her? Not even for comfort?'

'What would you like me to say?'

'Tell me how it started.'

'She has a flat in Hammersmith Grove, the street where you and David used to live. I walked the dog down there. As much because of David as anything else. One night I rang her bell.'

'Just like that.'

'I'm skipping the inessentials,' he said. 'You knew what was happening, but you chose to ignore it. As if it suited you. There was a phone call one night. She thought I'd started drinking.'

'So?'

'I'm not supposed to drink,' Matthew said. 'She rang Josephine in the middle of the night and persuaded her to phone our house. You found me downstairs, talking to her on the phone. It was all there. But you refused to see it—'

That was when everything came back. Not like a sneeze at all. More like the lights going on again after a power-cut. With the resumption of normality, she immediately missed the purer state in which she knew only what he had told her and what she had intuited. After the darkness, the electric light was crude and intrusive.

'—until one afternoon, it seems like months ago, but it was only last week, I told you about her.'

'Why?'

'You said I was treating you as if I hated you,' he said.

For the next few minutes, as he spoke, she saw how the shadow of David overlapped the image of Matthew, how her memory of her brother and her sense of this man were almost synonymous. She struggled to accept that the two of them were separate, that one could no longer be the vessel of the other.

She listened, forcing herself to be attentive. But she was preoccupied by the simple fact of having him there, of how glad she was to have been run over if, at the end of it all, she could have him so deliciously at her mercy, so prone. She remembered how badly she had wanted to be touching Matthew while Bill had been touching her. She remembered the strange smell which was not fear and the electricated sensation in Tamsin's flat. She remembered the wiry man in his angry van and the woman in brown leather.

'At half past three that morning, you were cycling around West London. You visited Josephine. I don't know what you did after that.' Matthew paused. 'I—. I took a drink after you left. Then I had a few more. Then I lost count. I thought you'd gone. I met my friend Victoria – for dinner.'

She wanted him to lie so she could catch him out. She wondered whether he had remembered to call Jim and Jennifer to cancel the weekend. Her mind was filling up with trivial questions – had he fed the cat? had he picked up the car? – when she should have been angry with him for cheating on her with his marketing executive.

Now that she had her memory back, she more-than-recalled the past. She had supposed that remembered things were faint prints of the original experience, copies which sacrificed some element of definition, of thisness, in return for being recorded and reproducible. Since their return, her memories were more pungent and palpable than anything current. Her recollections were her true possessions, more convincing and grasped than her clothes or her hair. But, like the murdery nightmare during her amnesiac fugue, they seemed to belong to someone else.

'Shall we have a cigarette?' she said, wanting the tobacco smell, to round out the rest of his Matthewy odour.

He longed to skip the part about being too drunk to do what he would otherwise have done to Victoria. He was tempted to reframe it as a form of self-denial. That, after all, had been part of the truth. The desire to make love to Victoria had been disabled as much by thoughts of Alison, as by the first drink and the drinks thereafter. Well, it had, hadn't it?

'I was missing you,' he said. 'I was very drunk.'

'What kind of excuses are those?'

'I didn't tell her what had happened,' he said. 'Between you and me, I mean. I tried to, but I couldn't find the right moment. It all seemed wrong. Char was scratching at the door. I was wondering if you were all right. I was pissed. Tory thought it was funny. I failed to embrace her point of view. I got dressed somehow and stumbled down the stairs. I made it to the pavement and fell over. It was raining. Char ran out into the street.'

He stopped. She was stroking his hand.

'Don't go on,' she said. 'I don't want to hear this.'

'I was crouched on the pavement,' he said. 'I was so drunk I couldn't get up. I saw the bicycle coming towards me. I don't think I've ever seen you on a bicycle. I didn't connect it with you. Perhaps you were on your way to Victoria's, to find me. You swerved into the road because I was blocking the way. The car was out of control. You saw it too late.'

'Enough.'

'Char was dead. I panicked. I ran away. When I woke up

in the morning there was blood on my hands. I couldn't work out where it came from.'

'I've heard enough.'

'You could have died there, on the street.'

'Stop it,' Alison said.

'But it could have been the end.'

'Do I have to ring for the nurse?' Alison said. 'Will you please shut up. Please?'

'I'm sorry.'

'What I am begging you to do is say nothing at all,' she said. 'Do you understand?'

When Matthew stood up, she grabbed his hand and gripped it in her own.

'You're blushing,' he said.

'There was plenty of room on the pavement,' she said, eventually.

'You remember?'

'Shut up, will you?' She tugged at his hand. 'I was on Tamsin's bike because the car was clamped outside her flat. That fucking car. I've always hated it. I was raw and alone. It was terrifying. Like tripping and being a child, all at once. As soon as I drove away from the house, I wanted you like mad. I had this flame between my legs and nothing would put it out. I couldn't bear being alone. I went over to Bill's. I did my best to fuck him, but I couldn't stop thinking about you. I made my escape and cycled back towards Tamsin's. I had a half-formed plan about going to Victoria's and stirring up trouble. One way and another, I ended up in Hammersmith Grove, standing outside the old flat. I was in a rage with David. I was furious about what he did to us, to himself. The stupidity, the vanity. He tangled us up in his death just like he embroiled us in every aspect of his life. I wanted to strangle him.

'But you can't strangle the dead. I was more angry with

myself than anyone else. When I saw you on the pavement, legless, it was so David, such a typical fuck-up. I saw the driver careering down the street, bashing into things. I thought of your parents dying in their car accident. I thought of David, bumming out on us. In that split-second I made a proper decision for once in my life. Right, I said to myself, I'll show the lot of you how it's done. And I steered out into the road.'

Matthew sat beside her in silence. She was breathing hard, surprised that the thrill of her decision was so fresh, still tangy with the rich flavours of that night. After some careful manoeuvring, he found a way of lying beside her on the bed. His lips were against her cheek. Her nose ached and his hair tickled her face. Her arm was under his neck and she reached round and stroked his shoulder with her hand. 'If it's a boy—' she said.

'No,' he said. 'No way.'

'That's what I meant.'

He listened to her breathing as it evened into a pattern. She fell asleep. And then, some minutes later, he slept too.

He awoke in darkness. His throat was itching – a mild symptom of withdrawal. He eased himself off the bed. The dead hour passed slowly as Alison slept. Distant sounds of traffic on the Fulham Palace Road faded into silence. He lit a cigarette and stood at the window, looking down on the silver trees of Hammersmith Cemetery under moonlight. He leant closer to the pane of glass. His exhaled smoke spread out across the window like a curtain. He saw partly his own reflection and partly the world beyond the glass. In the faint image of his own face he saw the lineaments of his father's. A face with kind eyes and an unhappy mouth. A man balding and grey before his time. A man with Matthew's chin and Matthew's jaw. A struggling man.

He found the car keys in her handbag. He wrote a

brief note which he left propped on one of her casts. He took a taxi to Warwick Road. He paid for the clamp, the impounding and the parking ticket. By four-thirty in the morning he was starting the engine. He lit a cigarette and put the Miles Davis tape in the machine. He drove through the dawn, light swelling out of greyness.

When he arrived at Longacres he was greeted by yet another agency nurse.

'Mrs Kerrigan,' he said. 'How is she?'

'And you are?'

'Her grandson.'

'Let me check the register.' The nurse slid shut the hatch which permitted communication between her office and the hall. Behind the hatch, he heard lowered voices.

'What shall I tell him?'

'Tell him she's asleep.'

'When did she die?'

'Couple of hours ago. They'll be cleaning her up.'

'Hold on. Isn't that Mrs Curtain?'

'God knows. I just came on.'

'Kerrigan's the old bat upstairs.'

The hatch squealed open. He was offered coffee. When the drink came it was sour and unsugared. He took it out into the carpark and lit a cigarette. Then he walked through the lounge and took the stairs to her room.

'It's time?'

'I came back, Gran,' he said. 'It's Matthew.'

'You will hurt me, Matthew?' She was in her chair, facing the television. She did not turn to look at him. 'Old Mrs Curtain gone and another waiting to replace her. As there is another waiting for my chair, my bed, my view. If you can call it a view. No shortage of us queuing for the last days. It makes me less afraid. Each one I survive is a victory, a defeat. You hear me?'

'You'll outlive them all.'

'There you are, threatening me.'

'I came,' Matthew said. 'To beg your forgiveness.'

'You have nothing on your conscience.'

'Not for me,' he said. 'For my father.'

'It's no business of yours.'

'Would it be so very hard?'

'You know nothing of hardship.'

'Do you imagine it's any easier being forgiven?'

'You were always strange,' the grandmother said. 'You and that dog.'

He parked on the main road, some yards from the turning. He walked down the rutted lane, crossing the bridge over the stream which – swollen in torrent – had killed his mother and his father. He passed his childhood home, transformed now by an extension built on to the drawing room. He trod carefully, leaving the sleeping undisturbed. He followed a line of oaks along the side of a field. Ponies raised their heads to watch him pass. He had planned to walk up the hill to his grandmother's cottage and look back over the valley. Without any consciousness of choice, he found himself continuing along the floor of the valley. He passed through a tunnel under a disused railway line. Here, he had once incited his dog to bark and listened to the ringing echo against the bricked arch.

He scrambled through a copse, where fallen branches slowed his progress. He came out by a newly-cut drainage ditch and could walk no further. He looked out across a much wider valley which extended to the foot of the South Downs. Broad swathes of meadow were submerged under spring rain. The drainage ditch at his feet ran fast. A mile away, close to the Downs, a triangular field lay at an angle to the lake of waterlogged pasture below it, a stage sloping away from the auditorium of the valley. At its centre stood a mature oak. He lowered his head to light a cigarette. When he looked up, the sun had cleared the ridge to the east. Beams of ochre light painted a shadow of the solitary oak across the triangular field. The elongated silhouette stretched to the hedgerow at the western edge of the pasture.

Alison did not wake up until a nurse came in with her breakfast tray. 'Where is he?' she asked.

'Left in the night,' the nurse told her. 'Said he'd be back soon.' The nurse straightened Alison's bedclothes. Holding up a slip of paper, she said, 'Do you want this, or shall I chuck it?' The nurse slipped her arm under Alison's shoulders and wedged in extra pillows to bring her upright.

'Show me, please.' The note was from Matthew.

Four in the morning—. When I wake beside you I know that I have arrived at a place for which I have always searched but, seeking it, never found. Whether deserved or undeserved, sought or unsought, I will always be yours. And you will be mine. Neither of us can possess the other in the way that David possessed us. That is our freedom and our bond. We have earned the right to bury the dead. They've had their ceremonies.

One day we might have ours, but no man, woman or god can inflate or diminish the love I hold in my heart. Before I feel differently, I want you to know that I am glad of all the sorrows and mistakes, if they have brought us to this. David is dancing. Even my old Gran may offer some small gesture of acknowledgement. But they are as nothing. There is you and only you.